HAMMERED BY LOVE

KACI LANE

For my mama.

I feel like you could use a good laugh about now.

AUTHOR NOTE

Hammered by Love is the third book in the Bama Boys Sweet RomCom Series. All books can be read on their own, but if you'd like to read from the beginning, check out *Hunting for Love*.

If you want to keep up with all my books and get updates about opportunities to receive Advanced Reader Copies as well as backstories on my content, join my newsletter.

Happy reading!
Kaci :)

HAMMERED BY LOVE

CHAPTER ONE

Jonah

Junior year of high school, we went cow tipping at Mason Magill's place. That was the first and last time I've trespassed.

Until now.

I duck under the yellow caution tape surrounding the front porch like a crime scene in a John Grisham novel. After almost tumbling off the front steps, I reach for my flashlight.

The large wooden doors are enough to make me drool. They're no doubt original, and so detailed that a quick coat of lacquer will bring them right back to pristine condition. But I'll totally update the clear doorknob. I jiggle the tiny crystal ball, and the door creaks open. Awesome. No need to break out my tools.

I cross the threshold and shine my light around the room. The ceilings have high wooden beams, and there's a step down into the living area. Full on eighties vibe, including floral wallpaper and shag carpet. But the bones are good. No, great. All of this can be fixed with more labor than money, which works in my favor.

Somewhere between building things with my daddy and listening to Carolina go on and on about designs and remodels, I got the bug to renovate houses. And possibly build them in the future.

So when the one of the largest homes in Apple Cart went into foreclosure, I made it my mission to buy it. I've got plenty of money saved up, thanks to living frugally and working at my family's hardware store since I was old enough to organize nails. I just pray I'm the only one wanting this old place.

Growing up, we'd ride four-wheelers by here and imagine what it looked like inside. The original owner was a local pharmacist who passed away about a decade ago. He left it to his granddaughter, who got in some financial trouble and lost it. She ran off to California with a guy she met on TikTok, and it's sat vacant for almost a year.

I step down and tiptoe across the stained carpet. Aside from a few creaks in the floor, it's eerily quiet here. Too quiet. My senses are heightened like a hound dog, which alerts me to the faint sound of a vehicle pulling up outside.

I shine my flashlight through the window and get a blue light in response. The cop car blinks, and I duck under the window. With my reflexes in overdrive, I make it into the hallway and cut my light before Bradley's voice belts out, "Police! Stay where you are!"

Oh, I'm staying where I am. That is, until I can manage to make a run for my truck parked down the road.

I'm not a bit scared of Bradley or worried he'll try and arrest me. Well, maybe a little worried. He likes to toss around his authority now and again. And he's always happy to remind me he has a few years and a few pounds on me whenever we're competing at something, be it poker or target shooting.

My breath catches in my throat as his footsteps grow louder. I should be scanning the kitchen by now, then heading home to change. Not playing hide and seek with Barney Fife.

I inch farther down the hallway as he passes the opening, shining a Maglite back and forth. He's headed toward the back of the house, away from me.

Before I can make a run for it, I see the light shine toward the front. I backpedal toward a doorway at the end of the hallway. Slinking against the wall, I inch my way toward an open door. I'm almost completely in the shadows when my back pocket buzzes. My fingers fumble to grab my phone before . . .

Crap. Too late. Carolina's ringtone blasts through the empty house.

Bradley's light shines my direction as I squat into the opening. I expected a room, not a wooden staircase. I roll down like a tumbleweed, my lanky limbs landing in a jumbled mess.

Somehow, I manage to uncurl myself and stagger toward the edge of the room. I hide in the corner and listen to Bradley descending the steps. His light shines above my head, but I'm hidden behind some boxes.

Apparently, so are a family of rats. I snarl my nose at the varmints. I'm not a fan of rodents, but at least they don't scare me. I shift my weight so I can back away from them. Judging from their size, they've been here a while.

The light shines my way again, and Bradley is close enough for me to smell his overpowering cologne. I hold my breath and pray I don't sneeze.

The good Lord answers my prayer, just not in the way I expected.

Between the dust and cologne swirling around, I let out the granddaddy of all sneezes. The noise scares the rat family into running from behind the boxes. They trample toward Bradley like a bucking horse out of the shoot.

I swallow back a laugh as Bradley screams like a little girl. The light shakes as he hobbles toward the staircase. I peek around the box and watch him stumble toward the top of the stairs. The largest rat stares back at me, his yellow eyes glaring. If I could, I'd high five him.

Instead, I stand and dust off my jeans and wait for the sound of Bradley's cop car peeling off before I turn on my own flashlight. Without Bradley to worry about, I shine the light over my body to check for any cuts. A normal scratch for anyone else can lead to a puddle of blood for me thanks to hemophilia. No blood, I'm good. But if my throbbing leg is any indicator, I'll have a big bruise tomorrow.

The rat stares my way once more, then I swear he nods before scurrying off into the darkness. I guess it's a he. I didn't get close enough to find out.

My phone dings with a text message from Carol.

CALL ME. NOW!!

Wow, all caps and two exclamation marks. I better get on that.

I sigh and climb the steps to the main floor, then take one last glance around the main room. Yeah, I'm gonna make this place something special. I've just gotta buy it first.

Carolina

We have Earl Ed as a stand-in for Jonah. My side hustle as a wedding planner is all but doomed. I can only hope none of Bianca's people find out he's an ex-convict. Of course getting incarnated for stealing mail is more of a white-collar crime, or in Earl Ed's case a no-collar crime. Like many on his mail route, my family was directly affected by losing our Netflix account back when they mailed DVDs. We all found it strange that only Tanner's Adam Sandler DVDs never made it to the house. Now we know why.

To most people, the best man going AWOL wouldn't be such a big deal, but to me, this is unacceptable. Especially since the best man is Jonah.

That stinker knows better!

I grind my teeth behind my fake smile as Earl Ed stands by Jack in a pair of board shorts. Never mind that it's the end of December.

Jonah's ringtone echoes from my purse on the front pew. I rush over and answer. "Where are you? What in the world is going on? You're never late."

"Calm down, I'm on my way."

My nerves unravel knowing I can fire Earl Ed in a minute. He has nothing to do with this wedding except for driving Bianca's matron of honor and her husband here. Then he volunteered to fill in for Jonah so I could check where everyone needs to stand.

Very kind of him to volunteer, but I'd much rather have pulled someone from the crowd. Like anyone but him.

"Are you okay?" I should've asked Jonah this first, but I'm a little ticked he's not here.

"Yeah, but I didn't have time to change."

"Don't worry, you can't look worse than Earl Ed."

"Earl Ed?"

"Yeah, it's a long story, but . . ." My words trail off as the double doors to the sanctuary swing open.

Jonah emerges between them, huffing and puffing like the Big Bad Wolf working double shifts. His clothes are dirty, and his shirt is unbuttoned in the center. His brown hair resembles a pile of pine straw.

He jogs up to me and exhales heavily. "I'm here."

I blink, still shocked at his tattered state, then reach out and button his shirt. "Did you get in a fight with Mason Magill's crazy bull or did Sasha get ahold of you again?"

"Haha, you're hilarious. Let's get this show on the road."

My face morphs into an evil grin at the Sasha jab. She all but beat him up when he ended things with her. I tried to tell Jonah and my brother she was crazy. But no, they wouldn't believe me. She was "too sweet" and "too hot" to be crazy. I countered that someone as hot and sweet as her could afford to be crazy. And guess who was right.

Jonah marches toward the front and taps Earl Ed on the shoulder. Earl Ed droops his shoulders and staggers to a pew near the front. His time in limelight has ended. Why he's staying, I have no clue. But I've got a wedding to run here.

"Okay, now that Jonah's here, we're going to run through the walkout again. Jonah, you're walking back with Ariel."

I motion toward Bianca's best friend, who halfway smiles at Jonah in a very "bless his heart" fashion. She's dressed like the boss in *The Devil Wears Prada*, and her husband is sporting a three-piece suit. Not the usual attire for a wedding rehearsal in Apple Cart, or even for a wedding in Apple Cart. But they're high-class Atlantians, so I'm certain this is quite the culture shock.

"Jack, Jonah, and Brother Johnny, if you will, step near the doorway where you'll come out once the processional music starts." I have everyone else follow me back to the sanctuary doors. Then I divide the groomsmen and bridesmaids. I've worked with a few weddings before, but never one with such a diverse wedding party. Even Lacie's husband, who's an Atlanta surgeon, didn't have as fancy of friends as Bianca.

Bianca's side of the wedding party could pose for the cover of *Vogue*, much in contrast to the groom and grooms-men, who resemble an Outdoorsmen Oasis sales paper. Except for Jonah, who's more like that dirty kid from the *Peanuts* cartoon.

I bite back a laugh at the difference in Bianca and Jack's worlds, and how she must feel about moving here. She must really love him to turn her world upside down like that.

"We're ready, Mrs. Bromwell," I say. The older lady wiggles on the piano bench and strikes the first chord. I turn back to the wedding party. "When you hear that chord, we'll start."

Once all the bridesmaids and groomsmen have found their places, I walk backwards, instructing Taylor on tossing the flowers as she trots down the aisle. Taylor makes it to the end, grinning at me with her front tooth missing. I return the smile and pat her on the back. No doubt, she will steal the show until the bride makes an appearance.

The ring bearers are Jack's labs. Brother Johnny agreed to let them take part, but made me promise we'd take them out as soon as their part ended. Bradley gets the honors of that job, and it didn't seem necessary to have him or the dogs at the rehearsal. Those hounds would run to Jack anywhere, anytime.

I don't mention the ring bearers tonight. Bianca's people have endured enough initiating for now with Earl Ed.

With everyone but the bride in place, I cue the piano player to switch songs. I tighten my ponytail and nod to Bianca. She grins at me, then shares the sweetest glance with her dad before gliding down the aisle. My heart pings with excitement. As much as I enjoy planning and decorating, the end effect is the best part. Seeing a couple's reaction to their new home or a bride shine on her perfect day. The fact that I had a shred of something to do with it warms my heart.

I stand back while Brother Johnny goes through the motions of Bianca's dad giving her away. A tear tugs at his deep-set eyes, even though we've practiced this part twice already. He pats her hand before joining his wife on the front pew. I try to ignore Earl Ed sitting a few feet away from them, legs sprawled in his board shorts.

Nothing ruins an intimate family moment like an overweight redneck proudly displaying his thick white thighs.

I return my focus to the front before I lose my cool and jerk Earl Ed up by the ears. Every event will have a few hiccups. Earl Ed sticking around has nothing on the time his aunt hijacked the microphone at his cousin's wedding. Of course, goats also ate the flower arch at that one.

My point being, I should overlook Earl Ed.

Everything runs smoothly except for a minor debate over where to stand during the communion. Southern weddings tend to last a little longer than most. We try and fit in anything and everything, from unity candles or sand-pouring to the Lord's Supper and a special song where the couple simply stares at one another. I try to plan for the special song to play in the background of the communion and unity rituals, so the couple isn't standing and staring awkwardly for too long.

Not that a soon-to-be husband and wife wouldn't want to stare at one another. However, something about everyone in the county having a front row seat to this makes it a little less special. At least in my opinion.

When it's time for everyone to walk back down the aisle, I nod at Mrs. Bromwell. She licks the tip of her finger, turns a page of sheet music, and starts the recessional song. "I need the groomsmen and bridesmaids to link arms when you meet. Guys on the right, please."

I point for Jack and Bianca to lead the way. Taylor follows them, and one by one, the wedding party steps out and links arms when I point.

Ariel hesitates before looping her satin-sleeved arm through Jonah's dusty elbow. But she's a good sport about it, only wincing momentarily. She struts like a runway model, which only highlights his disarrayed appearance.

Jonah narrows his eyes when they pass me. I'm sure my cheeks are shaking as I try hard not to laugh. Once the last couple reaches the foyer, the music ends.

"Thanks, everyone. You can head over to the Gamer's Paradise lodge. We have dinner set up."

"Great, I'm starved." Earl Ed stands and pats his big belly.

Seriously? Why is he still here?

CHAPTER TWO

Carolina

I plunge my fingertips into the front of my hair, no longer caring what it does to my ponytail. That's the great part about being behind the scenes at events. I don't have to worry about looking Pinterest perfect as long as my designs do.

Of course, on wedding days and design reveals, as well as meeting clients for the first time, I dress like a professional. Tonight, I'm in a low-key sundress, wavy hair pulled back, and flip-flops on my feet. They're cute flip-flops, though, even sporting a slight heel.

Studying the page in front of me offers a little relief. Something about checking off a to-do list loosens the pressure from my shoulders—literally and figuratively.

I'm midway through making another checkmark beside "flowers" when Jonah's hand lands on my binder. He starts shifting it away from me, so I push the pen firmly onto the paper to stop him. It doesn't work, and my purple gel pen streaks across the page as he slides the binder out from under my arm.

I sigh and drop my pen. Before I can raise my eyes to him, he pushes a full plate of food in front of me, then pulls out the chair beside me. I prop my chin in my hand and scan his dusty shirt.

"Now can you tell me what made you late?"

Jonah shakes his head. "After you eat something."

"I'll eat after tonight ends. I'm busy making sure everything's set for tomorrow."

Jonah crosses his arms and scoffs. "Bianca has a dozen minions running around here. Besides, you've gotta eat."

I glance toward the kitchen, where a team of Atlanta caterers and Mrs. Mary swarm around like busy bees. Paul slinks out of the kitchen with an armload of to-go boxes.

"Seriously? Paul?" I start to stand, but Jonah braces his large hand on my forearm and forces me to sit.

"Don't worry about him. Everyone's already eating but you."

I close my eyes and slump my back against the wooden chair. Jonah is always my voice of reason when I get worked up. I turn my eyes toward him to say he's right. But as soon as I open my mouth to speak, he grins and shoves a deer popper in my mouth.

The warm, melted cheese oozing in my mouth causes me to choke a little. He pats my upper back like I'm a toddler who's stuffed her mouth with one too many Goldfish crackers. I cough, then chew and swallow.

"See, deer poppers are better than Xanax."

I arch my brow at the odd comparison, then immediately laugh at Jonah's goofy expression. He has more dad jokes than a middle-aged guy with a minivan.

He takes a bite of his own food and leans back against his seat.

"You know, you should really sit near the head table since you're the best man."

He shrugs. "I wouldn't say I'm the best." One side of his face tugs into a smile. "Besides, I'd rather hang in the back with you than be in the middle of all that."

I return his smile before studying the plate in front of me. Jonah filled it with all the foods I like and even put my chicken tender sauce on a small dessert plate. He knows I hate it when sauces touch other foods not intended for them.

We met the first day of kindergarten and buddied up immediately. Over the years, he's become an extra brother to me. And out of all my friends and family, he puts me at ease the most.

He really is the best man.

"Thanks for fixing my plate."

He nods while biting into a dinner roll.

I take a few bites of my food, and we eat in silence for a minute. It's the most peaceful minute I've had all day. Funny how Jonah was the one to both cause me the most stress and bring me the most peace. Well, that's not entirely true. Earl Ed and Paul sure know how to push my buttons.

Jonah's still dusty from whatever he did before rehearsal. A long streak of dust outlines his jaw, wiggling as he chews. I glance around and realize he didn't get us any napkins. Typical guy. I rest my hand on the side of his face and rub his jaw with my thumb. The slight stubble tickles my hand.

"What?" He turns my way.

"You have a big line of something above your neck, but I got it." I move my hand and rub my thumb against my fingers to thin out the residue. Then I wipe my hand against my skirt. A little dirt can't hurt my twenty-dollar Target find.

"Thanks." His eyes scan my face, and his own morphs

into an unfamiliar expression. It's rather serious for him. Instead of allowing it to concern me too much, I jump in and ask again what I've wondered all night.

"Now can you tell me why you came to rehearsal half an hour late, covered in dirt?"

He takes a huge gulp of his tea, as if needing to wet his mouth before a long explanation. After he lowers his Mason jar back to the table, he widens his eyes toward me. And yes, we have Mason jars. That was the compromise I suggested when Bianca wanted everyone to drink sweet tea and lemonade from goblets and Jack preferred red Solo cups.

"I was at the Vanderburke Mansion."

I scrunch my face in confusion. "Why? Did you go in there? And isn't it roped off? Maybe even condemned?"

Jonah raises a hand to stop me. Whenever the wheels in my head start turning, my mouth catches up and spits out words faster than a hot knife slicing ice cream.

"I went in to give the place a good look over before I buy it."

I choke on the food I'm chewing, and Jonah reaches over to pat my back again. His long fingers stretch across my upper back, dislodging the food hung in my esophagus. I drink some lemonade once I regain my breath. "You're buying it?"

His hand slides across my bare shoulder, just slow enough where I can feel the callouses on his palm. "Yep. I'm gonna flip it." Jonah crosses his arms and stares at me smugly.

"That place is a mess."

He furrows his brow. "How would you know?"

"I drive by that way from time to time. They've had it roped off for months."

"To keep people like me out."

"Exactly." I laugh.

"Because they're getting ready to sell it. The bones are

great. All it needs is a proper cleaning out and a facelift. Maybe open up a wall here and there."

I shake my head. Jonah's mentioned wanting to build houses one day, but this is renovating the largest house in Apple Cart. One that's sat vacant for a while. If building a house is like buying a new car, fixing up this place would be equivalent to buying an eighteen-wheeler overturned in a ditch, with trees growing out the window.

"You think it's a bad idea, huh?" His brown eyes go all puppy-dog sad.

I eat a bite of my chicken, then shrug. "I have total faith in your ability to do it, but Jonah, that's a big project, no matter what shape it's in. And who around here will buy a house that big?"

"I'm sure someone will. I can get it cheap enough to sell it reasonably and make a huge profit. Some small-town doctor wanting a bunch of kids or some show-off like Samuel is sure to buy it."

I puff out my cheeks, then exhale. At least he has buyers in mind, but still . . . "How are you going to pay for this? It can't be *that* cheap."

"I've saved up money my entire life. From working with Daddy at the store and Jack at the lodge. I hardly spend anything, you know that."

"Yeah, I'm pretty sure you've had those jeans since high school." I glance at his faded Wranglers.

Jonah rolls his eyes. "We haven't been out of high school that long."

"So you have had them since then?" I smile, happy to call him out on it.

"The last thing I bought besides food and gas for my truck was that painting in my kitchen."

"Ugh. I told you to take that down."

He laughs. "And that's why it's worth every penny."

"What is it with you and Tanner decorating with animals? First his cow print, then you hang a pig butt above your sink."

"Hey, that's a perfectly acceptable accent piece for an older mobile home in Auburn."

I lift then lower one shoulder. "Eh, whatever. But what is your plan for this house? Hire someone to do the work or wait until the summer?"

We both graduate in May. I'm technically done with classes, but interning full-time at a design firm my last semester. I took a lighter load last year as well to work there part-time. With any luck, they'll offer me a real job and I can have some say in my designs. Drawing up someone else's plans is getting pretty old.

"I managed to get all my classes Tuesday, Wednesday, and Thursday. I'll work on it myself every weekend. Then I'll sell it before we graduate."

I laugh so hard, my rib catches. "Ouch." I bend forward and rub my side. After I recover, I look at Jonah. "You think you can take on a project that big by yourself and have it market-ready in a semester?"

"Nope. That's why you're gonna help me."

My limbs tingle. Did he really just suggest we Chip and Joanna this place together?

Jonah

"Ugh." I coil over and clutch my stomach. Nothing like a surprise shot to the gut to wake you up.

"Ha-ha, gotcha." Earl Ed lifts his helmet and laughs.

Most of us have on goggles, but he's protected by one of Michael's welding helmets.

An airy thud blows behind us, and Earl Ed lets out a blood-curdling scream. He bends at the waist, and Bradley smiles at me over his head. "You are welcome."

He lifts his goggles, smudging the eye black he applied right after tying a black bandana around his forehead, Rambo style. That completed his full camo attire, making him the embodiment of a video game soldier. Leave it to Bradley to take paintball way too seriously, like everything else he does.

I laugh, sending a tickle down my still tender skin. Without thinking, I instinctively rub my stomach, then regret it when my hand sticks to hot-pink goo. "Five o-clock." I nod to Bradley as Michael and Kyle stalk around a tree, army style. However, neither dressed for the part like Bradley.

Michael is in jeans and a faded shirt that reads, "I Played Hard at Goldstrike Casino and All I Won Was This Shirt." Sometimes I forget he's Earl Ed's first cousin. Then I'm reminded that he started dating his wife when she was pregnant with someone else's baby. They met when he took Earl Ed to the casino to celebrate his parole. Kyle has on his usual blue jumpsuit with his name sewn on the pocket. Despite running his own mechanic business, he chooses to wear a uniform.

Before I can draw my gun, Bradley takes them both out, then laughs hysterically. I know this is a paintball game, but I'm impressed by his reflexes. It gives me more confidence in his role as county sheriff.

Kyle steps up and pops him on the back of the head. "This ain't a drug bust, buddy."

Bradley shrugs. "I can't turn it off, big dog."

I glance around at the group before me. "I guess that's

game over, then. Jack and Tanner got hit first." Much to my delight, as I can rag them about it later.

"Son of a—" Bradley grabs the back of his shoulder and grits his teeth.

"That's game over," someone says in a deep growl from behind the trees.

JoJo steps out of the shadows. His broad shoulders and stern, bearded face are enough to make me cower a bit, even though I'm clearly marked by a bright pink glob like a scarlet letter across my midsection. I swear this guy never smiles. He's a little older than the rest of us and gives off a vibe that he thinks he's tougher than everyone else—and he probably is. He's not known for playing well with others, but we needed him to make the teams even.

When Tanner arranged a paintball war at Double Drive, we assumed Earl Ed would run things, since it's his business and all. But he just had to play, throwing off our numbers. JoJo happened to be there the day we booked the party, checking out some pine trees Earl Ed hired him to clear. Tanner mentioned him playing as a joke, but to our surprise, he agreed.

Earl Ed stands and stretches enough for his shirt to rise above his belly. "Woo, those things hurt. I think I better get some waivers made before opening this attraction."

"Yeah, if you want to offer it to kids," I say.

"Or anyone besides us," Kyle adds, wiping down his foggy goggles.

"Duly noted." Earl Ed wipes a hand across his sweaty face and hobbles toward the building. We fall in line behind him, our boots crunching pine straw as we finagle toward the mini-golf course. After JoJo finishes clearing trees, this place could compete with any paintball course in the state.

We climb the porch of the building, which houses an arcade and small diner. Earl Ed instructs us to leave our guns, ammo, and goggles in the bin beside the back door. I'm relieved to see he has a lock on it. With the only beer joint around a few yards away, I'm sure questionable characters have wandered this way late at night.

Earl Ed swings the door open to Tanner and Jack sitting in a corner booth across the room. I pass the various arcade machines and main area where people pay to ride go-karts and play mini golf. Then I elbow Tanner to slide over and let me in the booth. He and Jack have helped themselves to some chips and soft drinks from the snack bar.

"How long have y'all been in here?" I ask.

"Long enough to watch two reruns of *The Big Bang Theory*," Jack answers as he nods at the TV.

The rest of our motley crew staggers over like they're the last ones standing in the apocalypse. Bradley props his hands on his hips and grins at Jack. "Last night a free man."

Jack sighs. "Let me guess, you won."

Bradley's cocky smile turns downward. "Well, almost."

JoJo steps behind him, towering several inches over his six-foot-three frame. He slaps Bradley's shoulder, causing him to wince. Then he holds up a lime-green hand and . . . I lean forward to make sure this is happening. Oh my. JoJo Culp has cracked a smile. A very faint, tiny tug at the corner of his mouth, with the slightest sign of teeth peeking out between his mustache and beard. But yep, I'll call that a smile.

I take a photographic memory in case I never witness this again. If we hadn't eaten ribs earlier, I'd wonder if the dude even has teeth.

The moment fades soon enough, and his face straightens. Then he's back to mumbling behind his beard. "Sheriff here came in second."

Jack laughs. Tanner rolls his eyes and pulls a five from his wallet. These two will bet on anything. Like the time they had a ten-dollar wager on whether I would wear a cap or cowboy hat to the Auburn rodeo. Such children.

Even though I'm the youngest one in the room by a few years, I can't help but feel the most mature at times. Well, except for JoJo. Aside from that small jab at Bradley, he hasn't exactly joked around tonight.

"So what's next on the agenda since paintball has ended?" Bradley raises a brow to Tanner. Jack and I exchange a knowing look. Bradley hates to lose more than anyone. I'm certain he's ready for revenge.

Earl Ed hooks a thumb behind him toward the snack bar. "I can throw a few pizzas in the oven while you guys ride the go-karts if you want."

Tanner turns to Jack, who shrugs. "Sure. Might as well make a night of it."

Earl Ed disappears into the kitchen opening, while the rest of us make our way to the track. I suspect Tanner will have an unfair advantage, as he comes here often with his girlfriend and her daughter.

I lag, leaving me with last pick of the cars. I haven't slept much the past few days, thanks to worrying about the old mansion property. Part of me wishes Tanner had suggested we call it a night. But I can't leave to go to bed. They'd never let me live that one down.

I'm lowering myself into a car when Michael speaks from the other lane. "Hey, man, you can't drive the cars in that lane. We've gotta work on them."

"But there's none left."

Michael frowns. "Then you gotta ride with someone." He drives off before I can answer.

I stand and yell for Jack to wait. "Hey, Jack, hang on!" Too late. He's peeling out of the parking lane after Tanner.

"Get in," a gruff voice calls behind me. I turn to JoJo pulling over.

"I thought you'd left already."

"I did." He strokes his fuzzy beard. "Already made a round."

"Oh." I climb in next to him, my narrow hips sandwiched between his broad body and the car frame. He lays on the gas as I'm trying to buckle my seat belt. My head jerks forward, and I abandon the seat belt efforts in favor of holding on to the bar in front of me.

We zip and zag around everyone, bumping into fenders and cutting between cars. I'm both amazed and terrified at how we're the only car with two people, one of us the largest here, and we still manage to outrace everyone.

My life flashes before me on the third loop when we come close to flipping sideways by Kyle. Of course, my side is the one to momentarily go airborne. I white-knuckle the bar and silently recite what I can remember of the Psalm about sheep lying in the grass peacefully while we hang a curve.

Just as I'm sure this stupid metal bar is the only thing keeping me alive, the loudspeaker on the side of the building comes on.

"Jack, party of seven, your order is ready." Earl Ed's voice is loud and clear, and surprisingly professional.

JoJo stomps on the brake, bringing us to a screeching stop. He hops out of the car and starts toward the building, leaving me to roll backwards down the hill where we've stopped. I sit in a daze for a few seconds before realizing what's happening. Then I slide over and give it enough gas to make it back up the hill and park.

Everyone else drives their cars in line around mine. They unbuckle and get out as if they've ridden a kids' merry-go-round.

"Jonah, you coming in to eat?" Tanner pats my windblown hair on his way toward the building.

I manage a nod. "I just need a min—" Talking was all it took to dislodge my shaken-up guts and spill them all over the track.

Note to self: If I ever get married, don't let JoJo come to the bachelor party.

CHAPTER THREE

Carolina

I fight the urge to check on the lodge as I drive past. We left the place in good shape last night, and there's still plenty of time to finish decorating for tonight's reception.

First, I need to see a guy about a tux.

I park my Mazda in front of Jack's house and pull the suit bag from the backseat. Sunlight flickers through the pine trees surrounding Jack's yard, and a bird chirps someplace in the distance. I breathe in the crisp winter air and anticipate the day ahead.

I've led the decorations for half-a-dozen weddings so far, and this makes the third I've also coordinated. For a side gig that started as a favor to a family friend, it's turned out pretty well. And I've enjoyed it, for the most part.

The downside is dealing with all the minor details that can slip through the cracks on a wedding weekend. Like the fact that my brother forgot to pick up his tux in Tuscaloosa and texted me last night at ten to do it for him.

My ballet flats creak over the wooden steps as I climb Jack's porch, careful to hold the bag high so it doesn't hang on anything. I beat on the door before noticing the doorbell. That must be new. It's been a while since I've come out here. I hit the button and watch it light up, then listen to the ding.

After no response, I hit it again and hear the dogs bark. The curtains are drawn, so I can't see inside. They'd better be here. I just drove an hour one way to pick this thing up.

I knock on the door once more, so hard that my knuckles tingle. I'm rewarded with a gruff, "it's open," from the other side.

I open the screen door, then the wooden door, and cross the threshold. Chocolate and Brownie greet me, tails wagging. "Hey, girls." I pat them both on the head with my free hand, still holding the tux bag high. "Sorry, I don't have a treat."

As if they understood me fully, both lower their heads and trot back toward the couch. My eyes follow them to a mound of covers with a mop of hair peeking out of the top like an abandoned bird's nest. I'd recognize that shaggy mess anywhere.

"Jonah?"

The covers slowly lower to reveal his face, and he blinks. "Carol?"

I lift the tux bag even higher and cock my head toward it before folding it over my other arm. "I brought Tanner's tux. Is he still asleep?"

Jonah sits up. "They all went to Waffle House around five or so. I told them to let me sleep." He yawns, then shakes his head, animating the wild hairs standing straight up on the side of his head. "I had to get my beauty rest so I could be fresh for when the bank opens."

"Uh, news flash. The bank opened two hours ago."

"What?!" Jonah springs to his feet, abandoning the covers and giving me a front row view to his Auburn boxer shorts.

I shade my eyes with my free hand as my cheeks heat up. Not exactly the way I planned on starting this morning. The heat travels from my face down my neck as I chastise myself for peeking through my fingers. Jonah's always been an attractive guy, but I've never thought of him that way. Nor have I ever seen him in his underwear.

"Oh, my bad." He stares down at himself as if he's just now realized he's wearing almost nothing and snatches an afghan off the top of the couch.

I lower my hand as he wraps it under his arms and tucks it at the corner. A small laugh seeps out of me as he stands there with a grandma blanket wrapped around everything except his ankles, feet, and arms. He looks like a modern-day Joseph in a sleeveless coat of many colors. Well, not too modern, considering that quilt was probably made in the sixties.

He crosses his arms over himself, and I bite back another laugh. If I'd brought my phone in, I'd have taken a dozen blackmail photos by now. Jonah would be my slave for life. We'd be in our eighties, and I could make him come change out the tennis balls on my walker and turn my TV antenna all because of this one photo I took six decades prior.

"I'm actually glad you're here because I want your opinion on something before I go to the bank," he says.

"What?"

"I'm going to open up a line of credit at the bank for any remodeling on the mansion."

"You don't even own the thing yet."

He points a finger my way and narrows his eyes. "Yet. But I will come Monday, and I need to be prepared." He runs a hand over his messy, short hair. "Come look at it with me real quick before I go to the bank. I need your opinion on decorating costs."

I sigh. "I've got a lot to do today. *We've* got a lot to do today."

"I know, like go to the bank for mansion money."

I shake my head. "Fine. But we can't take too long. Go change while I hang this somewhere."

Jonah salutes me, then marches toward the spare bedroom with the afghan still wrapped securely under his arms. I glance around for a place to put the tux. It needs to be high enough where the dogs can't sit on it, but obvious enough where Tanner can't miss it. I decide on the ceiling fan above my head. Hard to miss there. I shoot him a quick text to let him know the tux is there waiting for him when they return.

K. Thx.

I raise my brows, shocked that he replied right away. Worst case scenario, he forgets I told him. However, someone should notice a long black bag hanging in the middle of the living room.

Jonah emerges from the back in a T-shirt and jeans. His hair's still a mess, but he grabs a cap off the couch arm and covers his head. "Let's go. I'll drive."

I follow him out, locking the door behind us. I grab my purse from my car and climb in his truck. We pass the lodge on the way out, and I crane my neck to get a better view of the people working in the backyard. My shoulders relax at the progress they're starting to make.

Bianca hired a whole team of caterers and decorators out of Atlanta to come down and do most everything. They're all staying at the lodge this weekend too, which makes it extra convenient. Still, I need to come right back and make sure everything is up to par with her plans so she can enjoy her day stress free. Not that I've ever come across a stress-free bride. But it's my job to run interference on as many obstacles as possible to at least lessen their stress.

"Why the hurry on all this house stuff?"

Jonah's laser focused on the road ahead as we pull out of the long drive from Gamer's Paradise onto the main road. "The house goes to auction Monday morning at the courthouse."

"Oh." I widen my eyes at the realization of how serious he is about this. Jonah has talked about renovating houses since we were teenagers, when all those home remodeling shows got popular. I assumed this was another one of those random conversations.

"Why do you need me to look at it? You're the one who will be doing all the work. You know better than me how much materials will cost." I mean that too. He grew up in a hardware store and can build or make anything from a pile of scraps.

Jonah sighs and turns toward me for the first time since we left Jack's yard. "Because, Carol, you know your stuff too. You're great at decorating places and picking out flooring and all that stuff. I need you on this. I trust you more than anyone, and I value your opinion."

My lips curve into a smile at the compliment. He smiles back before staring ahead again. My insides warm. Nobody's ever said they value my opinion before. At least not in those exact words. I get asked my opinion a lot on decorative things or details for events. People say I do a good job and refer me to others.

But the word *value* . . . For lack of better wording, I put a lot of value on that word.

Jonah

"Watch your step." I offer my hand to help Carol maneuver through the yellow crime-scene tape wrapping the porch.

She squeezes my hand and ducks under the taping while dodging a mudhole. "Are you sure it's okay that we go in here?"

I scoff. "I'm sure it's *not* okay. That's why we're making it quick."

She drops my hand and shakes her head. I laugh. Carolina isn't one to bend the rules, which makes it that much more fun to put her in situations like this one. I can't resist sneaking a glance at her face when I jiggle the crystal ball handle and the door creaks open. Her mouth morphs into a large O shape, and her eyes widen with terror.

I smirk and push the heavy door open. "Ladies first."

She frowns and tiptoes inside, then stands beside the door. Its comical how cautious she's being. I slam the door, causing her to jump. Then I laugh, earning a slap across my back.

"Ouch."

"We're trespassing," she whisper-yells at me.

"We won't be long. Besides, there really aren't any current owners."

I'm now rewarded with the scowl she usually reserves for Tanner, and occasionally her oldest brother, Matthew. Good to know I've made it to brother status.

Clearing my throat, I step down into the sunken den and focus on the floor joists rather than Carolina brother-zoning me for eternity. Part of me is flattered, really. But the other part of me wants to be something more.

That's the one secret nobody knows about me. Not my family, including Jack—especially Jack. Not Tanner. And certainly not Carol.

She slowly follows me across the living room, then freezes momentarily when I jump to test the flooring. "Still intact," I comment as Carol holds a hand to her chest and sucks in a breath.

My eyes trail the crown molding around the ceiling, which I couldn't see last night. The wooden beams I could see, but they're even more impressive in the daylight. I wish I could say the same for that hideous wallpaper and carpet, but those can easily be fixed. Apparently, what I mistook for stains last night were patches of squash-yellow among brown in the carpeting. Gross.

I knock around on the wall and step toward the kitchen. Carolina's footsteps shuffle behind me at a close distance. The kitchen entrance is easily marked by the change in flooring. Squash carpet transitions to mustard tile beneath the small opening. I suspect a door once blocked the entrance and was later removed for easier entry into the main living area. Linoleum would've been much easier to replace, but I expected tile from a house of this stature. Of course, the countertops have a wooden chopping-block finish. Typical eighties. Carolina stands in the center of the kitchen and crosses her arms.

"So what do you think?"

She scans the room and wrinkles her forehead. "It's just so brown and yellow."

"I know. It's hideous, and I love it." I scratch the stubble on my jawline and study the wallpaper. This room is decorated in fruit rather than flowers. I walk through the small archway that leads into a very green dining room. "We could knock out the wall between these two rooms."

My boots squish against some loose carpeting. I tug at the corner and pull a piece up. Carolina gasps. "Jonah. You can't do that. You don't own this."

I bend down and pull a little harder, then smile up at her. "This will be easy to pull up."

She shakes her head. "We should go."

"Not until you've seen the rest. I want us to get a good look at the place before I literally drop my life savings on it."

"Okay . . ." Her eyes trail toward the lacy curtains hung across the dining room windows.

"Come on." I exit the dining room and weave back through the living area. "I think the bedrooms are this way."

We cross the main area to the hallway where I hid from Bradley the night before. Between that and the paintball war, I'm a little sick of hiding from him. Maybe that's why I'm running through here now like I own the place. Carolina stays a few feet back as I comment on changes I'd make in every room. I catch her staring at me, her brown eyes soft.

"What?"

"You're really passionate about all this."

I waver my head. "I guess you could say that. I mean, I see a lot of potential in this place."

One corner of her mouth lifts. "I wish I had that much passion about my work."

"You like decorating and planning designs, right? And this wedding stuff?"

She laughs. "Stuff is not quite the S word I'd use. Maybe 'stress' or something even more colorful. But yes, I love decorating and designing. The coordinating *stuff* is just an extra paycheck. Plus, I've been told I have a knack for bossing people."

I narrow my eyes. "No comment."

She laughs again.

I tap my hand on the wall and nod toward the staircase across from the room we're in. "Let's go upstairs." We step back into the hallway.

"Wait, what's in that room?" She motions toward the doorway to the basement.

"Just a friendly family of rats and some boxes."

Carolina winces.

"The basement."

She passes me, taking the stairs two at a time, as if Papa Rat can open the basement door and attack us. Maybe he can? He sure charged Bradley. I chuckle. "Slow down or you'll—"

Before I can finish my sentence, she tumbles back, and I catch her. I hoist her petite body into my arms and continue up the stairs.

"Thanks." She wraps one arm around my neck, and I breathe in the citrus smell her hair sends my way. I swallow back the rush of adrenaline that holding her like this creates inside me.

This is the same girl who caught crickets with me in kindergarten. And less than an hour ago, she caught me drooling on the couch in my faded underwear, which I quickly covered with my great aunt's quilt. She has zero reason to find me attractive.

I reach the top of the stairs a little slower than necessary, all out of my selfishness to prolong this moment. We lock eyes briefly as I set her on her feet. I all but bite a hole in my tongue to hold back articulating my true feelings.

Every time I come close to telling her how I really feel, I think back to middle school.

In eighth grade, I tried to make a move on her at a school dance. She didn't catch on and made it clear she'd already friend-zoned me. Then she danced the rest of the night with the playboy of middle school, who broke her heart a few weeks later. From then on, I vowed to watch out for her. Even if I couldn't have her whole heart, I didn't want others breaking off pieces of it.

Somehow, that protectiveness earned me an unofficial brother badge in her eyes and Tanner's. So now I'm twenty-three and worse than friend-zoned. I'm brother-zoned. That leaves me with soaking up friendly hugs and relaxing in her citrus scent whenever possible. In a non-creepy way, of course.

"Wow." Carolina's eyes dart around the spacious area, which is basically one huge master suite.

"It's nice, huh?" I comment, just as stunned as her. I never made it up here yesterday. There aren't any curtains, which highlights the beautiful views of the front and back yards, complete with a covered porch on each side and a pool in the back.

In true split-level fashion, the room sinks down a few steps and leads to a door. Behind it is a spacious bathroom with a garden tub and one of those weird privacy windows with the square tiles. The floor is pink. Quite the contrast from yellows and browns everywhere else.

On the other end of the bathroom is another door. We open it and step up into what I assume was a study. Maybe even a home office or workout room. It's hard to tell without furniture. The floor transitions back to brown carpeting to match the bedroom.

We walk the outline of the room and stop in front of the back window. "It's got over five acres," I say as I stare at the overgrown field scattered with oak trees. I glance at Carol beside me.

"It's a beautiful view," she comments, without taking her eyes off the yard.

"It sure is." My throat catches when she looks up at me. I

jerk my gaze back toward the window and silently pray she doesn't get what I really meant by that.

Out of the corner of my eye, I notice she's still looking at me. I ease my face toward hers, contemplating if she read my mind.

Should I fess up? It's been ten years since I've tried. Would she feel the same way?

The Auburn fight song interrupts our ambiance, and the moment is gone. Carolina reaches into her back jeans pocket and answers her phone. "Hello?"

I watch her face transition into worry mode as she listens to whoever's on the other end of the line.

"Thanks, I'll be right there."

She shoves the phone back in her pocket and sighs. "I'm needed at the church. ASAP."

CHAPTER FOUR

Carolina

My door is barely closed when Jonah jerks the gear shift into drive and races toward the main road. I tip over in my seat trying to buckle my seat belt.

"What exactly happened?"

"I don't know. It was Bianca's friend Ariel, and she sounded a little hysterical. All I made out was something about the piano and that they needed me as soon as possible." I chew on the end of my fingernail. "I knew I should've already been there."

Jonah releases one hand from the death grip he's holding on the steering wheel and pats my arm. "Hey, it's okay. We're almost there." He glances at the truck radio, then at me. "I've still got an hour before the bank closes."

I nod and pull back my hand, immediately regretting the chip I made in my pale pink polish. Even though I'm not in the wedding party, I always aim for a top-notch appearance at the actual wedding.

Jonah gives my arm a tight squeeze before clutching the wheel again. I sigh and muster a half-smile. A dozen or so worst-case scenarios run through my brain while we drive the short distance from the mansion to the church. Thankfully, we were already close to downtown.

He angles the truck in front of the porch steps and puts it in park. I hop out and look at him through the open door. "Go on to the bank, I'm fine." I even fan my hand like I'm shooing a stray dog to encourage him to leave.

Whatever's going on in there, I can't be responsible for him missing out on that house. It's his dream. I've never talked about or looked at anything the way he has about it. Well, except for maybe a fresh strawberry Bundt cake.

He cuts the engine and gets out. "Nope, you may need help."

I press my lips together. There's no use arguing with the man. It will only waste more time. He's as stubborn as me, if not more.

We jog up the front steps in tandem, my legs working overtime to keep the pace with his six-foot self. He opens the door, and I bolt in like lightning. I don't stop until I reach the piano. Bianca and Ariel are sitting on the bench. Ariel's arm is around Bianca's thin shoulders, and both wear a weary expression.

"What happened?"

"It's Mrs. Bromwell," Bianca answers. "She's in the restroom throwing up."

My jaw unhinges and I stand there like a largemouth bass taking the bait as my mind funnels for a proper response. "There's more than one piano player in town. I can call around."

Bianca's mouth twitches as if she wants to smile but can't

quite make it happen. "Thanks," she mummers with the enthusiasm of a robot.

I pull my phone from my back pocket and scroll through my contacts. Once I dial Mrs. Maudy, I massage my temples with my thumb and forefinger while I wait for an answer.

"Mrs. Maudy? This is Carolina Nash. Do you still play the piano?" I bite down on my thumbnail once more, then stop when I remember the polish.

"No, dear. I quit giving lessons five years ago."

"Yes, ma'am. This isn't for a lesson. Could you play yourself, for Jack's wedding?"

"No, dear, I'm afraid not. My arthritis caused me to quit altogether."

"I see. Thanks anyway."

"Maybe try Roxy Adkinson. She was a great student of mine and still plays. Give me a minute and I'll fetch her mother's number."

"Thank you, Mrs. Maudy."

I make eye contact with Bianca, who clinches her teeth with anticipation of news. I raise a finger, signaling her to hold that thought. Then I search the back of a few pews until I find a pen and prayer request paper in the hymnal holder.

Mrs. Maudy returns to the phone a little winded, but she is pushing eighty. I jot down the number she gives me and thank her. Then I circle back to the front of the sanctuary to give Bianca the not-yet-good news.

Her face falls slightly, and I force a fake smile to try and cheer her up. "Let me call this number and then some more. Okay?"

She nods, and I excuse myself to call Roxy's mom. She answers right away. Unfortunately, Roxy is in the mountains with her friend's family. I thank her mom for answering and browse my contacts for anyone local who plays.

I call the Apple Cart High School music teacher, who

informs me she only knows brass and woodwinds, then the choir director for Wisteria Worship Center. He would love to help, except he has a broken arm from falling off a horse over the holidays. Great.

That leaves me with hooking my phone to the sound system and an iTunes prelude, or possibly seeing if Paul has one of those keyboards that plays by itself. I puff up my cheeks and shove my free hand into my hair. A warm hand squeezes my shoulder, causing me to jump.

I turn to face Jonah's chest. "You scared me."

"Sorry. No luck?"

I drop my eyes and shake my head in defeat before looking back at him. "Think Bianca would settle for non-live music?"

"I'll do it."

I half laugh, more from shock than amusement. "You're kidding, right?"

"No, I'm not. You know I can play."

"Yeah, but you *hate* playing. And you haven't played in years."

"That doesn't mean I can't play."

Jonah's mother was big on making sure he and his sister diversified their activities. His sister loved dance, so his mom made her try outdoor sports for a while. Nothing really stuck until she tried archery. Now she's like the Katniss of Apple Cart.

Jonah was big in FFA and all things outdoors. So in order to "culture him"—her exact words—Mrs. Elisa had Jonah take music lessons. He purposely chose an instrument he couldn't play in the school band, for fear she'd push that too. God forbid he have something else to do during high school football games besides paint his chest bright red and wear a fake armadillo shell in honor of our beloved mascot. The result was three years of piano lessons every week. Like his sister, he found he had a hidden talent. Unlike his sister, he hid his.

I tilt my head and stare at the piano behind us. "Are you sure?"

He shrugs. "Yeah."

"But you hate playing the piano, and hardly anyone even knows you play other than Tanner, me, and your family."

"But you need me."

"You'd do that for me?"

Jonah reaches out and wraps his massive hands around my elbows. Tingles shoot up my arms and my anxiety starts to fade. This time when I smile, it's relaxed and not forced through gritted teeth.

"You'd seriously play the piano, in front of literally everyone and their mother, for me?"

"I would." A mischievous grin crosses his face. "But let's let Jack think it's for him."

The shred of worry still hanging onto my gut comes out in a nervous laugh. Without thinking, I fall into his arms and hug around his waist. He wraps his arms around me and gives me a gentle squeeze. I'm still hanging on when he peels me away.

"You're welcome. I gotta run to the bank. I'll be back later."

I open my mouth to respond, but Jonah darts down the aisle like a runaway bride. As soon as he disappears behind the sanctuary doors, I let out a deep sigh and turn to Bianca. Her face is full of questions. I give her a thumbs-up and smile as relief washes over her, bringing instant color back to her cheeks. Ariel grins and pats Bianca on the knee.

Crisis averted. I collapse on the pew behind me and laugh with relief. A happy bride means a happy wedding. I can't believe Jonah is willing to embarrass himself to save the wedding. To save *me*!

I owe him big time.

Jonah

Did I really agree to play the piano? At my cousin's wedding? In front of the whole town? And a bunch of Atlanta socialites?

Yeah, I did.

Despite my loathing for instruments and the fact that I haven't played anything other than maybe three songs since middle school, I couldn't let Carol suffer like that. She needed help. She needed me. And the way she embraced me made it all worthwhile. Only this house could peel me away from a hug like that.

Luckily, Christmas was only a week ago. Every year I play for my mama, since she's the only one who appreciates my musical talent. It doesn't even matter that neither of us care too much for Christmas music. I play the few songs I remember, and it always makes her smile.

"Great Balls of Fire," "Benny and the Jets," and the theme song to the *Peanuts* cartoon. In that order.

I also remember "Amazing Grace," which was my grandma's favorite. After my grandparents died, I'd play it now and again in their memory when I was alone with a piano. I guess that's what I'll be playing today.

I wince. Jumping Jupiter, I don't know that stupid wedding song.

Once I park at the bank, I shoot Carolina a quick text before getting out.

Can you get me some music for the wedding song?

Three little dots appear as I step down and lock my truck.

Yes, we have music for the march.

My nerves unbuckle. Somehow, I still remember all the keys, even without regular practice. I push open the glass door to the bank and almost cough at the overpowering heat.

I don't get this place. In the summertime, they keep it freezing, and in the winter, they make it like a sauna. Apparently, Ashley is hot too.

Well, she's definitely hot, but I mean in a temperature sense. Even though we live in mild-weather Alabama, most people don't wear low-cut, sleeveless shirts in December.

She smiles and sets down the stack of cash she's counting when I cross the glossy tile floor. "Can I help you, Jonah?"

"Yeah, I need to talk to Samuel, I guess."

"What you need, sugar?" She slides the cash in a bag and folds her hands on the desk in front of her before batting her eyelashes at me.

"I've got to talk to someone about a line of credit, and I know Mrs. Bromwell isn't here today."

"I can help you."

"Oh, really? Good."

She motions to the chair across from her desk. I sit and wipe my hands on my jeans. "I didn't know you did this."

"Why, of course. I'm in training to be a loan officer myself."

"Cool." I nod, not really knowing what that entails. All I know is Bethany Bromwell usually sits at the desk, while Ashley does deposits.

Ashley smiles my way before turning to the computer screen. "Sam said Mrs. Bromwell's playing the piano for Jack's wedding later today."

I scratch the side of my neck. It's itching with the realization that I am now the one playing in the wedding.

"That's what I heard." I clear my throat, hoping this is answer enough to sidestep the question.

Ashley's eyes pop out and she blinks a few times. "Wow, nice bank account."

"Thanks." If my glossing over the question didn't do it, my savings account did.

Ashley's thin eyebrow arches as she looks at me. "Why exactly do you need a loan?"

"I plan on buying a place, but it will need renovations. I'm not sure how much I'll have left from the sale, so I want to open a line of credit to cover any repairs."

She nods. "I see." After clicking the computer mouse a few times, she gives me a flirty grin. "You could always wait to fix it up. Who knows, you might meet a nice woman and get married. Then she could give you all the input on how to decorate it." Her eyelashes flutter with the last few words.

"Nah. I've got Carolina to help with that."

"Oh." Slight shock washes over her face at my quick, dry response. "Well, of course you do." She shifts in her seat and types a few things on the keyboard.

"Let's see. You don't have a business and you don't own a home." She types a few more times and stares at the screen. "You have a perfect credit score and no debt. With that, you should get a personal line of credit easily."

"That's good, right?"

She laughs. "Yeah, you're doing great."

I nod and smile. It's nice to hear that from someone who doesn't know me well. Ashley has no reason to not shoot it to me straight.

"How soon are you wanting to repair this home?"

"As soon as possible."

She sighs. "I see. We can get this started for you. Only thing is the interest rate on these personal lines of credit aren't the greatest. You can possibly get a home equity loan after purchasing the house."

I nod. "How do I do that?"

Ashley flashes her big teeth at me once more and flips her blonde hair behind her shoulder. "Just come see me again."

"Okay."

She stands, still smiling. Then she turns quickly and pulls some papers from a nearby printer. "All you need to do is sign these to get you going."

Ashley sits and shuffles the papers between us. She fishes a pen from the coffee cup on her desk, or Mrs. Bromwell's desk, and points to a line with a very long, very red fingernail. I sign and date the line, and she flips the page.

We continue the point, sign and date, flip the page routine several times. With each page, she gives a brief overview of what it says. I'm assuming she can be trusted, as I don't care to read all the fine print. Once we're at the end of the papers, she restacks them and staples the top.

"Any questions?"

I pause for a moment and drop the pen back in the cup. She covered all the important details, like when and how much money I can get if needed, as well as the interest rate. "No, I think I'm good. Thank you, Ashley."

She smiles again and stretches her slim arm across the desk, extending a hand. I shake it, surprised at the firmness of her grip. Multiple bracelets jingle like sleigh bells when we shake hands.

After releasing her grip, I stand and nod to the few tellers counting down cash at the windows. Then I walk out either richer or in debt. The sale and condition of the mansion will determine which.

CHAPTER FIVE

Carolina

The sun lowers behind the oak trees surrounding Apple Cart Baptist. After the piano incident, I ran home to grab lunch and change for the wedding. The bridal party should get here in about an hour to change for photos. According to the schedule Bianca and I made, they had a late brunch at the lodge, followed by hair appointments at Cut and Dry Salon.

I pull around back and park near the entrance to the basement. I need to stuff my purse and emergency bag in the bridal room before going upstairs.

Yes, I carry an emergency bag. After the first wedding I helped coordinate, I quickly learned what all could go wrong and what all we might need. A sewing kit, snacks, stain wipes, nail file, lip gloss, hair spray, water bottle, bandages, and Tylenol are just some of the items in this bag. After every wedding, I seem to add something else.

The bridal suite doubles as a prayer room for the church,

with comfy couches and several Bibles lying around on end tables. It's now sparsely covered with dress bags, open makeup bags, and several floor-length mirrors that I bought at Dollar General last week.

I tuck my purse and bag behind one of the mirrors, keeping out only my phone and planner. As I start out of the room, I stop and check my appearance in one of the mirrors. I smooth the skirt of my dress and stand a little taller. Then I rake my fingers through my wavy, shoulder-length hair.

Bianca's dress hangs from a coatrack beside the mirror. Before I can think better of it, I close the door to the prayer room and pick up the dress.

It's heavy with beading from top to bottom. A fitted mermaid gown. I'd go for a more classic look, perhaps an A-line with minimal embellishments. But this dress fits Bianca's high-society persona. I hold the hanger below my chin and sigh as the beads shine beneath the florescent lighting. Imagine how exquisite it would look in good lighting.

Carefully, I hang it back on the rack. My fingers trail the beading and outline the curve of the waist. I glance toward the door and listen to the deafening silence. Nobody's in the basement but me.

My lips curve as my eyes scan the dress once more. I've never worn a wedding dress before. Not even playing around in a store.

I trace the beading back to the hanger and gently unhook the strings hanging it up. The dress is strapless, and I'm a bit surprised those tiny satin straps held so much weight. I drape the dress over the couch and unzip my own. My dress falls around my feet, and I step out, leaving a cotton-and-lace puddle on the floor.

Cold tingles dance across my fingertips as they carefully unzip the champagne gown. I'm sure some of the older ladies in town will draw crazy conclusions about Bianca not wearing a stark white gown. They know everything about tradition and nothing about fashion. I, for one, think this gown is perfect for her.

I slide it over my head, the heaviness of the beads weighing on my small shoulders. Bianca is taller than me, and a bit slimmer. I'm more petite and have what my grandma refers to as "childbearing hips." Either that's her way saying she wants great-grandkids, or that my butt is big. Probably both, knowing her.

Those hips do me no favors as I tug the dress over them. It goes, but barely. I suck in my stomach, as if that will somehow magically make my butt smaller. Then I bend my arms behind me to zip the thing. Halfway over my butt cheeks, I hear a slow ripping sound. I gasp and jerk the zipper back down. It catches on a bead, and I want to curse, cry, and die all at the same time.

Just when things couldn't get worse, I hear the faint sound of heels clicking down the basement steps. I drop my hands from the zipper and shuffle fast as possible, taking tiny steps toward the door. I never knew speed tiptoeing was a thing until today. Maybe they should add that to the Olympics next to speed walking. I'd totally be a shoo-in for competing, since I make it across the room in a few seconds.

I lock the door and lean against it to drag in a quick breath. Exhaling helps my anxiety a tad, but the relaxation is short lived when the footsteps get heavier. I lunge away from the door and shimmy my hips like a belly dancer.

All the Pilates in the world couldn't have prepared me for this moment.

By some miracle, the dress eventually shakes to the ground. I stumble backward as I try and step away from the beading. My thigh slams into the edge of a couch, but I prefer that pain to doing any more damage to this dress.

The footsteps grow even louder, and I dive to the floor

and scoop up the dress. I untangle the bead from around the zipper, wincing at the loose thread. Then I zip the stupid thing and return it to the hanger. No sooner than I've hung it back on the coatrack does the door handle start to jiggle.

I swallow and reach for my own dress in the floor. The door swings open when I'm squatted on the floor, wearing nothing but heels, a padded bra, and bright pink panties. I close my eyes as someone gasps and pray under my breath that it isn't a man.

"I'm so sorry."

Relief washes over me when I hear Bianca's voice. I stand, pulling my dress up with me, happy to see she's shut the door behind her. The last thing I need is for everyone in town to hear I gave a peep show in the Baptist church basement. "It's fine. I was just changing for the wedding."

"I see." Bianca is staring at the carpet like the lady she is.

I shrug into my sleeves and zip the side of my semi-formal Target attire. "Done."

She lifts her eyes and offers me an awkward smile. "The others should be here soon. I'm a bit nervous, so I came in early."

I step toward her and put my hand on her arm. "It's fine. All brides feel nervous. At least all the ones I've been around."

Her smile softens. "That's good to hear. You've done great with everything, by the way."

"Thanks. Your hair and makeup look beautiful." I nod to the dress that caused me momentous stress moments earlier. "And that dress is perfect for you." Not for me, but I keep that fact to myself.

She sets her purse on the couch nearest the door, along with a small keyring. I swallow as I recognize the church logo on the keyring. That would explain her getting through the locked door.

Bianca crosses the room to her gown and runs her hands over the beading, like the way I did before the incident occurred. She turns the dress on the hanger and examines the back, then gasps.

My stomach bottoms out when she picks at the loose bead. "My word, I didn't notice this until now."

"What?" I ask as innocently as I can, while chewing any remaining polish from that poor thumbnail that's taken all the beating today.

"There's a bead hanging by a thread."

I blink back any fear and put on a brave face. "I have a sewing kit in my bag."

Bianca drops her hands from the dress and leaps toward me, wrapping me in her willowy arms. "Oh, Carolina. You're the best."

I pat her back and let out a nervous laugh. If she only knew.

My fingertips are still numb from stitching the loose bead back on Bianca's dress. Talk about nerve-racking!

It's times like this I wonder why I continue directing weddings. All the little details that can go wrong usually do, making the bride—and me—a bit crazy. But after I zip the dress up Bianca's back and catch her reflection in the mirror, I remember why.

She dabs at the corners of her eyes and fans out the skirt as she turns to get a view of the back. It's the satisfaction of somehow playing a role in making a bride's special day come together that makes it all worth it. Even if I'm responsible for some of that stress myself.

Note to self: No more trying on wedding dresses.

Well, at least not for now. Hopefully, I'll find my own

Prince Charming one day and try on dresses for myself. Not sneak on my client's while she's at the salon.

"You look amazing," I say.

"Thanks." Bianca's red lips curve into a wide heart shape. We both stand in awe as she turns slowly for us to admire every inch of this gorgeous dress.

The moment is short-lived when the door opens and Misty Mayberry bursts inside. Excuse me, Misty Miller. In my defense, the woman's been married so many times, I have a hard time keeping track of her last name.

"Bianca!" She puts her hands to her mouth and gasps. "Let me touch up your cheeks."

Before either of us can respond, Misty rummages through a makeup bag on the couch for some bronzer. She finds a brush large enough to dust an ancient bookshelf in one fell swoop and starts swiping Bianca's cheeks. When she's done, we all turn to the mirror. To my surprise, she made Bianca look even better.

"Misty, I didn't know you were coming." That's my Southern belle way of asking, "What the heck are you doing here?"

"Oh, yeah. I've been helping Adrianne out at the salon some when she has to do events."

"Okay . . ." I allow my voice to trail off before I say something stupid.

Misty is a nice woman, but a little eccentric. Besides having a grocery list of exes, she has a ton of kids and a loud, flirty personality. She's also the only woman over fifty I know who wears pants with words on the rear. I haven't noticed the back side of her today, but her pants are black leather, which says enough.

"Anyway, I came down to tell you that the photographer is about ready for Bianca and Jack."

"Thanks, Misty." I offer a tight-lipped smile.

"Sure thing, darling." She slides toward me and runs bright red fingernails down my hair. "I can't wait 'til you get married. I'll fix you up right pretty, you darlin' thing."

I hold my breath until she releases my hair, then force myself to keep a polite face. That offer alone is enough to make me plan on eloping. Even before I plan a wedding—or find a groom.

"Ready?" I ask Bianca. She smiles and nods. Misty disappears, and I hold Bianca's train so she can go first. We use the elevator to avoid any slips or falls up the wooden staircase. It's only one floor, but I don't want to chance losing any more beads. We ride in mutual silence to the only other floor in the church. Then I gather the end of her dress before we exit.

Jack is waiting in the foyer with Tanner. His jaw drops when he catches the first view of his bride in her wedding gown. Goosebumps populate my arm as I witness their interaction. This is my favorite part of working on weddings. Tanner and I both walk toward the sanctuary to give them some privacy.

The florist is adjusting a few arrangements on the ends of the pews, while the photographer takes photos of the decorated stage. Everything is simple and sleek but in an elegant manner. Very Bianca.

It's a good thing too. Jack would just as soon marry in coveralls outside the dirt pile where he and my brother shoot targets all the time. Bianca's good for him. The man needed a little culture in his life.

I continue toward the front of the church, admiring the colors that dance on the floor as the lowering sun shimmers through the stained-glass windows. My eyes follow a trail of yellows and blues to the window near the piano. The light ends at Jonah.

He's standing by the window, hands in his pockets. A

smile tugs at my lips, as I haven't seen him wear a tux since our senior prom. Even the so-called formals at Auburn aren't formal.

I study him for a moment, noting how different he looks from five years ago. Though still slim, his shoulders are broader and his face fuller. His hair isn't quite as shaggy, and his features more mature. He really is a handsome man and will make a great husband for someone.

My stomach knots at the idea of Jonah marrying. I wish him happiness as much or more than anyone. He deserves it. However, I hope and pray whoever marries him treats him well. And I selfishly hope I like her. Nobody wants their best friend to marry someone unbearable.

Even worse, I hope that she likes me, whoever she is. I can't imagine a life without Jonah in it.

"Carolina? Did I do my tie wrong or something?"

I blink. Jonah's staring at me like I've lost my mind. "No."

He leaves the window and stops about a foot in front of me before wiggling his bowtie. "You sure?"

I straighten it and nod. "Yeah, you did great." He takes a step closer and smiles down at me for a beat. A weird vibe surges between us, so I do what I do best, which is talking to interrupt. "I have the sheet music for the piano."

"Yeah, I saw that, thanks."

I smile and nod again, before realizing I'm still holding the corners of his bowtie. I drop my hands and wipe them down the front of my skirt, as if that would erase the awkwardness of holding on to him like I've got him on a leash.

"Wedding party. I need you guys up front." The photographer's voice booms through the sanctuary. She's mighty loud for a wiry woman. I turn to find Jack and Bianca already in place.

"Oh, I better get up there." Jonah cocks his head toward the stage.

"Yeah." I smile and take a seat in the front row. The photographer snaps photos of all the attendants with the bride and groom, as well as several group photos. I pull my phone from my dress pocket and check the time. We'll unlock the church doors in about an hour. Weddings are big in Apple Cart, as we don't have a lot of everyday events.

For the rest of the photos, Jack and Bianca barely keep their eyes off one another long enough to face the camera. My insides warm at the amount of love they have for each other. Then I fight off that nagging voice that creeps in my head now and again. The one that suggests I will never find someone to share such mutual affection with.

I've had several boyfriends over the years, but either I liked them more or they liked me more. Not that I'm an expert by any means, but I personally believe true love is when each person loves the other as much as he or she can love.

Since I'm only twenty-three and focused on graduating and starting my career, I haven't given it much thought lately. All I can say for sure is the last guy I dated wasn't the one.

The photographer announces she's got all she needs, and I hurry toward the stage. I shuffle Jack toward the door by the pulpit and Jonah to the piano. "You sure you're okay with this? I have a playlist on my phone—"

"Carol." Jonah grabs both my hands in his. His big, warm hands soothe my small, shaky ones. "I promise, it's fine." He strokes the backs of my hands with his thumb, then gives me his signature goofy grin.

I shrug. "Okay. Thanks again. I owe you big time."

"Yeah, you do," he laughs.

"Is that why you agreed to this?"

He drops my hands and plays a melody on the piano

before smiling back at me. I shake my head and laugh, then hurry Bianca and her bridesmaids out of the sanctuary and into the hallway toward the basement. Once I have the flower girl and ring bearers—or should I say ring dogs—in place, I signal for Tanner to open the doors.

Half of Apple Cart is waiting outside. They begin shuffling in and I peek my head into the sanctuary. I point to Jonah, and his fingers dance across the keys. "Amazing Grace" fills the air as Tanner and the other groomsmen start escorting guests to their seats.

Jonah's on his third round of "Amazing Grace" when it's time to seat the parents. I should've tossed a hymnal up there or something. Why isn't he playing anything else? I take my phone and shoot him a text. I know he'll get it. The man practically sleeps with his cell phone.

The faint noise of a dog barking echoes from the sanctuary. Everyone looks back at Chocolate and Brownie, but they're fine as frog hair in the hallway, living their best life as Taylor feeds them flower petals. I shut down the petal pushing, then pet the dogs for acting civilized. Almost as soon as it starts, the barking stops.

"Amazing Grace" ends . . . for the fourth time. I line up the parents and open the wooden doors to the sanctuary. Jack's parents cross the threshold as the music resumes.

Jonah's fingers are banging down on the keys to something much livelier than before. *Is that . . .*

I gasp. "No!" I whisper-scream loud enough to gather the attention of the wedding party and the people sitting in the back two pews of the sanctuary.

Jonah turns his head and makes eye contact with me. He smirks while continuing to beat out the notes of "Great Balls of Fire." Is this some kind of sick joke? The noise muffles against my pounding head as I walk backwards into the hallway leading to the basement. I slide down the wall until I'm sitting cross-legged on the floor . . . in a dress.

"Carolina?"

Afraid to see who's asking, I slowly lift my head from staring at the wooden floor. It's Ariel. "Yes?"

"Is he playing—"

"Oh yeah." I crane my head around Ariel's legs to see Bianca's reaction. She's literally clutching her pearls. With her other hand, she fans her face, then she takes a deep breath. I'm not sure if it's the music or her nerves causing this reaction. Whatever it is, I need to check.

I push myself to standing just in time for Jonah to switch music. The familiar "Canon in D" plays like a healing balm. I instruct Taylor and release the dogs to admiring "aws" across the crowd. They obediently swish their way toward Jack, pillows on their backs. Who knew Jonah would embarrass me more than the dogs today? Bradley emerges from the front pew and leads them out a side door.

One by one, I tap members of the wedding party when it's their time to walk. Bianca steps up beside me after Ariel starts down the aisle.

"Bianca, I had no idea he'd play that."

She laughs and shakes her head. "It's fine, Carolina. Nothing could ruin today."

She winks at me before making eye contact with Jack. Jonah seamlessly transitions into the wedding march, and I rub Bianca's arm. "Your turn."

"Finally," she whispers, without taking her eyes off Jack.

I sigh as the beautiful bride takes her father's arm and glides down the aisle like an angel. I could strangle Jonah right now, but it will have to wait. He needs to live long enough to give the best man's toast.

CHAPTER SIX

Jonah

I survived another wedding. Not that I attend them regularly. Come to think of it, I only attend weddings I'm in. That would make one college friend's and now Jack's the only weddings of this decade.

I wiggle a finger under my bowtie and loosen it, then unfasten my top shirt button. That's better. Why the women get to have bare necks while we choke to death is beyond me.

Puffing up my cheeks, I find a chair near the wall. The lodge hasn't had this many people ushered through it since Outdoorsmen Oasis had its grand opening at the back of the property. Plenty of people stopped by Gamer's Paradise before leaving, boosting Jack's business big time. Not that he needed it after selling off the land to the store.

The store's owners mingle around the crowd, dressed like western royalty. Ronald fit right in wearing a bolo tie to the wedding. He pulls off the look much better than Paul.

Maybe Ronald can retire to Apple Cart if he ever bores of Texas.

I lean back in my chair and watch the crowd. We have quite the diverse party at this shindig. Half Apple Cartians and half Atlanta elite. It's not hard to tell who's cut from what cloth, even with all us Alabamians dressed in our Sunday best.

Speaking of Sunday best, a red flash darts past a group of Atlanta men and women who are wearing mostly black. I follow it down to recognize Carolina's legs.

Yes, I can pick out her calves in a crowd. And the back of her head, as well as her feet, hands, elbows, and other parts I wouldn't dare name. I'm *that* pathetic. She marches across the room, getting lost now and again behind people who aren't so small.

My eyes follow her to the cake table, the photographer, and finally the kitchen. That's when I decide to follow her with my feet too.

When I get to the kitchen opening, she's literally counting pieces of shrimp on kabobs. I bite back a laugh. It's cute when her OCD goes into overdrive. Tanner thinks I find it funny like him, which is why he keeps buying hideous animal decor for his house. I do it to bring out her passion for making all things perfect, simply because I enjoy seeing her passionate. Even if it does result in her swatting at my head when I pick up random thrift-store finds and leave them around my trailer.

That's why I need her help on this mansion reno. I can fix floors and walls, spruce up the yard, and clean out the pool. But I don't know a hill of beans about decorating.

"Hey, Carol, got a minute?"

She holds up a finger. I wait a few seconds before she lifts her head, still mouthing numbers. "What's up?"

I glance around at the random waitstaff Bianca hauled in,

all wearing black slacks and white coats. Mrs. Mary stands by the stove in her usual checked apron spotted with grease stains, with her hair in a neat bun. Again, quite the contrast between these two worlds. I don't care to have a serious conversation about the future in front of them.

"Come on." I grab Carol's wrist and tug her toward the kitchen door. We step outside onto the edge of the patio.

Someone taps her on the shoulder and asks about where to leave a wedding gift. She directs them with her finger and gives basic directions before turning back to me. People around us are starting to dance, and I instinctively wrap one arm around her back and hold her hand. If we're dancing, it will be much easier to hold her attention . . . I hope.

She smiles up at me, and I pull her the slightest bit closer. Flashbacks from middle school plague my brain. We're grown now, both out of braces, and instrumental love songs have replaced the Justin Bieber tune that was the unfortunate background to our one and only dance.

Carolina doesn't go to many parties, and the few times we've been at the same event where dancing occurred, one or both of us had a date. Prom, birthday parties, events in Auburn she attended. I haven't danced with her in ten years or more.

The same anxiousness overtakes me for a moment, as if I'm convinced the middle school bully will swing by any moment and cut in.

Pushing that thought aside, I focus on her pretty face. "Carol, I've got something I need to ask."

She smiles and laughs a little. "There's no need to say it."

I wrinkle my forehead. "No, I need to ask you this before—"

She covers my entire mouth with her palm and leaves it there for a beat before putting it back on my shoulder. It takes all the willpower I can muster to not kiss her hand.

We're super close and have hugged or held hands many times as friends. I've even held her hair back when she got sick, but I've never kissed her. Aside from her shushing me like this, our lips are forbidden fruit.

Energy surges through my lips, and I couldn't talk now if I wanted to. She smiles at my silence and continues.

"There's no need to apologize for playing 'Great Balls of Fire.' I've already had half a dozen people come up and compliment the unique and riveting choice of music, including a few from Bianca's side."

My jaw drops. It never occurred to me that playing it wasn't a good thing. I rocked that song. "I wasn't going to apologize. Well, except for maybe not having my phone on silent during the wedding. But you were the one to text me mid-song and make my phone bark."

Her mouth twists. "I knew that wasn't Chocolate and Brownie!"

I laugh as she rolls her eyes. When our eyes meet, I go serious again. "I was going to make you a proposition."

"A proposition?" One eyebrow shoots up as she gives me a wondering look.

"Business proposition," I correct, realizing how that sounded. Not that I haven't considered making one of those cliche marriage pacts with her before. But we're only twenty-three, so I doubt she'd throw in the towel so soon and agree to betroth herself to me by thirty.

She raises her chin in acknowledgment, so I continue. "I got the line of credit at the bank. Depending on the sale price, I may not even need it. Either way, I should have plenty to renovate however I wish."

"That's great, Jonah."

"Thanks." I grin at her genuine happiness for me. "Only I don't know the first thing about decorating."

"So that's where I come in, I'm guessing?"

"Yep."

"You know I'll help you any way I can, but I'm in Auburn all week this semester for my internship."

"I know, weekends are fine."

"Then sure, you know I'll be happy to help." She smiles.

I laugh nervously and drum my fingertips against the back of her lacy dress. "See, here's the proposition. You've been talking about having your own business for over a year now."

She stops swaying and cocks her head. "One day, not now."

I keep talking as if she didn't just stall out. "So have I."

"Well, duh. Your daddy's all but said he's ready to retire."

I turn us slightly so she starts swaying again. The moment we end our dance, someone will come take her away. If not some middle school jerk, then the photographer, or a bridesmaid, or a caterer. I want her to myself for just a few more minutes. She's the only one I want to talk to about my future.

"I'm not going to take over the store."

"You're what?"

Now it's my turn to stop swaying. I turn my back against the house and tug my tie again to loosen it all the way. Carol stands beside me, arms folded.

"I want more than anything to build and renovate houses. I know I can do it, but Daddy wouldn't hear the end of it if I didn't prove myself first. That's why I'm buying this house and flipping it before I graduate."

Her eyes bug and she stares at the stones beneath our feet a few seconds before looking at me. "Jonah, you know I think you can do that, but before we graduate? By May?" Her voice grows higher with every word.

"Yeah, it's just now starting the year. That gives me over four full months."

She shakes her head. "Then I guess you're hiring help, right?"

"Yeah." I chuckle and turn toward her with my shoulder on the wall. "I'm hiring you."

Carol shakes her head. "I'm not accepting payment for decorating your house."

"I know you won't. That's where my proposition comes in."

Her eyes narrow. "Oh yeah? What is it?"

"First, I'll pay you for your work after the sale, and you have to take it."

"Sounds fair."

"But wait, there's more," I say in a mocking tone to emulate those late-night infomercials. "If we manage to finish the renovation and flip this house for double the money I've got in it, you have to move home after graduation and start your own business."

Her mouth drops, then shuts quickly. She pinches the bridge of her nose and sighs. "Jonah, I can't do that."

"Why not?"

"Because." Her arms open wide. "I don't know the first thing about running a business."

"But you know about design."

"I've never even worked anywhere full-time until now."

"And you may not have to if you do your own thing."

She folds her hands over her stomach and stares out at the crowd. "I don't know. I always thought I'd work someplace a while and build up clients first."

"Everyone in Apple Cart already comes to you for anything design related."

"Yeah, but . . ." She bites her bottom lip.

"If you opened an LLC, it might help you quit doing things for free."

She shoves my shoulder, and it scratches across the wall.

"You're one to talk."

"Cutting limbs for old ladies isn't the same as redecorating for all the debutantes in the Garden Club."

She sighs. "Bianca is paying me well for this wedding."

"See." I give her shoulder a gentle push. "Another service you can offer."

"I told you weddings are stressful."

"Oh, don't act like this weekend hasn't been fun. Between Earl Ed, dogs in the wedding, and my riveting performance, who wouldn't want in on this?"

"You're to blame for two of those things, you know." She shoves me harder this time, and I seethe, faking an injury.

I laugh. "You. Are. Welcome."

Her eyes slowly meet mine, and when they do, she smiles. "You really think I can make a decent living doing my own thing?"

I nod. "Uh, yeah. Especially in Apple Cart, with the low cost of living. The Pig hasn't raised its prices in some time."

She tries to keep a straight face but ends up laughing. I lift my hand and hold out my ring finger. It's a silly gesture that means nothing to anyone but us. Something we've done since the fourth grade.

That was the year we learned about a vein that runs from the third finger all the way to the heart. Carol suggested instead of doing pinky promises like everyone else, we should give a heart swear using our ring fingers. That way our hearts would be accountable for keeping whatever secret or bet we had conjured up at the time.

I later read in a random magazine at the doctor's office that many veins from our hands go to our hearts. However, since this vein was discovered doing so first, that's why people wear a wedding ring on that finger. After learning that fact, I decided to never tell Carol any different.

"You have to make double for me to move back, huh?"

I inch my finger closer to her. "Double."

"You know I'll most likely get an entry position at Home-Sweet-Home Designs."

"That's why I said double."

She studies my finger like it's an exotic animal, then lifts hers. Right before her hand meets mine to curl our fingers and seal the deal, a teenage girl taps her shoulder. Carol drops her hand and turns around.

"Carolina, you're needed in the front yard."

"What's happening?"

The young girl winces. "Earl Ed is insisting on sending the couple off with a twelve-gun salute."

Carol gasps. "I'll be right there." She turns back to me and wraps her finger around mine. "Fine, heart swear." Then she rushes off, jerking my hand for a split second before dropping it.

I watch her hobble across the dark yard in her heels to save the day. Perhaps I'm selfish for making this bet with her to come back to Apple Cart. A twinge of guilt washes over me, but it isn't strong enough to make me regret this deal.

"Because it's not appropriate to shoot off a dozen guns without first running it by the bride and groom."

"But it was gonna be a surprise."

I shake my head at Earl Ed. "No. You're not doing it. If you wanted to surprise Jack, you should've done it last night at the bachelor thing y'all had."

"We did surprise him. With a paintball sneak attack."

I prop my hands on my hips and give him my most intimidating stare. He's twice my size, but I've learned it's not so much how you look as it is how you look at the other person.

He slumps his shoulders in defeat when he realizes I'm not going to back down. "Fine. But can't we do something?"

"Yes. As a matter of fact, we have sparklers to light their way to the getaway car. You can help light those."

"Super-duper." Earl Ed winks and pats me on the head like I'm his new rescue pup.

A perfectly tuned engine hums behind us. I turn toward the antique car Ronald's driving beside the lodge. "Come on," I motion for Earl Ed to follow me.

We walk side by side toward the car. The engine stops and Ronald steps out. Apple Cart unofficially adopted him after he and his business partner, Macon, started the store behind Gamer's Paradise. Macon usually leaves the visits from Texas to Ronald, since he is a longtime bachelor who doesn't mind the travel. Ronald once told me the only thing waiting for him back in Texas was his favorite steakhouse.

He tips his suede Stetson at me and nods to Earl Ed. "Car's all primed and ready to take the lovebirds to their honeymoon nest."

"Thanks again for letting us borrow it." I mean that more than he knows, as Jack contemplated landing a helicopter in one of his green fields for their getaway.

"Much obliged, Miss Carolina."

I smile. "You can drive it about a hundred feet from the entrance while I get everyone out here."

"Yes, ma'am." Ronald grins.

Earl Ed stares at me like a fat kid anticipating a candy bar reward. "You can come with me and help," I say.

"Yes." He pumps his fist in the air and follows me up the porch steps.

I lead him to the laundry room to retrieve a large box of sparklers and a few grill lighters I stashed away last night. "Earl Ed, grab that tub, please." I motion toward a metal tub with my head.

He grabs it from the corner of the room and follows me back onto the porch. I open the sparklers and spread them inside the tub. He rocks on the balls of his feet, staring at the grill lighters like an impatient arsonist. After arranging the sparklers in an attractive array, I hand him a lighter.

"Wait until Jack and Bianca toss the garter and bouquet. Then you can light sparklers for everyone."

He nods, a little too enthusiastically. I press my lips together and almost regret handing him the lighter as I open the front door to make an announcement.

"May I have your attention please?" Though I am small, I am loud. Grandma always said that the two biggest things about me were my hips and my lips. Again, another jab at my Beyonce booty, I'm sure. Every head turns, even Chocolate's and Brownie's.

"The bride and groom are leaving in a minute. After they toss the bouquet and garter, you may get a sparkler. We will light them. You can line up out front to send the couple on their way. Exit through this door. Thank you."

After a beat of silence, the talking resumes as guests shuffle toward the door. I open it and stretch to reach the top latch that holds it open. Despite wearing heels, my five-foot-four stature isn't quite enough. A large hand reaches above mine, grazing my fingertips as it latches the top.

I'd know that hand anywhere. It's attached to the finger I almost dislocated when I ran off during a heart swear. "Thanks." I lower from my toes and smile at Jonah.

"No problem." He grins with all the confidence in the world, like he didn't just make an impossible bet with me.

Now that I stop and think about it, I'd love to work for myself. And I'd love it that much more if Jonah could double his money and do what he wants. But I don't subscribe to the same mindset as he and Jack. They all but had a thriving hardware store handed to them on a silver platter and pushed it aside for other ventures. Of course, given the recent success of the lodge and Jack selling some land to Ronald and Macon for the outdoors store, I'd say it paid off.

I'm not a risk taker, though, and it shows in every area of my life. My car is factory white, my wardrobe mainly jeans and T-shirts, and even my design tendencies lean toward neutrals and classic decor. Tonight's red dress is a rarity for me.

My daddy and Matthew work at the mines, while Tanner works for a large poultry supply chain. My mom stayed home with us. Entrepreneurship isn't exactly in my bloodline.

I brush past Jonah as a metaphorical signal to shift my mind back to the wedding. "Single women on the left, and single men on the right," I call to the crowd.

A mixture of all ages gathers in their designated spots. Some kids jump out front for the sheer joy of trying to catch something. Paul struts toward the center of the men's group, holding his customary to-go boxes. I bite back the snark dancing on my tongue. He's only holding three boxes, which is light for him. Plus, he was invited tonight.

One of the older church ladies asks me to hold her cane while she squares off in front of the porch. I hate to break it to her and Paul, but they're way past their prime. At least Misty isn't out there. She's now married to this Woody guy who works with Daddy. He's a nice guy, so I pray this one sticks.

Jack and Bianca join us on the porch, hand in hand. I pull a rocking chair in front of the steps for Bianca. She sits, and people yell and whistle as Jack removes her garter. He stands and holds it on his fingers like a slingshot. The men lunge in anticipation, only for Jack to ball it up in his hand. He walks over to Tanner, who isn't even in the lineup, and stuffs it in his shirt pocket.

"That was rigged!" Paul yells in protest, while other guys sigh. I laugh as Tanner takes a bow. By the surprise on his face, I can assure them it wasn't planned. My brother is a horrible actor.

Tanner jerks it from his pocket and shoves it at Jonah's chest. This sets off a mixture of moans and cheers from the crowd. Tanner announces that he no longer needs it and dips Hannah. She blushes as he kisses her, making even the moaners cheer. Leave it to my brother to steal the show.

I shuffle past the women as Bianca starts to stand. By the time she's turning to toss the bouquet behind her, I'm standing beside Ronald at the car.

"Why ain't you out there, darlin'?" he asks.

I shrug. "I've never been a fan."

"But you want to get married someday, right?"

I shrug again. I do, but I've always wanted to take care of myself. Settle my career and make my own way first. Besides, it's not like I've found that special spark with anyone yet. But I forego all that in favor of sarcasm when responding to Ronald. "I didn't see you out there for the garter."

"Touché, Miss Carolina, touché."

"Besides, I had to hold Ms. Eunice's cane." I smirk at him as I start back toward the front, instructing those not in the lineup to go ahead and form a line on either side of the car, stretching toward the porch.

I hand Ms. Eunice her cane, which I'm quite certain she doesn't need. Although Daisy may need it after the way Ms. Eunice elbowed her to the ground.

"Thank you, dear," she says in the sweetest voice, as if she didn't just go all WWE over a handful of roses.

Adrianne shuffles past the others to Bianca, for a picture with her prized bouquet. She had a height advantage on most. The photographer snaps a few photos of Adrianne and

Tanner with the bride and groom while I instruct Earl Ed to start lighting the sparklers.

He smiles like a Miss Apple Sauce Pageant contestant at the county fair as he lights each sparkler for passing guests. I grab the other lighter and stand on the opposite side of the porch steps, doing the same to speed up the progress. The few remaining guests file in line, and within minutes, the driveway is lit up like Woody and Misty's RV on Christmas Eve.

It would've saved time to let everyone light their sparklers from the one in front of them. However, I once witnessed an older woman's hair catching fire when a teenage boy lit her sparkler a little too close to her head, setting off the hairspray fumes on her gray curls.

After that, Adrianne changed to non-aerosol hairspray for her older clients that come in for a weekly "hair set," as they call it. I also made a note to never allow self-lighting of sparklers at any event I'm facilitating.

I light my own sparkler last and spread my arms to move back some of the people crowding the makeshift aisle of light. The photographer walks backwards in front of Jack and Bianca as they strut through the crowd. I'm impressed that someone can walk backwards in the dark, all while taking photos. I can barely walk backwards in the shallow end of a swimming pool while playing Marco Polo.

Sparklers start fizzing out as Jack and Bianca reach the old car. I hurry to grab the tin, making sure people put the extinguished remains inside. Ronald opens the back door for them, then hurries to the driver's seat. People cheer, clap, and whistle as the couple settles inside and Jack closes the door. He rolls down the window, and they hang out, waving to their guests.

If Apple Cart ever had celebrities, it would be these two. Jack, a self-made millionaire off outdoor ventures, and

Bianca, an Atlanta socialite moving to rural Alabama for love. If that's not a story fit for *Southern Living* . . . or at least the local paper.

Once the car is out of sight, guests start toward their own cars. I prop the bucket of sparkler remains on my hip and head inside. Earl Ed meets me at the porch and hands me his lighter. "Thanks again for letting me help light."

"You're welcome." A slight laugh escapes my lips. This dude is like thirty. He shouldn't be so enthusiastic about lighting sparklers.

I drop his lighter in the bucket with mine and climb the steps. Thankfully, it's the last day of December. Otherwise, the place would be crawling with bugs from leaving the door propped open that long.

Jack and Bianca wanted to marry on December 31 to start the New Year together as a married couple. Several people in their families complained that it interfered with people's holiday plans. As my job to advocate for the bride, I countered that most people would still be off work and that the wedding would end in plenty of time for everyone to enjoy New Year's Eve. On a personal note, I find it rather romantic that they would want to start the New Year as one.

Deep down, I know that's the real reason I keep agreeing to these weddings. It's the fairy tale that five-year-old Carolina hangs on to. Too many Disney movies and pampering as the youngest child and only girl led me to romanticize my life. I've got everything planned out for my own wedding. Except the groom.

Only a few people remain inside, all workers or family members. I pass through the kitchen to discard the smoky sticks in the large trash bin outside. The back door opens before I can reach for it. Jonah stands in front of me.

"Here." He takes the bucket and hands me the lighters before dumping it all with the plates and napkins inside the trash. "I'm gonna run to Jack's house and change. Then I'll come back and help you clean all this."

I lift a hand. "I think Bianca has enough hired help to do it all."

"Yeah, but Jack left me in charge of the lodge, so I want to make sure everything is in place."

"Thanks." I smile, the OCD part of me mentally high fiving him.

"And I don't want you working yourself crazy."

I laugh. "Oh really? Mr. Hey Come Design My Mansion."

He points a finger in my face. "You agreed to that."

"I did."

He shoves his hand in his pants pocket and pulls out the garter. "Take this thing. I'll go get changed and be right back."

Jonah jogs down the hill in the direction of Jack's house. I watch him disappear into the darkness, then stare down at the garter. My stomach pings at the idea of Jonah getting married next.

A lot of people thought he might marry Sasha. They dated for a while, and everyone went on about how sweet she was. She was okay, but not right for Jonah. I could tell he wasn't sold on her. Even if nobody else could.

I curl my fingers around the garter and ball it in my fist. Like it or not, Jonah will get married one day. It's likely that whoever he marries, no matter how she feels about me as a person, she won't want her husband having movie nights and random dinners with another woman.

It's time I face the fact that one day I'm going to lose him. Not completely, but a big part of him. I sigh and shove the garter into my own pocket. That gives me more reason to help him with this project. One last great adventure guaranteed with my best friend.

CHAPTER SEVEN

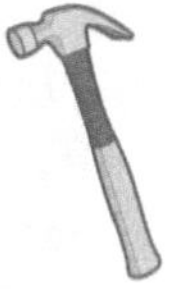

Jonah

It's the first Monday of the New Year, and hopefully the day I become a homeowner. I park my truck in front of the court-house and straighten my cap. Nothing like joining a bunch of old men for a good old property auction.

I climb the front steps to find three older men and Bradley already out front. This is my first official time attending an auction, but I have overheard some a time or two while walking downtown to or from lunch. I had to call and get accepted to come bid, and the mayor's secretary sounded delighted that a new person would be joining the usual crowd.

For the past few years, I've kept my eyes peeled for a project like this one. So when I saw the foreclosure tax sale notice in the *Apple Cart Weekly*, I called that day.

Wendall Jenkins peers at me from under his CO-OP cap. He's an old farmer from Wisteria, always looking to buy land. His beady eyes let me know he thinks I'm direct competition. I open my mouth to say I'm not here for land, but the door to the courthouse opens.

The probate judge makes a rare appearance, his shirt pressed stiff as a two-by-four. It's not doing him any favors by highlighting his protruding belly.

Judge Wright is old as dirt and doesn't care to socialize with anyone. Nobody's ever seen him outside of his home or the courthouse. He and his wife don't go to church, and she does all the shopping and errands. Rumor has it he's still working to keep up her affluent lifestyle.

He'd be the type to buy the mansion himself, except he already owns one a few miles from the Vanderburke home. Right on the edge of the Apple Cart golf course, which doubles as a cow pasture half the time. Yep, even our rich residents are rednecks.

Judge Wright shuts the door behind him and straightens his tie over his stomach. It falls halfway down his shirt. I clear my throat to keep from laughing as his bushy eyebrows come to a point on his forehead, making him resemble the fat red bird on *Angry Birds*. If his shirt were red rather than blue, I'd have no chance at withholding laughter.

Bradley leans against the wall as the judge greets us. I'm not sure if he's here to feel important or for backup in case a fight breaks out. As a passerby, I've never witnessed these auctions get out of hand. But I also never cared to pay much attention until now.

Wendall pulls a sweaty checkbook from his front overalls pocket. He's about a buck fifty soaking wet, so I'm not sure how his checks got so sweaty in this mild of weather. Maybe he's nervous. He cuts his eyes my way again, daring me to bid on land with his death stare.

I smile in return, and he scratches the side of his head in

confusion. I couldn't give two turnips about the land, and Wendall will find that out soon enough.

The judge goes over a few rules, all of which I ingrained in my brain the day I talked with his secretary. I've made darn sure that nothing on my account will keep me from purchasing the Vanderburke place.

After coughing up what sounds like a lung, he makes a gurgling sound and pulls a pair of glasses from his front pocket. They're the kind Clark Kent wears, but the allure is lost on Judge Wright's full face. He pulls a piece of paper from the same pocket and holds it out enough to rest his hand on his stomach the way pregnant women do.

"We'll start with the items in order of foreclosure."

My palms sweat and I shove them in my pockets. I have no idea when he will call out the mansion, but I want to make sure I'm ready to bid. Every time his mouth opens, my ears perk up like Chocolate's and Brownie's when Jack pulls a Popsicle from the freezer.

Most everything is land, much to the pleasure of Wendall. It only takes my silence through three properties for him to soften his glare at me and realize I'm not the threat he suspected. Wendall buys all three fields, and another man buys an old parking lot.

A house in town comes up, but nobody wants it due to zoning regulations. If I'm not mistaken, it will become county property at this point. Which is what I don't want to happen to the mansion.

"Last, we have the former Vanderburke residence. House with five point seven acres." My stomach churns as I wait for someone else to bid first so that I can outbid them.

Nobody says a word, so I raise my hand and make an offer. The three old men, Bradley, and Judge Wright all study me like I've lost my mind. It's not a crazy offer, but I'm wondering now if I've bid too high.

The judge glances around at everyone and asks, "Any other bids?"

Wendall opens his mouth. He would be the one to outbid me. Instead of speaking, he spits a lug of tobacco off the porch. Once it's clear he's not bidding, the judge turns to me.

He holds out a hand. "Looks like you got it, son." I shake his hand. He tightens his grip. "That is, if you have the money in place."

"Yes, sir, I do."

"All right, those of you who purchased property can come inside and sign the paperwork."

I fall in line behind Wendall and the parking lot guy, and Bradley comes in behind us, shutting the door. "Dude, you got that place for a steal," he whispers behind me.

"You think so?" I had thought so until everyone gave me weird looks.

"Absolutely. Word around town was you were gonna come up here and bid way more than that."

I stand still and exhale through my nostrils. It had to be Ashley and that stupid line of credit.

Bradley pats my shoulder. "Good thing Wendall didn't want it. You would've had to loosen those purse strings."

I climb back in my truck, a new homeowner. I've owned the place a matter of minutes, and I'm already itching to sell it. All in the name of proving my ability to get this home-building/flipping/renovating/whatevering business off the ground.

Before I leave the parking lot, I reach for my phone and select Carolina's contact. She answers after a few rings.

"Hello?"

"Hey, Carol. I got the house."

"You got the house!" She goes quiet for a moment, then speaks a muffled "excuse me." I hear a door open before she speaks again. "Sorry, I was in my cubicle. I'm outside now."

I chuckle. I forget she's working in an office all day now. Being the overachieving perfectionist that she is, she finished her classes before me and lined up a full-time internship at the place where she'd worked throughout college.

As a business major, I preferred to come home and work with Daddy or Jack, which satisfied my advisor. We both graduate in May, but I'm having to take two classes right now to finish.

"I got it for a good price too. Depending on how the reno goes, I might not have to take out a loan."

"Jonah, that's awesome."

My heart swells as I hear the smile behind her voice. I picture her pretty face and can't wait to have her working on the house with me.

"That means—" I stop myself before saying that it will take less money than I thought to win our little wager. I don't want to bring that up or jinx myself in case the rehab on the place sucks more money than I planned. "You have more money to work with on the design." I park in front of my new home and hop out of the truck.

"Good to know." Her voice is still cheerful, so I saved myself on that one. "I just hope we can pull this off in a few months."

I rip the caution tape from around the porch banisters and reach for the doorknob, preparing to jiggle it. Then I remember I have a key in my pocket. My trespassing days are over.

"Of course we can. You and me, we're perfect together." I push the door open and swallow. "Working together," I add, to not give away my true feelings.

I leave the front door open to air out the musty smell.

The sunlight streaming in highlights all the dust circulating. I walk to the kitchen and stop under the doorway, resting my arm on the top molding. "Besides, this house has good bones."

When I drop my hand, the molding comes down with it, almost hitting my head.

"Jonah, what was that?"

"Nothing." I clear my throat and kick the broken wood aside with the toe of my boot. "I just wanted to call and give you the good news." Sawdust flecks my face, and I blink up at the rotting wood above my head. I think I'll start with knocking down this wall.

Carolina

My first day as a full-time intern did not go as planned. I've worked part-time for this place the past two years, mainly keeping the front desk and answering phones. Now that I'm an actual interior design intern, I expected to jump right in and do real work. Not that answering phones and making coffee isn't work, but that's not exactly what I'm going to college for.

Perhaps my boss, Audrey, put this false hope in me. During my interview last month, she raved about what an asset I'd been all this time and how she loved all my projects she'd seen so far. I'd asked her opinion on several occasions before starting a design assignment for class. Other times, she'd asked what I was working on, offering advice and complimenting my natural talent.

Once she called to tell me I got the internship, I practically flipped with joy. If part-time receptionist was sticking my foot in the door, this job would shove the door wide enough to fit at least my full leg inside. All I need is to get my hip in the door to hold it open.

This morning, my face lit up like a June bug when Audrey invited me to come to a design meeting with her and her top two designers. Then she had me get everyone's breakfast order and run to the mall Starbucks. When I returned, they were finished with the actual meeting and chatting about their holiday.

She then gave me a ton of spreadsheets to check, asking that I update the data in our client database. I'm totally good with that, since I'm young and technically not even an employee. However, the day ended with me asking if she wanted to see some of my new designs, only to have her shoo me away, saying, "Please work on your projects on your own time." She's never not had a minute to glance at one of my plans.

Maybe it's her time of the month or she's still upset about how this season of *Sweet Magnolias* ended. Whatever the case, this internship is shaping up to be barista and file shuffler with a bump in pay. Which would be totally fine, if I could somehow regain Audrey's attentiveness.

I park outside my apartment and sigh. I shouldn't get so down. It's only the first day. I should be grateful for decent pay and an opportunity. I'm certain Audrey doesn't have much for me to do yet after coming off the Christmas holidays.

Grabbing my purse and cardigan, I climb out of my car and lock the door behind me. Once I get to our apartment, I hear the TV. My roommate, Kendra, loves any reality show to do with weddings. Cake decorating, finding a wedding dress, flower shops, planning weddings. You name it, she's watched it. I'd bet my bottom dollar she's got one on right now.

Sure enough, I open the door to TLC and a woman in a bridal shop. "Hi." I greet Kendra first, as she's engrossed in the world's largest binder. It's filled with magazine clippings and notes and washi tape in floral patterns.

"Hey, welcome back," she answers, without looking up from studying a page filled with flower arrangements.

I've tried to convince her to set up some Pinterest boards to store all her wedding ideas. She looked at me like I'd proposed she cut off her arm. We've roomed together the past three years, and even before she got engaged, she had a wedding planner.

She claims that she started it in high school when she first discovered bridal magazines. Then after getting serious with her fiancé freshman year, she amped up the clippings and notes. I find it a little obsessive, but who am I to judge. I have my own planner—be it much slimmer and less subject specific. Not to mention that I haven't had anything to do with a man since . . .

"Hey, Carolina."

I carefully turn my gaze from the TV, where a woman is wearing a hideous feathered dress with a veil made of sequins, to the voice belonging to the man in my mind.

"Daniel?"

"Yeah, what's up?"

"You're here . . . in my kitchen." I press my lips tightly and enter the kitchen area, setting my purse and cardigan on the countertop.

"Kendra let me in a few minutes ago. I hope you don't mind."

Keeping my lips closed, I shake my head and stare down at the stone surface in front of me. Not wanting to meet his eyes, I turn back toward the couch. Kendra looks up at me and wiggles her eyebrows. "He wanted to surprise you."

"Well, he did that," I say, as if he's not standing right behind me.

Daniel circles the counter and sits on the stool beside me, Diet Coke in hand. Why is he drinking my drinks?

He takes a large gulp, then sets the can behind him and leans back, resting his elbows on the counter. "I wanted to take you to dinner since I haven't seen you in a few weeks."

My mouth goes dry. I thought I made it pretty clear that I didn't want to see him these past few weeks.

Daniel is one of those cliche "looks good on paper" guys. He's an engineering student on scholarship from Illinois. He's athletic, but not to a dumb jock, annoying level. He played football in high school but was better at academics. He's also an Eagle Scout and worked as a church camp counselor last summer. Add to that sandy blond hair and muscles, and yep, he's a real catch.

I'm sure he's had plenty of other bait dangled in front of him, so I'm not sure why he keeps swimming around my pond. I'm also not sure why I keep tossing him back. Guys like Daniel don't come around every day. If I had better sense, I would've fried him in peanut oil and covered him in cocktail sauce by now.

Instead, I urge him to float downstream while I focus on my career. Well, that's the excuse I give. In all honesty, there's no spark there. No blinking lights in my face saying, "He's the one." Plus, I don't want to end up in Illinois. There's no way I can say pajamas like they do.

"Can I take you to dinner?"

My mouth is now dry as a bone, and swallowing only makes it worse. I reach for the Diet Coke, which is mine anyway, and down about half of it. I sigh and wipe the residue from my lips with my finger. "Sure. It beats eating cereal."

"Great." Poor guy. He's grinning like a possum. Not like I just agreed to go for free food and to escape another episode of *Say Yes to the Dress*.

I snatch my purse and cardigan, then follow him out our door. Kendra meets my eyes when I pass and gives me a thumbs-up. I clinch my teeth into a pitiful smile and slam the door behind us. Daniel leads me across the parking lot, toward the side of the building. Of course he parked in the overflow lot to not take any spaces designated for residents.

Always the Midwestern gentleman, Daniel opens his car door for me. He also drives an old, restored Mustang in fire red, which only adds to his impressive resume. Seriously, why is he wasting his time trying to woo me? Maybe he likes playing hard to get or he's one of those rare unicorns who is perfect in everyone's eyes but his own. A ball of insecurity because he can't see how great he is.

That would still make him saner than me. I *can* see how great he is and I still don't want to be with him. Ugh. Maybe I should stay home and eat Cap'n Crunch while listening to Kendra go on about bridal shower themes. That would make me appreciate this golden-haired stallion taking me to eat hot food.

Soon as I sit, he shuts my door. I buckle my seat belt and settle my purse by my feet. "Where are we going?"

"I was thinking maybe Italian."

"Sounds great." That's the most excited I've sounded since approximately 8:05 this morning, when Audrey asked me to join them in the conference room. Maybe a plate of Alfredo will turn this day around.

Daniel talks about his week on the way to the Italian diner in town. I feign interest in stories of watching his nieces play in the snow and giving sled rides to little kids on his family farm. My mind is split between my new job and Jonah buying the house.

After today, I get why he needs this project to prove his skills. If I can decorate and design it fit for an affluent family to purchase, then I could prove my worth as a designer to Audrey. Prove I have an eye for more than simply color-coding spreadsheets.

"I hate that I couldn't go to the wedding," Daniel says.

"Oh, you'd have been bored." That was my excuse when he'd hinted for an invitation. We hadn't gone on a date in more than two weeks when he ran into me on campus and asked about my holiday plans. I happened to mention the wedding, and he started asking questions. Five minutes later, he was saying things like, "That sounds fun," and "I've always wanted to see where you grew up."

I tend to be forward with people I know best and dance around directness with others. That's why I haven't flat out told Daniel I just want to be friends. Instead, I've tried to leave him hints to let him down easy. After enough hooks in his jaw, I'd assumed, he'd swim away a little scarred, but smart enough to stay downstream.

Instead, this dumb bass keeps coming back for more.

"I'm sure I could've found something fun to do. It was at that hunting camp place, right?"

"The reception was. The groom is the owner."

"Is that Jack?"

"Yeah, Jonah's cousin."

"Oh yeah, Jonah." Daniel's voice sours a tinge when he says Jonah's name. "How is he?"

"Good. He's about to renovate a house."

"Oh."

"Yeah . . ." My voice trails off and I awkwardly stare out my window.

"You know, I'd really like to meet your parents sometime."

"Why?" The word falls out before I can stop it. I know why. I just don't understand why.

Daniel looks at me, his blue eyes perplexed. "Haven't you ever wanted to meet my parents?"

I slide toward the window and shrug. "I haven't given it much thought. I mean, we've only gone on a handful of dates, like a month ago. We've only kissed twice."

"Three times," he corrects me quickly.

He flips his blinker on and turns into the restaurant. I face the front, my stomach tightening. No amount of free pasta is worth this.

"Daniel?"

"Yeah?" His baby-blue eyes bore into my soul. Even under the parking lot streetlight, he's hot.

I tuck a loose strand of hair behind my ear and twist my mouth. What is wrong with me? Why can't I tell this guy straight up that I don't want him? Or better yet, why don't I want him?

"I really have to pee."

"Oh." His eyes widen like a can of biscuits bursting open.

"Can you get us a table, and I'll meet you inside?" My hand is already on the door handle.

"Of course." Daniel starts opening his own door as I open mine, get out, and slam it shut.

I scuttle across the parking lot in my ballet flats, not stopping until I'm within the safety of a bathroom stall.

CHAPTER EIGHT

Jonah

I'm back in my trailer heating up a Tupperware of lasagna Mama sent with me when my phone barks. I'm starting to enjoy Carolina's new ringtone a little too much. I answer the dog before it howls, which is indication the call is about to go to voicemail.

"Hello?"

"Jonah." Carolina's using her infamous whisper-yell. "I need you." Her voice is rushed, which means she's stressed.

I give myself a glorious second to relish in the words "I need you" coming from her lips. I'm brought back to reality too quickly by a whooshing sound in the background.

"Is that a toilet flushing?"

"Yes, I'm in the bathroom at the Italian place."

I wipe a hand down my face as the microwave beeps. "You know I don't mind, but can you please check that thingy on the bathroom wall before I run to the gas station for tampons?"

"No, not Code Red!" This time her voice is more yell than whisper.

I sigh with relief. I've had to get her tampons twice before. One time when she couldn't get Kendra on the phone, and one time in high school when she was too embarrassed to tell anyone else.

"Then what's the problem?" I take the lasagna out of the microwave and fumble it onto the counter, shaking out my hand from the heat. I need to invest in a fish mitt like Jack's, or just steal one of his.

"Code D."

"Ah, date gone bad?"

"Date, Daniel, Dinner, Desperate. Whichever D you want to use."

I shake my head and hold the phone to my ear with my shoulder as I carefully open the container. When will Carol learn? I told her a month ago to pee or get off the pot with this guy. She'll go on a date with him and brag about his credentials, then shy away when he wants to see her more.

Not that I want her to like him in that way, but as president of the Carolina Nash fan club, I sympathize with the dude.

"What do you need me to do?"

"Show up here, come talk to us, and I'll invite you to join us."

"Can't I just pick you up and take you home?"

"No. I don't want to hurt his feelings."

"And inviting me to crash as a third wheel won't do that?"

"No, he's way too nice. I need time to think of how to tell him I don't like him like that."

And that's all she needed to say for me to agree to this

crazy scheme. "All right. Give me five minutes." I stare down at my boxers and bare legs. "Make it ten. I gotta put on some pants."

"Thank you, Jonah. You're the best."

"Yeah."

I hang up and re-cover the lasagna, then toss it in the refrigerator and go to my bedroom. This isn't the way I envisioned my first date with Carol, but I'll take what I can get.

I step into the jeans I took off thirty minutes ago and run my fingers over my hair. The place isn't all that fancy, but Mama raised me to not wear a cap in a restaurant.

On my way out, I grab my wallet and keys from the dresser and turn out all the lights. My next-door neighbors are sitting in lawn chairs, drinking cheap beer. I wave to them as I climb in my truck and drive the few minutes to the Italian place. It's Papa's Pasta, but I rarely hear anyone call it that.

Before even one song ends on the radio, I'm looking for a parking spot. I find a space near the back, as its now prime time for supper. My stomach growls and I huff. I could be on my couch eating lasagna right now. Instead, I'm going to have to pay for lasagna that isn't as good as Mama's. Oh, and I'm having to wear pants.

Not bothering to lock my twenty-year-old Ford, I shut the door and hurry toward the restaurant. I enter behind a group of girls and a few families, then shuffle toward the dining area.

"Jonah." I turn toward Carol's voice and smile. Natural as I can, I stroll up to the booth where she and Daniel are sitting.

"Hey, guys."

"Hello." Daniel gives me a forced nod. I hold my hand out, daring him to shake it. He stares at it like I've covered it in dog poop.

At last, he gives it a quick shake, then slides his hand under the table. He faces Carolina, who widens her eyes at me. "So what are you doing here, Jonah?"

"The same thing you guys are. I came to eat." I chuckle, and Carol joins me with a nervous squeak. I'm so better at playing it cool than her. She gets her bad acting skills from her brother.

"Why don't you join us?" She smirks at me, then smiles at Daniel.

"Well, I mean, I was gonna just get something to go." I thumb toward the counter where people place the takeout orders.

"We don't mind," she says.

Daniel frowns at her, then puts on a slightly more pleasant face for me. "It's fine by me, if it is with Carolina."

I shrug as if I'm not about to purposely ruin this date. "Sure."

As I lean toward Carol's side of the booth, I decide to have a little fun with this. After all, she's the reason I'm missing out on Mama's lasagna. I step in the other direction and slide in next to Daniel.

His big, muscled arm tenses as I brush beside it. Carolina sips her Diet Coke, her cheeks shaky. That's her "I'm trying to hold back a laugh" face. I scoot back against the booth in case she loses it and spits her Coke on me.

Daniel stares at his menu. I lean toward him. "Let me see what's on here." Carol laughs a little. I don't look at her, or I'll totally lose it.

"Have you decided on an order?" I raise my eyes to a waitress old enough to be our grandmother. In sloth-like fashion, she writes out their orders on a pad. Then she turns to me just as slowly. With all the enthusiasm of someone who's about to have a kidney transplant, she says, "You weren't here before."

"No, ma'am. So I'd also like a sweet tea with my order." I add a pizza, since any pasta I eat will be a letdown compared to what's waiting for me at home.

She takes her time writing my order too, before saying, "I'll get that right out." Then she shuffles away slow as molasses, making me doubt our food will be "right out." I'd best settle in and make Code D count.

I lean back against the booth. Daniel sits stick straight, as if he's afraid one sudden move might cause him to touch me again. I should've pulled up a chair on the end, or even sat with Carol. But this is way more entertaining.

"So, Daniel, how's engineering treating you?"

"Good, thanks." He turns his head toward me, then briefly snaps it back to face Carol when he realizes how close we're sitting. "Carolina says you're renovating a house."

"About to—I just took ownership this morning."

"Good for you," he replies, before taking a huge gulp of his water.

I haven't been around him much, but I've never witnessed him drink anything but water. An awkward quietness hangs in the air a few minutes. Then Carolina starts sharing about her day at work.

"That doesn't make any sense. She knows how talented your designs are," Daniel says, not taking his eyes off Carol.

"He's right," I add. "I tried to tell her she could start her own business."

"She really could," Daniel agrees.

He smiles at me and doesn't snap his head away this time. I scoot even closer to him, and then he looks forward. This game is quite amusing. A few more inches and I could have him climbing the wall.

Grandma Snail tiptoes back with our order. I'm impressed that it didn't take long at all, and glad to have something to do besides chat about my day with Daniel.

He's an all-right dude, I guess. I've never heard of him being anything but respectful toward Carolina. He's just all wrong for her. And clearly, she agrees with me, or she wouldn't have enacted Code D.

We started the codes back in high school, when one of us needed out of a jam. She's pulled Code D way more than me. A guy gets drunk when he's supposed to drive her home. A blind date turns out way wrong. Typical guy drama.

I must admit, it surprised me that she pulled it on Daniel. He doesn't strike me as the type a girl would want to be saved from. However, I'd crawl through a barbed-wire fence naked if Carol needed me to. So what's sharing a little Italian with the Mustang Stallion?

Daniel got a pizza too, but he blots the top of it, then sets the greasy napkin aside. I eat mine as is.

"Want my roll?"

"Well, yeah," I answer Carol, grabbing her roll.

She doesn't like the ones here since they smother them with lots of garlic butter. I love their rolls and always eat hers. We've eaten so many meals together that we know one another's preferences for most food items, including the restaurants we frequent.

Daniel glances at the roll in my hand as I bite off half of it. I hold it up to his nose. "Want a bite?" I ask with a mouthful of bread.

He shakes his head and inches toward the wall. Carolina raises a napkin to her mouth, even though she hasn't yet taken a bite of her pasta. She's hiding a smile. I can see it in her eyes.

The next half hour goes just like that. Me pushing Daniel's patience for no other reason than to get another laugh, smile, or anything else I can out of Carol. Pretty much the same reactions I'd want from her if this were a date just between the two of us.

Maybe one day, it will be.

Carolina

By the time the waitress brings our checks, I can't decide if Daniel has loosened up or simply given up. Either way, I'm hoping this proves I've paved a permanent parking spot for him in the friend zone. I'll have to commend Jonah for sitting beside him. That was a nice touch, and one that almost made me spit Diet Coke across the room.

Just in case he hasn't gotten the hint, I drop my debit card on top of the check when the waitress comes back. "Put the Coke and Alfredo on this card, please."

"Okay," she answers, long and drawn out.

Daniel starts to protest as she turns away, but I reach across the table and put my hand on his arm, then shake my head to stop him. He frowns at me. "Carolina, I told you I was taking you to eat."

"And you did, but you never said anything about paying."

"I always pay on dates, you know that."

"You never said this was a date." My neck itches with the guilt of throwing this back on him.

Of course Daniel meant for it to be a date. I should've politely declined and ate my cereal at the kitchen sink like a single mother on Saturday morning. Instead, I let my stomach get the best of me. I also didn't want to hear Kendra scold me all night for turning him down.

Daniel's handsome face falls into a lost puppy sort of state. I jerk my hand from his arm like it's a poisonous snake.

Just great. In trying not to hurt him, I've hurt him. Meanwhile, Jonah sits there, staring at me as if silently asking what he should do.

We sit in silence for a moment before Jonah speaks. "So Daniel, what did Santa bring you this year?"

I slump down in the booth, my head cemented against the back cushion as Daniel gives him a bewildered look. Like a lot of people, he doesn't get Jonah's humor. I can't say I get it either, but at least I know when he's attempting to be funny.

It finally clicks and Daniel goes into detail about the new stereo system his parents bought him, which his dad helped him install in the Mustang before coming back to college. I turn my head and sigh in relief when the waitress creeps toward us, papers and cards in hand.

"Keep the change." Jonah grins at her.

She smiles back and nods. "Thanks, son."

Ninety percent of the time, he pays with cash. Jack does the same. I'm not sure if it's because both their parents did the same or because they don't want to leave a paper trail. Who knows with those two?

She holds out the remaining two receipts and slides her glasses up the bridge of her nose with her forefinger. "The Alfredo," she mutters more to herself, handing me my receipt and card.

I scribble in an amount for the tip, then sign and hand it back. Daniel signs and returns his slip as well.

As soon as the little old waitress scoots away from our booth, I stand and grab my purse. I start toward the door, both guys following me. I'm almost propelled forward when I push the door open. I glance back to Daniel holding it open behind me, smiling.

How should I take that? Is he trying to convince me this is a date after all, or is that just the typical Daniel gentleman act? Jonah meets my bewildered look from behind him and shrugs.

"Thanks." I give Daniel a smile as I step into the parking lot. I'm afraid it's more of a "bless your heart" smile than one of genuine gratitude.

Daniel stops once we're all away from the door and stares at Jonah. "Nice seeing you again, Jonah."

Jonah grabs his hand and gives it a firm shake. Daniel clinches his teeth like it pains him to shake his hand. I'm sure it has nothing to do with wiry Jonah giving a death grip, but rather Daniel not wanting to touch him.

"Carolina, are you ready?" Daniel focuses on my eyes, his mouth now relaxed.

I freeze, not sure how I need to play this. Jonah senses my hesitation and takes the lead. "I can drop her off at her apartment."

"I planned on taking her home," Daniel contests.

I take a step back as the two guys lock eyes and size each other up. One tall and thin, the other short and stocky. If they were peacocks, feathers would be fanned out and flying high.

"I just want to be friends!" My lips tingle when the word "friends" leaves my tongue. There, I finally said it—or shouted it.

Both guys snap their heads my way, as does everyone else in the parking lot. The numbness on my lips travels to my tongue and throat, preventing me from saying anything further. Not that I need to.

Daniel's crystal eyes glisten with sadness, like puddles of teardrops gathering. *Please don't cry.*

He doesn't, which eases my guilt a smidge. Daniel is way too put together to spill his emotions out on the asphalt like I just did. Plus, it's not like we have this grand history together.

Jonah's face is an emotion I can't quite interpret, which is odd. I can read all his faces. Happy, sad, mad, sleepy, stressed. So basically, any emotion used to name one of Snow White's Seven Dwarfs. But this face is new. I'd have to say it might be a concoction of frustration and worry, with a pinch of relief for garnishment.

He's encouraged me to just be honest with Daniel. "Sit down with the guy and tell him you don't want to date. It's that simple. Just tell the dude how you really feel."

That's easy for Jonah to say. It's not him. He doesn't understand what it's like to not ever want to let anyone down. As the only daughter who followed both a perfect child and a free spirit, I wanted nothing more than to please my parents and live up to my sweet princess status. My streak of perfectionism carried over into every area of my life the older I got.

Even to the point that I couldn't find it in me to admit to anyone I didn't want to date a perfect guy like Daniel. Anyone except Jonah.

My head pounds as if my heart is beating between my ears. The people passing by eventually get in their cars or turn their heads. Daniel's sad eyes go a little cold, and an overall shock covers his face. Jonah inches toward me as if he may need to prop me up for whatever happens next.

"I can drop her off," he says low enough so that only Daniel and I can hear him.

Daniel's eyes shift to Jonah and study him for a long minute. He draws in a breath, and I swallow, anticipating what might happen next. In true Daniel fashion, he relaxes his shoulders and exhales, then nods his head and walks away.

No harsh words, no thrown punches, no anything.

I drop my own shoulders and lean against the car behind

me. Once my butt hits the hood, the horn goes crazy and the front lights flash. I squeal and hop up.

"Hey!" a middle-aged business guy yells as he marches outside.

"Come on," Jonah grunts at me as he snatches my wrist and pulls me toward his truck. We climb in and screech out of the parking lot like Bonnie and Clyde running from the law.

My heart pounds in my chest as I scramble to buckle my seat belt, then plaster my head against the headrest. Jonah turns down a back road so that the guy can no longer see his truck. When he slows down and turns toward my apartment, we both burst out laughing.

No matter what, I can always count on Jonah to save me from my own craziness and lighten the mood. He's my true ride or die.

Jonah

"You should probably leave," I belt out to an empty kitchen. The sound of my sledgehammer hitting the wall adds an offbeat acoustic to the Chris Stapleton song pulsing through my earbuds.

I didn't like how closed off the kitchen was to the living room. So when the molding crumbled, I made an easy decision that this wall needed to come down. I'll add two wooden beams where it's load bearing. Maybe a third if I decide to take out the wall to the dining room as well. Regardless, I plan on expanding that opening too.

There's something primal and therapeutic about beating things to shreds with a sledgehammer. I graduated top ten in my class in high school and do well in college, but I've always preferred working with my hands. I get it from Daddy, I guess. He enjoys building things and helping people find all the right tools for every project in the store. We both have a business mind too. I think that has a lot to do with him assuming I'd take over the store instead of Jack.

However, Jack's proven himself with the lodge. And I intend to do the same with this house flip.

A few more swings of the hammer, then I let loose again, joining Chris for a duet on the chorus. A clapping noise rings out when I stop singing. I turn my head to see if it's Papa Rat tap dancing on the tile. Instead, I find Carol leaned against the counter, applauding me.

I flinch, both shocked and embarrassed to see her. I jerk the earbuds out and dip my head.

She laughs. "I didn't mean to scare you. The door was unlocked."

I lift my gaze, taking in her ripped jeans and Armadillos sweatshirt. She's dressed to work. "I left work early and decided to come by and see if I could help."

"Thanks." I smile, trying to ignore the heat in my cheeks at her catching my pathetic concert.

She picks up a bag of Doritos and a bottle of sweet tea I haven't noticed until now. Carolina is the only thing that could keep my attention from Doritos.

"Trade?" She holds them toward me. I hold up my earbuds.

"Nope, that." She nods to the hammer in my other hand.

I stick the earbuds in my pocket and hand over the hammer in exchange for something equally as satisfying as slamming things. And way easier on my joints.

The hammer weighs down Carol's hand, making it obvious she didn't expect it to be so heavy. She lifts it to elbow height and hits the wall. A few flecks of drywall fall, and she hits it a few more times, grunting.

"Ugh," Carolina moans as she drops the hammer on the floor. The tile chips and she gasps. "Jonah, I'm so sorry."

I laugh around a mouthful of chips and fan my hand her

way. "Do you seriously think I'm gonna keep this yellow tile?"

She shrugs.

"The yellow brick road will be the next to go." I nod. "And it looks like that needs to be your job."

A slight smile crosses her lips as she wipes her brow with the back of her hand. I set the bag of chips back on the counter and take a sip of tea. Then I cross the shattered floor to her.

"Stand back," I warn her before wiping the cheesy chip residue down my pants and picking up the hammer. "If you're hitting the wall, you need to come up and swing down. Like this." I lift the hammer over my head and beat down against the wall, creating a dust storm of drywall as huge chunks hit the ground.

Carol coughs and fans her face.

"Sorry. I guess I'm used to this."

She half-smiles to show she's accepted my apology. "Can I try again?"

"Yep." I hold out the hammer, and she takes it. This time, she uses two hands so it doesn't weigh her down. She struggles to lift it over head.

Carol's always been on the smaller side and isn't exactly athletic. Of course, Tanner took full advantage of this growing up by slinging her over his shoulder and body slamming her on the couch whenever she aggravated him. The sheer fact she survived two decades of that toughened her a good bit. Yet it did nothing to help her lack of upper body strength.

"Here, let me help." I step behind her and wrap my hands around hers, then lift the hammer above our heads.

Her shoulder blades press against my chest, and I suck in a whiff of her citrus shampoo. I'd gladly stand like this for hours, holding a metal weight above my head, so she could stay snuggled against me.

"Now what?"

Her question snaps me out of my citrus coma, and I bring the hammer down toward the wall, breaking more sheetrock to shreds.

She laughs as I lower our hands away from the wall, my arms wrapping around her when I do. I swallow back my desire to squeeze her tightly against me and unfurl my hands from around hers.

Before I can step away, she turns around. Our eyes meet, and I want to kiss her. I often want to kiss her when she's this close to me. But never as much as now. Something has shifted between us, and I search her eyes for permission.

I'm struggling for the appropriate way to act when she pushes the hammer toward my chest. My eyes lower to it, killing whatever vibe we had between us. I take the hammer and drop it behind me on the tile, not caring if it cracks.

I've missed my window of opportunity like a coward. Or like a smart businessman and loyal friend? I choose to believe the latter. Harboring a secret crush since middle school might come off cowardly, but not so much when I consider it might cost me my best friend. Plus my new business partner.

Carol leaves my side, and I stare at the ugly tile, mourning the moment.

"We're going to make this place look great," she says. I raise my eyes to her standing a few feet back with her hands on her hips. She's scanning the room, her eyes wide. That means she's in planning mode.

I sit on the countertop and follow her gaze around the room. "I can't wait to see what you do with it."

"Well, I'll do what you want, of course. It's your house."

"Yeah, but I granted you total creative control, remember?" I lift the corner of my mouth in a crooked grin.

She drops her arms and joins me. Her arm brushes mine when she pushes herself onto the countertop and scoots back. I stare down at her tennis shoes dangling beside my calves. After letting out a deep sigh, she puts her hand on my knee.

My chest tightens. *What is she doing? Should I reach out and hold her hand?*

"Thank you for that."

"For what?" I ask like an ignorant moron.

She pats my knee, then draws her hand back to her lap, sucking a string of electricity from my body when she does. "Giving me creative control."

"Of course. I told you I needed you to make this house a home."

She smiles with her mouth, but her eyes stay sad.

"What's the matter?"

Carolina shakes her head and draws her lips into a slight pout. "Nothing."

"Come on, Carol." I nudge her arm with my elbow.

She fixates on her hands as she picks at her pink fingernails. A minute later, she looks up. "I'm afraid I glamorized working at Home-Sweet-Home, or any design studio."

"What do you mean?"

Carol shifts on the counter. "I naively assumed I'd go in there and hit the ground running since I had such a good relationship with the owner."

"And?"

"I needed to be knocked down a few notches, I guess. I mean, I'm only interning." She lifts then lowers one shoulder, grazing her arm against mine. The hairs on my forearms stand at her touch.

"There's nothing wrong with wanting to do more."

"I know, and it's not so much the whole internship thing as I'm not sure it would be any different as an employee."

"How so?"

"I get the feeling I'd have to move way up the ladder to have any of my ideas considered."

"Ah, that shouldn't be such a problem."

She wipes her hands down her face and blinks up at the ceiling. "This may sound terrible, but I'm not sure that's something I want to pursue."

I wrinkle my brow, unable to imagine Carol doing anything other than designing and decorating. She's always been artistic and fell in love with interior design after our college career day in high school.

She continues, obviously attuned to my confusion. "I want to design and decorate and all that. It's just I'm not sure I like having to deal with the bureaucracy that comes with working at a firm. What I enjoy most is sitting down one-on-one with the client and talking out their vision. Not designing a portion of a large rebrand for an office building or remodeling a spare room for a dog nursery."

"People have dog nurseries?"

She laughs. "Apparently so, since one of the partners asked me to help sketch out her plans."

I shake my head. "Some people have more money than brains."

After smirking, she adds, "I love giving a family their dream home or a bride her perfect setting. Helping make lasting memories for people. That's what I want to do."

I glance at the popcorn ceiling before smiling back at her. "You can start with this house." I hop off the counter and grab the hammer. "One tile at a time."

She stands and takes the hammer from my hand. Our fingers brush momentarily. I'd prefer to help her swing at the wall until my arms go numb, and I have no other reason than wanting to wrap them around her and rest in her embrace. But that's not what she needs right now.

Right now, she needs to smash something.

I nod at the floor where she accidentally chipped a piece earlier. "Go ahead." Then I pick up a crowbar and go back to the wall.

If I can't hold Carol, then I need to smash something too.

Carolina

I pull my ponytail tighter and smooth out my sweatshirt before bounding downstairs to the kitchen. My daddy is semi-retired, taking most of the summer off to travel. In the cooler months, he still works at the mines full-time. My mama happily fills her days cooking and researching new places for them to visit when summer rolls around again.

Mama stands in the kitchen, pouring a cup of coffee. "Morning, sweetie. Want something to eat? Your daddy didn't leave any bacon, but there's some banana bread."

"That sounds good." I'm not a bit surprised about the bacon. When my brothers still lived at home, they'd stand by the stove and eat it as soon as Mama dropped it on a plate. Naturally, they got that from Daddy.

She reaches for a plate, but I stop her. I pull off a paper towel. "I'll eat in the car."

"Where are you going this early?"

It's not terribly early. Though I guess it is for a Saturday, which is the day I tend to sleep in.

"I'm helping Jonah with a project."

"The house?"

"Yeah." I wrinkle my nose. "How did you know?"

Mama wipes her glasses with the tail end of her shirt and

readjusts them on her face. They tend to fog up when she's cooking. "Through the grapevine."

"Uh-huh. You mean the apple orchard."

She laughs. That's my way of making the old gossip cliche a little more specific to Apple Cart.

"It may have started there, but I heard it in Mary's Diner from Sheila, who heard it at the salon from someone who heard it at church."

"Church? A Sunday hasn't even come and gone since he bought it."

"No, but a deacon's meeting and Wednesday night service have."

I shake my head. "Oh, the apple orchard."

Mama half grins, reading my irritation. She hints often how she can't wait for me to move back, even though I speak more about staying in Auburn than not. Truth is, I love small towns. I just think it'd be nice to start over in one where half the town hasn't either changed your diaper in the church nursery or tried to get you to date someone in their family—some both.

I take a bite of my bread and sigh as I chew. Mama smiles widely now, her thin face growing fuller.

"Sure you don't want some coffee?"

I shake my head. "No thanks." I grab a water from the refrigerator with my free hand.

Mama doesn't keep enough creamer on hand for the kind of coffee I prefer. I'm also not a fan of sweet tea, which makes Daddy say if he didn't play such a major role in my coming into the world, he'd swear I was adopted.

"Do you need to pack a lunch?" Mama pats the back of her short hair and stares at the refrigerator.

"No, ma'am." I glance at the time on the microwave. "I need to get going." Jonah's such an old man, he probably beat the sun there.

"Okay, love you, have fun."

"Love you," I call as I head out the back door to my car.

Mama never tells us goodbye, always, "Love you, have fun." If it's dark outside, she adds "watch for deer," no matter what time of year it is. Tanner jokes that he's going to put "have fun and watch for deer" on her tombstone. Nobody thinks that's funny but him.

I balance the piece of bread on my lap as I drive to the house. Our neighborhood is more downtown, and the mansion is on the golf course. If you could call it that . . . I snort. It's an open field owned by the county. They cut it for hay and intermittently put cows on it. When the hay isn't overgrown and it's sans cows, it serves as a golf course to the well-off people living nearby.

For some reason, the wealthiest in town like the illusion of living at a golf course, even if it is a cow pasture.

The apple orchard isn't far either, which makes for a nice backdrop to the houses beyond the field. However, the Vanderburke Mansion sits squarely in front of the "golf course" for the full effect.

I park out front beside Jonah's truck. I wad the paper towel of breadcrumbs into a ball and stuff it in the trash bag I keep under my seat. My oldest brother, Matthew, swears I'll get it stuck on the pedals one day and cause a wreck. He's forever parenting me. It's not like a few napkins and Diet Coke cans could weigh down a gas pedal.

Music fills the air when I open my car door. As I walk toward the house, I notice the windows are open. It's still a little crisp outside, and I hug my arms around my waist to combat the breeze.

I turn the tiny doorknob and let myself in. Jonah is expecting me this time, which would explain why the only voice I hear is the one on the radio. I must've really scared him yesterday, or he'd have his earbuds in again.

As soon as I walk in, Jonah waves to me from the gap that was once a wall. I wave back and laugh. Sheetrock covers the floor in a heap around his feet.

"Good morning." I greet him as I step across a pile of debris.

"I see you got your beauty sleep."

I roll my eyes, unsure if that's a jab at my homely appearance or for showing up a little after eight. When he laughs, I hurl my water bottle at his head.

He catches it with ninja-like reflexes and chugs half of it. "Ahhh." He wipes his mouth with the back of his hand. "Thanks for that. Saved me a trip to my toolbox for a cold drink."

I shake my head and step back to assess the mess he's made. "You've done a lot since last night."

"Yeah. I got here around six."

"Of course you did."

He shrugs and tosses me my half-empty bottle. "Hey, I didn't tell you to come that early."

"True, and I appreciate that." I look down in front of me, then back at Jonah. "Is it safe for me to start cleaning and sweeping this up?"

"Yeah. I'm done pounding for now. But don't worry about sweeping. We still gotta pull up the tile and take down that wall." He points toward the dining room.

"All right. Where's the trash bags?"

Jonah brings me some empty boxes to discard all the bigger pieces, and I get to work. He takes measurements and makes calculations on the other wall and some of the studs left on the wall we destroyed.

I've never minded physical work and find it therapeutic in many ways. As I busy myself with picking up drywall and straightening up the work area, dozens of ideas flow through my brain for how to fix up this place.

And I'm getting excited about it.

At first, I only agreed to this for Jonah's sake. But I have total control over the look and feel of a mansion. How cool is that? Much cooler than designing office spaces or decorating spare rooms for affluent families, which is the norm at Home-Sweet-Home.

It has crossed my mind to look into bigger markets and apply to companies that specialize in home designs. Once or twice, I've considered asking Bianca for recommendations. However, I've never lived anywhere other than Apple Cart and Auburn, and I'm not a big city kind of person.

"Are you going to hire some help?" I ask once all the big pieces are stacked in boxes and my hands resemble a baker's after tossing around flour.

"I plan on splitting the profits with you."

I raise an eyebrow. "You do?"

"Yeah, fifty-fifty."

I blink. I never agreed to do this for the money, even after he said he'd pay me from the profits. But splitting all that he makes . . . "Jonah, that doesn't seem fair. You bought the house with your money."

"Doesn't matter. Your work is priceless." My lips curve at the compliment, and I can feel my cheeks blush. Before I can downplay his praise, he fans his hand. "Come here."

I cross the dusty tile to the kitchen counter. He's leaned over a notebook, staring at a rough layout of the house. And I do mean rough.

"Wow, don't quit your day job. You'd for sure starve as an artist."

"So funny." Jonah flicks my ponytail with his hand before picking up a pencil. "Now that we've torn down some walls, I want to think about flooring. Something that will bring the whole space together."

He carries the notebook to the living area, and I trail behind him like a kindergartener following the line leader.

"Some kind of engineered wood maybe. Definitely not carpet." Jonah kneels at the corner of the room and picks at the edge of the fuzzy flooring before looking back at me. "What do you think?"

"Wood is great. Darker hues to bring out the luxury feel, though not too dark or it will show dust."

"Like I said, your call. The design is up to you." He smiles, then reaches for his back pocket when his phone rings.

"Hello?"

I stand back and watch his face transition from cheerfulness over the remodel to disgust over whatever's on the other end of the phone.

"Yes, sir." Jonah returns his phone to his pocket and sighs heavily as he stands.

"That was Daddy." He cups the bill of his cap with his hand and frowns at me. "He needs me at the store right away. Sorry about this."

"No, that's fine." I offer him a sympathetic face and transfer the sheetrock residue from my hands to my sweatshirt.

"I'll come back soon as I can. Don't worry about staying. Just turn off the radio and lock the front door when you leave."

"Sure thing." I half smile and nod to assure him it's fine. Except I know it's not. Whether Jeremy Jackson has a real emergency or something mundane, Jonah isn't happy about it.

I stay in the center of the brown and yellow living room floor like I'm planted in sinking mud until Jonah drives away. For a minute, I debate going to Mama's house and falling back into bed for a few hours. Then I glance around and imagine what this place could be—will be—when we're finished.

A sudden burst of energy catches. Before I know it, I'm in the corner ripping up carpet, with Dolly Parton serenading in the background. Maybe I could be Joanna Gaines. But with less kids and goats.

CHAPTER TEN

Jonah

It's almost two when I make it back to the house. Seeing Carolina's car still parked out front is a pleasant surprise. I fully expected her to go home and sleep. Maybe she did. Although it would be hard to replicate the exact crooked parking job she did earlier.

Yes, I notice her car too. I huff at my obsessiveness and climb the steps. The windows are shut, but I can hear the radio.

I ease open the door, so I won't scare her in case she's in another part of the house. Even more surprising than the Mazda still out front is the bare floor. Well, almost bare.

She's kneeling in one corner with my crowbar, grunting as she pokes at the edge of the carpet. I laugh to myself before going to rescue her.

"Here," I say, reaching my hand down.

She stops and places the bar in my hand. Then she looks at me and wipes her fingertips across her brow, leaving a trail of dust on her forehead.

"You got a little something there." I wipe at the smudge with my thumb, lingering ever so slightly against her soft skin.

"I almost had it all, but there's a lot of glue under this part."

I laugh and scan the concrete surrounding us. "You're doing a great job. You didn't have to stay and do all this."

"Thanks." She blushes slightly, and I fight the urge to caress her pink cheeks. "What else was I going to do?"

"Sleep?"

She smiles. "That did cross my mind."

"I'm sure." I smirk at her, then bend down to finish the job. A few hard shoves and the carpet separates from the concrete. I drop the crowbar beside me and toss the edge of the carpet back. "There."

"Now how did you make that looks so easy?" Carol crosses her arms.

"For one, I'm twice your size. Plus, I've done this a lot more than you."

"Thank you."

"You're welcome. You did most of it yourself."

"No, I mean thank you for not saying because I'm a girl."

I frown. "Come on, you know I don't think of you that way. You can do whatever you put your mind to doing."

She smiles, causing my stomach to pit. What I said is true in the sense that I don't think of her as too fragile or incapable of strenuous work. Even if she can barely hold a hammer higher than her head. However, I very much think of her as a girl.

My eyes trace the feminine line of her collarbone poking out above her sweatshirt and trail up to her small facial features. Except her eyes, which are large and almond-shaped, framed by dark lashes. I could get lost in those eyes for hours. I settle on her mouth. Her thin, pink lips form a slight heart shape when her mouth is closed.

"Jonah?"

I blink. Oh crud, she's caught me staring. "Yeah?"

Carol's palm waves in front of my face. "You okay? You look a little dazed."

"Yeah, I'm fine. Just thinking."

"About what?"

I pick at the edge of the carpet. "Just this house," I lie, and try to cover it with a smile. Maybe the flush in my face won't give me away. "Have you eaten anything?"

"Not since this morning."

"Let me order a pizza. Sound good?"

"Yeah, you know what I like."

I nod and smile like a weirdo, then pull out my phone to order a large pepperoni from the Quick Stop. After I make the call, we work together, rolling up the bunches of carpet Carolina peeled away while I was at the store.

Daddy needed me no more than a politician needs a lie detector test. I'm fully convinced he wanted me at the store to introduce me to one of his new wood suppliers . . . with the intentions they'd be dealing with me soon. I shove the carpet forward to roll it together and try to release some of my frustration.

I roll it all the way to the front of the room, ending at a pair of cowboy boots. My gaze raises to Bradley.

"Hey, big dog."

"Bradley." I stand and extend my hand. When he grabs it, I squeeze, allowing the firm shake to communicate what I really want to say. *What the jiminy crickets are you doing in my house?*

"I got a call that there was some suspicious activity out here."

I turn to Carolina, who wrinkles her nose in confusion. When I face him again, he's staring at the floor. "Boy, you didn't waste any time getting to work on the old place."

"No." I press my lips together, curious as to how long he plans on standing here. Doesn't he have something better to do?

Oh right, he doesn't. This is Apple Cart County. The few and far between law breakers we have only work at night, and on the opposite end of town.

"Mind if I check out the basement? I caught wind there was some drug activity going on down there recently."

I shrug. "Sure." If there is a hidden meth lab or moonshine still, I want it gone. Plus, I'm really looking forward to a reunion between Bradley and Papa Rat.

Bradley's boots click across the concrete before he crosses into the hallway, which is still carpet. Just of a different color. People must've liked a lot of variety in the 1980s. Carolina joins me as I follow him into the basement.

Watching Bradley lead the way with a huge Maglite, taking each step with caution as he peers around for rats, is the highlight of my day. Unless I count studying Carolina's pretty face before she caught me staring.

I stay a step behind Bradley, and Carol a step behind me. If we were going any slower, we'd be going backwards. That is, until Bradley jumps, and I do go backwards, knocking into Carol.

"Are you okay?" I ask.

She nods as I grab her hands and help her regain her balance. I'm so caught up in holding her hands that I forget what we're doing until Bradley squeals and throws the light across the room.

I drop Carolina's hands and hurry down the next few steps and turn on the light. "What in the world?"

"I saw something," Bradley answers in a husky voice. I'm fully convinced he's overcompensating for his girl-like scream.

"What?" Carolina asks.

"Nothing." Bradley brushes it off as if he's made a mistake, which confirms he saw Papa Rat.

"I hear something," Carol says, and leans closer to me. She stays there just long enough for her citrus scent to waft under my nose before she walks to the back window.

I follow her and so does Bradley, stopping momentarily to retrieve the flashlight he abandoned.

We line the back wall and listen as voices mumble outside. Laughter, bickering, and bossing all at once. It could only be one thing: the old ladies of Apple Cart.

Bradley steps in front of Carol and opens the back door to Mrs. Maudy and two of her friends, Ms. Ethel and Ms. Dot. "Freeze," he says in a stern voice, as if we've just opened the door to the Fight Club instead of three gray-haired ladies perched on my pool furniture.

"I swear, Bradley, we haven't done any trading yet."

He relaxes from his intimidating stance and shakes his head. "Now, Ms. Dot, you know what you girls are doing is illegal. Don't make me write you up."

Ms. Dot opens her hands and shrugs to feign innocence. I catch a glimpse at what's really going on when Ms. Ethel slides her hand across the table. A prescription bottle is visible when she picks it up and shoves it in the front pouch of her walker.

"I saw that," Bradley scolds. "I've told you ladies twice now, swapping prescription drugs is illegal."

"But they're all legal pills," Ms. Dot protests.

"For the people they're prescribed to, not for each of you to share."

"But Bradley, we share many of the same ailments," Mrs. Maudy adds.

"What do you think Mr. Hubert would say if he knew you were doing this?"

"Oh, he knows." She pushes her glasses up her nose confidently. "He asked me to score him some back pills."

Carolina lets out a giggle behind me. I fight to hold my own laughter.

"You can't be doing this. Hand me the pill bottles and let me distribute them to their rightful owners."

Maudy and Dot slide over bottles, while Ethel turns her head toward the pond-like swimming pool. We all know she's hard of hearing, but we also know she's hiding a bottle of pills in her pouch. So my assumption is she's ignoring Bradley's request.

"Ethel?" He drags out her name loud and clear as he bends closer to her face.

Her shriveled lips pucker into a sour pout as she reaches into the pouch and pulls out the pills. She slams them on the table beside her and sighs.

"That's a good girl." Bradley sounds more like he's praising a puppy that's given him a half-chewed shoe rather than a seventy-something woman handing over prescription drugs.

Bradley reads all the labels and distributes them to their rightful owners. "Now, I'll walk you ladies to your car."

He glances around the—or my—backyard. At least it is for now. "Did all you ladies ride together?"

Ms. Dot shakes her head and points to a golf cart parked all cattywampus on the slope by the patio. Bradley shakes his head. She lives down the end of this road, near the apple orchard. Not a far drive on a golf cart. Unless you're an elderly woman in the dead of winter.

"Well, I can't park my car back here," she says. "The neighbors will see it and talk."

Bradley puts a hand on his hip. "That should tell you it's not okay." He raises the pill bottles in his other hand. "Being here or exchanging pills."

"I'm going to follow you ladies back to Dot's place with these pills." He points to Ethel and Maudy. "And I'm going to check in tomorrow and make sure you ladies didn't do any switching and swapping on your way back into town."

Ethel frowns but pulls herself up by her walker as Bradley leads the other women toward the car . . . and golf cart.

Once they're in their vehicles and destroying my grass one tire turn at a time, he turns to me. "Good luck, you two, with this house. Glad I could cut out the riffraff in this dangerous neighborhood." He winks, then shakes his head before walking to his cop car.

Carol and I stand in silence while the women, followed by Bradley, drive down the road. After Bradley drives out of sight, Carolina looks at me and we burst out laughing.

Once I catch my breath, I say, "I'd have been less surprised by a meth lab." Then we laugh even harder.

Carolina

I'd like to say I can't believe a bunch of grannies just got busted for trading prescription pills beside an abandoned swimming pool, but this is Apple Cart County.

Jonah and I laugh so hard, my ribcage feels like the cage on a dune buggy that's been recently flipped. When we finally settle down, a banging noise comes from the front. We exchange a look before walking around the house. A teenager holding a pizza has his nose glued to the front window.

"Can I help you?" Jonah asks.

The boy jumps back and almost falls off the porch, dropping the pizza box in the process. "Oh man, I'm sorry."

"That's fine." Jonah carefully picks up the box, which luckily stayed shut, even if it did land upside down. "How much do I owe you?"

He points to the box. "It's on there."

Jonah glances at the box, then back at the guy, who motions for him to flip the box. "Oh," Jonah says as he flips it between his hands. Then he pulls out his wallet and hands the guy a twenty. "Keep the change."

He smiles at the bill, then at Jonah. "Thanks, man."

"Sure thing." Jonah motions for me to follow him inside as the delivery boy climbs in his car and heads back toward town.

"Shall we eat on the kitchen counter or on the concrete floor?"

"Definitely counter," I decide. Call me a princess, but I always go for the smoother surface.

We walk to the kitchen, and I hoist myself onto the counter. Jonah sets the pizza box beside me, right side up this time, and heads back toward the front door. "I have a cooler of drinks in the truck. Let me go grab it."

"Okay."

I survey the space. The kitchen has a stove, which we will likely replace, as well as an outdated microwave. But no refrigerator. We will need to plan out what to do about the counter space and cabinets before I can officially shop for new appliances.

The sloshing sound of ice swaying in the cooler calls my attention back toward the living room. Jonah walks through and sets the cooler on the kitchen floor. "I put a few Diet Cokes in for you."

"Really? Thanks." I smile and hop down to grab one. I shouldn't be so surprised. Jonah is always so thoughtful. Unlike my brothers, who say, "help yourself to whatever you can find," when they know I'm a Diet Coke girl. Only my mama makes the effort to keep some on hand when she knows I'm coming.

He gets a jug of tea out and pulls a stack of red Solo cups from the cabinet nearby.

"I see you've bought china already. Or did the church give you a housewarming party?"

He laughs. "I bought it. Didn't seem right to register for china at the hospital gift shop as a single man."

I laugh, then straighten when the idea of Jonah getting married enters my mind for the second time in a week. Why should it matter to me? He's my best friend. I want him to be happy.

Just the thought of losing moments like this, I guess. I can't expect him to hang out all day with me when he has a wife waiting at home.

I hoist myself back onto the counter, pop open my drink, and take a huge sip. The cold liquid eases my mind a bit.

Jonah joins me on the counter and opens the box. He shakes his head, and I snort-laugh at the saucy dough circle. Thanks to the tumble outside, the toppings must've melted to the top of the box. Cheese slowly falls onto our pizza in clumps.

I grab a rogue pepperoni and pop it into my mouth. Jonah sighs at the goopy cheese and pepperonis piled across the crust like sand dunes at the beach.

"Would you like a piece with cheese, a piece with cheese and pepperoni, or a piece with sauce?"

His attempt to feign seriousness fails when he looks at me, and we both burst out laughing. I double over, holding my side, and almost fall off the counter.

Thank God for Jonah's cheetah-like reflexes, because his strong hand swoops under my side and hoists me back onto the counter.

"Careful there." His brown eyes lock with mine for a moment. They reveal concern and amusement at the same time.

"Thanks," I mutter, as I shift away from the edge so I'm sitting cross-legged facing the pizza, *Sixteen Candles* style.

Jonah stares down at the pizza and scratches the side of his head. "Hmm. It's already cut, so I guess just grab whatever toppings you want and toss them on a piece."

I snort again. "Fine with me. You know I love extra cheese."

"At least neither of us are germaphobes."

"True. And we've shared water bottles plenty of times before." Mainly because we were doing something beyond my athletic abilities, causing me to drain my own water, then reach for Jonah's like a camel on empty.

"And you sneezed in my face that time."

"Yeah . . ." I wince. "In my defense, you knew I was sick before you came over."

"Oh, so now it's my fault for bringing you vegetable soup while you were holed up in your apartment?"

I frown. "No."

He's right. Kendra is a germaphobe to no end and pretty much told me to fend for myself. She'd leave food by my door, but stayed gone as much as she could that week. Then she'd wake me up late at night by spraying down our bathroom with disinfectant spray. Nothing hammers a throbbing head quite like tiny tornado sounds swirling at two a.m.

My prediction is she'll stay sick her first full year of teaching elementary school. Maybe I'll buy her Lysol disinfectant spray for a wedding present.

Jonah fists a ball of cheese and plops it onto a piece of pizza. I enjoy watching the wad of cheese string from his mouth as he tries to take a bite off his slice. After he fails sloppily, I hold up my piece and fold it in half before I take a bite.

"How clever. See, I knew I needed you."

I catch myself grinning around a mouthful of cheese. Not half bad for a gas station pizza that's been through the wringer. The real reason I'm grinning, however, is Jonah. He has a way of making everyone in his life feel important.

With two older brothers, my opinion is rarely warranted. I think that's why I dove headfirst into design and now wedding planning. It's something my brothers know nothing about. They even show me respect on the matter.

Of course, my brothers love me. They're super protective and would do anything for me. Except honor the fact that I'm a grown woman.

Maybe it's because Jonah and I are the same age and grew up together, but he's always treated me as an equal. In every sense, not just with my career. That's one of the many reasons I enjoy spending so much time with him.

Every girl needs a Jonah in her life.

"Now that we've got the carpet ripped from the living room, I thought maybe we could go back to the kitchen tile," he says.

"Yeah." I lean over—but not too far this time—to get a better look at the flooring. "I know I'm getting ahead of things, but what are your plans for outside?"

"Obviously landscaping, but I'd love your opinion on flowers and such for around the porch and out back."

I nod and start on another slice of pizza sandwich. "I want to see how much room is out there around the pool and patio. I didn't get a good look earlier with all that was going on."

"Oh, whatever do you mean?" Jonah's straight face morphs into a smile after I laugh.

"With all the horror movies Tanner made me suffer through growing up, I was pretty much prepared for anything going into that basement. Anything but an elderly pill swap."

We share a laugh, and my insides warm. I've worked harder physically today than I have in a long time. But mentally, I needed this. Laughing with Jonah, the crazy unpredictability of Apple Cart folks. It's a good way to kick off the weekend.

After we finish the pizza, Jonah stands and wipes his hands down his pants. "You want to go look around back some before we get to work in here?"

"Sounds good to me." I unfold my legs and slide off the countertop.

Jonah closes the empty box and tosses it on top of our pile of sheetrock to discard. "I need to see about getting a garbage bin out here," he comments, more to himself than me.

I follow him outside and down the slight hill, rather than through the musty basement. A wise choice on his part, unless he wants me to sneeze on him again. I do not look forward to cleaning that floor. I'll suggest we save that for last.

My eyes wander across the property. This really is a gorgeous place. It has a decent-sized front yard, all flat, then a sloping hill that flattens out again at the back. There's close to four acres in the backyard, including the swimming pool and patio. Planting some blackberry and blueberry bushes along the perimeter would add to the appeal. I imagine this home attracting someone wealthy, wanting that country feel. It would make the ideal hobby farm for a young family.

Jonah stops at the edge of the concrete surrounding the swimming pool. "No cracks, that's a relief." He toes his boot at the slick surface. "A little pressure washing, and it'll be good as new."

I wrap my arms around my waist as a light breeze blows. The sun lowering over the horizon has made it pleasant until now. "I hope the pool's in good shape."

"Me too," Jonah comments as I pass by him toward the edge of the pool. "I didn't spend much time inspecting out here, as I was more concerned with the actual home."

I nod. Makes sense. Most people building a home have very strong feelings one way or another about pools. Yet for a house this size with five acres, it kind of makes sense to have one.

The water mirrors a pond with its murky surface. It's down about two feet from the top, so I can see the liner. At least around the edges. Who knows what's waiting at the bottom? Probably a snake and a few dead lizards. Maybe a turtle or two, and thousands of bugs. Ugh.

I shake off the queasiness of varmints lurking beneath the surface and squat down to get a better look at the dingy liner. It's not a liner at all, but rather teal tile. That's great, unless it's all cracked.

"Hey, Jonah." I glance over my shoulder to see him inspecting the light fixtures on the back wall of the walkout basement.

He turns and starts walking toward me. "What is it?"

"The lining of the pool is tile. That's fancy."

"Let me see." Jonah stops behind me and bends forward.

His chest and arms press against my shoulders, causing me to scoot up a little.

When I do, my shoe slips and I fall forward . . . into the pool. No, more like the tile-lined pond. My body tenses from slight panic at what all surrounds me and the sudden shock of submerging myself in January-weather water. An Alabama January, but still, too cold for this crap.

Thankfully, I'm not quite to the deep end. I stand, my nose barely surfacing above the water as I tiptoe on the slope. Before I take three steps, something scoops under my waist.

I scream and flail my arms like a feral cat in a room full of rocking chairs.

"Ouch, Carol, it's me."

I suck in an icy breath when Jonah's big hands cup around my ribcage and under the bend of my knees. When did he jump in and how did he get behind me without me knowing it?

I peer up at him, my teeth chattering. He's focused on the steps as he marches us up the shallow end. Once the bottom levels out, I'm fully above water except for my dangling feet. Thanks only to his height.

Squeezing my shoulders, I bunch my body against his chest and bury my face in his flannel shirt. He's just as wet as me, but snuggling up to him makes me warmer somehow.

My eyes stay shut, but I feel every movement as he steps out of the pool and climbs the slight hill to the front, then the porch steps. I don't look until we're in the house and he's laid me on the counter where we just ate.

"Stay here."

I watch as Jonah hurries outside, leaving soggy footprints to mirror the ones he made coming in. Then I face the ceiling again, since I can't afford to move too much. Apparently, everyday obstacles are a threat to my balance.

He returns with a pile of clothes and blankets. "Here, I

don't have anything to really fit you, but you can change into these."

"Thanks." I stare down at the bulky coveralls, which are sure to swallow me like the little brother on *A Christmas Story*. Wow, I'm full of eighties movie references today. I blame that on my mother. For every horror movie Tanner made me watch, she had an eighties movie to combat it.

"I'll let you change." Jonah leaves two thick blankets folded beside me, then disappears down the hallway.

I slide down from the counter and step farther into the kitchen, away from a full view of the hallway. Just in case.

Not that Jonah would look. He's the biggest gentleman ever. And it's me, not someone he'd want to see like that.

As I peel off my soaked jeans and toss my heavy sweatshirt to the ground, a shiver runs down my spine. Not from the temperature, but from the thought of Jonah seeing me in my underwear. I caught him in his faded boxers the other day.

My cheeks warm with embarrassment as I remember peeking through my fingers at his chest. It's not like I haven't seen him shirtless plenty of times before. Swimming, cutting grass, preparing to paint his chest for a football game.

Something was different the other day, and I doubt it had anything to do with his bottom half being only in boxer shorts. For the first time, I noticed him as a man and not Jonah.

I slide into the bulky, stiff pants of the coveralls and slink my arms into the sleeves. The fleece lining brings almost instant comfort to my icy skin and wet underwear as I zip the suit up to my neck.

"Decent?" Jonah calls from the other end of the house.

"Yeah," I call back before dropping my gaze. Decent is a stretch. Everything is covered except my bright red toenails and the tips of my fingers. I hold out my arms to shrug my hands out of the sleeves.

Jonah's laughter catches my attention. He's propped against what's left of the wall, arms crossed. Lucky him to have a pair of his own jeans and a T-shirt.

I push the sleeves of my redneck astronaut suit up to my elbows and muster a slight smile. Then I silently scold myself for pondering that Jonah might see me any way other than this.

CHAPTER ELEVEN

Carolina

I flip my Bible open and slump down in the pew. Last night, I passed out as soon as my head hit the pillow. I'm not so much sleepy as tired. Remodeling is much more strenuous than simply redecorating.

Jonah and I worked a few more hours after our plunge in the pool. The coveralls made for a comfy cushion when it came time to get on my knees and pull carpet from the other rooms.

Despite my offer to help with the tile, Jonah assured me he would take on the grunt work. However, he did let me bang the hammer on it a few times to loosen some of the pieces. More like drop the hammer, but I got the job done.

Ever the gentleman, he also offered me his new socks so I wouldn't hurt my feet on anything. He said it wasn't the first time he'd worn boots with no socks, and I can testify to that.

Although I can't say I've ever witnessed him doing so anyplace besides Broken Bridge . . . until yesterday.

The pew on the other side of Jonah is empty with Jack and Bianca on their honeymoon. It's funny how everyone tends to sit in self-assigned seats at church. People barely change spots. Tanner now sits with Hannah's family, and that was a big deal from day one.

I smile at the memory of the day he first sat with her. It was all a plan to make everyone think they were dating before they really were. A ruse to make old ladies quit trying to set them up with people. Now they're all but married themselves.

Hmm. Maybe I should find a handsome guy to sit beside? I scan the room. There's nobody new my age.

Samuel Covington makes eye contact with me from a few pews forward. I quickly dip my head. He's handsome and well off, but has his nose so far in the air, he's likely to drown next time we get a decent rain. Oh, and his extra-gelled hair and seersucker suits aren't exactly doing him any favors.

On second thought, I'll just stay by Jonah.

Brother Johnny calls out another passage, and I flip the pages of my Bible. As he recites a verse, an eagle screech belts out from beside my feet.

I fumble for my purse, dropping my Bible on the floor. Digging through my purse is like searching for a gold nugget in the Grand Canyon. A few screeches and millions of stares later, I find my phone and silence it.

Jonah is bent over collecting all the bookmarks and photos that fell from my Bible. I'm bad to stick things in there as placeholders. He stuffs everything back inside and sets my Bible on my knee.

I half smile, and he shakes his head. His lips curve at the corners, which means he's holding back a laugh. I allow myself to take in some of the scolding looks from our elders to keep from laughing myself.

We sit in silence the rest of the service. Questions flood my mind about the phone call. The Auburn eagle is my ringtone for Daniel.

I haven't heard from him since that awkward encounter in the parking lot the night he tried to take me on a date. Can't the guy take a hint? Maybe I need the eagle himself to fly above the stadium with a sign that reads, "Daniel: Carolina just wants to be friends."

My brain shifts between the sermon and Daniel-Gate like a swinging pendulum. Brother Johnny closes the altar call and that section of my brain. Unfortunately, the Daniel section kicks into overdrive. I pull out my phone and unlock it as soon as people start scattering.

"What the heck was that?" Jonah's voice is hurried, as if he's waited thirty minutes to ask me that. He probably has.

I hold the phone to his face so he can read Daniel's name on the top of the missed calls list.

"Seriously?" Jonah's eyebrows scrunch together until he resembles that yellow puppet on Sesame Street.

I nod. "He left a voicemail."

"Have you guys talked since that night at Italian?"

"No."

Jonah shrugs. "Weird." He drums his thumb against his own Bible, then glances back at my phone. "You headed to lunch?"

"Yep, meeting Mama and Daddy at Mary's. You should come. It's just us three today. The brothers both have plans."

"Thanks, but I want to get a head start on feeding all the animals at Jack's. I slept in this morning."

"You slept in?" I scoff. Jonah's the most morning person I know. Okay, so his whole family is, but still. I am so not.

"After a polar bear plunge followed by pulling up tile, I was beat."

"Hey, I offered to help with the tile." I poke my finger into his chest.

"And we'd still be there right now." Jonah rolls his eyes as he shuffles out of the pew.

I give him my signature stern look. He laughs. It never works on him. I've scared men twice my size and age with this look, but never Jonah. He sees through my facade.

I follow him out of the church. Most everyone is driving away or on the front porch steps, saying goodbyes and making lunch plans.

"Want to meet at the house later?" Jonah asks as we reach the gravel parking lot.

"Yeah, that's good." I shade my eyes from the noon sun and click on Daniel's number.

Jonah heads toward his truck, while I walk in the opposite direction. Some places have better service than others. It's like this all over town. A particular shade tree near the front of the church has the best service.

"Hey, Carolina. Thanks for calling me back," Daniel says as he answers the phone.

"Sure thing." I try to not sound so skeptical.

"Hey, Carol!" Jonah calls from behind my back.

I snap my head around to him. He's holding up five fingers, two on one hand and three on the other. He's mouthing something, but I can't make it out.

"What?" I ask.

"I didn't say anything," Daniel answers.

"Oh, sorry, Daniel, hang on."

"What?" I hold my hand over the phone this time and ask louder.

"Meet at the house at two-thirty."

"Okay, two-thirty." I give Jonah a thumbs-up, then put

the phone back to my ear. He waves and smiles, then continues to his truck.

"Sorry about that. Jonah was saying something to me across the church parking lot."

Daniel lets out such a laborious sigh that I can almost feel his breath through the receiver. "Yeah, that's why I wanted to talk to you."

"About Jonah's house remodel?" *Dear Lord, please don't let Daniel try to move here!*

"Not exactly. More like Jonah."

"Jonah?" I switch my phone to the other ear and watch his truck pull into the street. Why on earth would Daniel want to talk about him? "What about Jonah?"

"How he is with you."

"What does that mean?" My throat tightens as I'm ready to defend Jonah if need be. Daniel better not dare suggest he's violent based on that stupid parking lot encounter. If anyone was violent that night, it was me.

"I think the reason you want to be just friends is Jonah."

"Yeah . . . Jonah and I have always been friends."

"No, he's the reason you want to be just friends with *me*."

"Daniel, you're not making any sense."

"Carolina, the guy's in love with you."

I let out a huge belly laugh that ends with my infamous snort. Daniel's muttering something about how he knows this is true, but I'm laughing so hard that I can't understand him. I finally settle down and lean against the oak tree. Between working on the house last night and laughing so hard, I can barely hold myself up.

"And you're in love with him too."

Okay, that does me in. I push against the tree and let out a few more snorts. Daniel must be on one of his health cleanses. He isn't getting enough carbs to his brain. Come to think of it, he is a good representative of the Daniel Diet. That makes me laugh even more.

A few stragglers walking to their cars give me strange looks. I straighten and clear my throat. I hope they weren't visitors. My behavior has not been marketable material for Apple Cart Baptist this morning.

"You can laugh all you want, but I know it's true."

I roll my eyes and pick at my nails with my free hand. "Okay, Daniel. So neither of us subscribes to this idea of being in love, but somehow you know it?"

"Oh, I'm sure Jonah knows it too."

I roll my eyes again and slide down the tree trunk, not caring that my blouse is probably bark picked. Daniel spouts out all the telltale signs of why he thinks Jonah and I are in love while I sit in front of the tree and examine my nail polish. His closing statement is that I didn't invite him to Jack's wedding because I wanted to be alone with Jonah.

"Hold up, now. I wasn't alone with Jonah. I was running around like a chicken with my head cut off, making sure everything ran smoothly, while Jonah was the best man. Nobody was alone with anybody. The whole town was all up in my business all week. Which is precisely why you didn't need to come. Why would you want to endure Apple Cart drama while I worked?"

"To see where you come from, and to be with you."

I sigh and massage my temples. My stomach growls, commanding me to get off this stupid call and feed it. I'm sure my parents have long given up on me and ordered by now anyway.

"Fair enough. But you see my point in why I didn't invite you. And no, for the fifth time, I'm not in love with Jonah. He's my best friend who just happens to be a he."

"Fine. But he's in love with you."

I bump my head back against the tree trunk and immediately regret it. That'll make a knot tomorrow. "What makes you say that?"

"Why would he break up with Sasha if he wasn't in love with you?"

"I don't know, Daniel? Maybe she wasn't his type?"

Now it's Daniel's turn to laugh. I must say, I'm a little offended. Sure, Sasha's your typical hot girl, but Daniel was totally into me until the other night. Heck, until ten seconds ago, I think? Ah, who cares. The guy's a nut job. He thinks Jonah's in love with me!

"Daniel, thanks for all the intel. I really need to go now."

"Carolina, I just wanted to prepare you."

"Prepare me for what?"

"You'll never have a real relationship until you and Jonah figure out whatever's between you."

"Okay, have a nice day." I click the phone and thrust myself off the ground.

I gather my purse and Bible, then pick pine straw from my backside as I walk to my car. That had to be the weirdest phone conversation ever. Unless I count the time Misty called me thinking my number was this singles hotline. So the second weirdest.

As I buckle my seat belt and back out of the parking lot, the conversation replays in my mind. I shake my head. Daniel. What a moron.

Just because I'm not into him that way doesn't mean I'm in love with Jonah. I mean, I love Jonah, but in the same way I love my brother, or maybe even Bundt cakes. I've never been *in* love with anyone. Daniel's just trying to patch his ego.

Yeah . . . I'll go with that.

I settle on the windowsill and sip my Diet Coke. The conversation with Daniel haunted the back of my mind all through lunch. Thankfully, my mama didn't comment on my silence. Most likely because by the time I got to Mary's, my parents had almost eaten all their meat and threes. That left me feeding my face while they did all the talking.

Once we all got home, I busied myself changing into work clothes and packing up water and Coke for today. Daniel's words sit in the back of my mind like an old prom dress collecting dust in the back of a closet. I don't need it, don't want it, and I often forget it's there. But it sparkles from the corner of my childhood closet every time I crack open the door.

If only I could donate my thoughts to Goodwill.

Instead of donating the lion's share of my brain, I hurried to the mansion to pound out my frustration. On a wall or floor—not Jonah. I shake my head to try and dislodge any thoughts of me pouncing on Jonah and covering him in kisses. I've never imagined myself like that with him, and it doesn't weird me out the way I wish it would. My neck and face heat up, and I feel like I'm harboring a dirty little secret. Darn that Daniel and his crazy assumptions.

I take a long drink of my Diet Coke, and stare at the wall in front of me. That helps my brain transition to plans for paint colors after we rip off this hideous wallpaper. That thought bubble pops as soon as the door opens and Jonah steps inside.

My chest tightens when he smiles. *Nope. Not going there. Daniel is an idiot. Jonah's just happy his help showed up.*

"You're here early," he says.

I pull back my sweatshirt sleeve and stare down at the imaginary watch on my wrist. "Or maybe you're late?"

He checks his phone. "Nope. It's two twenty-nine. I'm a minute early."

I roll my eyes, also rolling away any notion of Daniel's conversation holding weight. "I've only been here a few minutes."

"Hey, I love punctuality in my employees."

I swallow, then brush off the word "love" like the dust that falls from that prom dress whenever I dig in the bottom of the closet.

"Since I'm your first employee, and all."

He wavers his head. "Eh, I've helped Daddy hire a few teenagers for part-time stock boys."

I laugh and down the last of my soda. "So, boss, what's on the agenda today?"

Jonah reaches into the back of his jeans pocket and pulls out a rolled-up piece of paper, which is a little flattened from being in his pants. Knowing Jonah, he sat on it driving here. He unrolls it like a Biblical scroll and lays it flat on the floor in front of me.

A drawing of the house interior that's even worse than his first attempt stares back at me. A kindergartener with a broken crayon could've done better. Maybe it's all the time I spend on actual computer drafting software or the preciseness of professional plans I work with daily. But I'll need to intervene when he gets an actual client, before he shows them something resembling a serial killer's stakeout.

"I'm guessing that's me?" I point to one of the two stick figures on the page. The one with a ponytail and not as tall.

"Yeah, I'll have you start in here. We're working on wallpaper now that the flooring is gone on the main floor."

I nod. If I open my mouth to speak, I'll laugh. He didn't have to draw us, but I needed this amusement. He runs his finger across the page, mapping out our plan for the day like he's prepping to find buried treasure. To be fair, if we were to find any buried treasure in Apple Cart, our best bet would be in an abandoned mansion that until yesterday also doubled as a site for prescription drug solicitation.

"I'll help you pull down wallpaper before I start working on the kitchen cabinets," Jonah says.

I nod again. By now, I'm sure I resemble one of those bobbing bird toys that dips its head in and out of water. Just when I think they quit making those, one shows up at Paul's store. Of course, he probably finds them used.

Jonah rolls his ugly art project back into a cylinder and heads for the kitchen. I pick up my empty Coke can and follow. He sets the plans on the counter, and I chunk the can in our trash box on the way to the dining room.

I snarl my nose at the wallpaper. I haven't paid this room much attention until now. "Wow, what kind of green would you call that?"

Jonah scratches his head and shrugs. "Somewhere between olive and puke."

"Eww."

"You asked."

"That, I did. But the pears are a nice touch, I guess."

"Yeah, a nice contrast to the citrus in the kitchen."

Sticking to routine, I nod again.

Jonah finds a seam in the wall and digs his finger into the edge. The wallpaper pulls back with ease. We both let out a sigh of relief. That is, until he gets a little too ambitious and rips it with both hands.

When he's made it to the edge of the wall, a long streak of paper remains. He picks at it with his short nails. "Well, ninnies. That didn't come off as easily as I'd thought."

I snicker. Jonah's made-up curses never cease to entertain me. "Nope."

"We'll have to put some elbow grease into this, as my grandma would say."

"Nothing like good ole arm sweat to make this place

beautiful." I raise an eyebrow at the opposite wall, still sporting a million pears.

Jonah scratches at the leftover paper again with no results. "Let me get a putty knife."

I tilt my head toward the window. A pale blue would be pretty against this natural light. I'll suggest something in that color scheme vicinity for this and the kitchen.

"Okay." Jonah returns from the kitchen with some ammo to prune the rest of these rotten pears. "These should work. If not, we can always wet the wall and then try it."

"Thanks," I say as I take one of the knives from him.

I start at the edge and chip away the corner, making no progress whatsoever. Jonah tries next and barely makes a dent in it. Well, unless you count the small dent he makes in the actual wall from shoving the knife so hard.

He steps back and rubs his chin. "We better wet this down and let it soak a bit before pulling more. Let's rip the rest first to see what all will be left."

"Okay, I'll take this wall." I step to the back wall and leave him with the one opposite the window. The fourth wall is now mostly opened to the kitchen.

We start tearing and pulling back paper, both walking backwards. I stop when Jonah bumps into me. Instinctively, I turn around, and so does he. My face falls inches from his chest, and the memory of him shirtless in Jack's house flashes through my mind.

I shake my head as if to dislodge the memory before my brain goes off the rails and starts crashing toward the Daniel diagnosis of Jonah and me having feelings for one another.

As I take a step back, my eyes lift to his face. He's giving me that goofy grin he wears ninety percent of the time. Only this time, it looks a little sexy. I'm so losing it right now. That's what I get for drinking Diet Coke too fast. Tanner always said it would fuzz my brain. I guess he's right for once.

"Careful." Jonah grins. I feign a smile and try to ignore the way his eyes sparkle in the sunlight. They're the color of newly lacquered wood floors. *Note to self: Pick out floors the exact color of Jonah's eyes. It will increase the value of this place immensely.*

I dip my head and finish tugging at the last of my paper before dropping it to the ground. Only two spots remain on the wall. Decently sized, but still, only two. Jonah managed to leave only one thin trail of paper on his wall.

"I'll rip the small corners of the last wall," he says.

"Want me to get some water?"

"Yeah, there's some buckets and stuff in the kitchen."

I exit through the new opening and glance around the room. The kitchen has become our designated place to store work equipment. Jonah keeps a toolbox here, as well as cleaning supplies. I find a gallon bucket and some soap, along with a few sponges.

My every move echoes through the vast room. The faint sound of paper ripping comes from the dining room, and a lone bird chirps outside. All this quiet makes the pipes sound even worse when I turn the faucet knob.

"Whoa, is that the sink?" Jonah calls from the dining room.

"Afraid so." I twist it off and stand back when he comes to inspect it.

He twists the knob and listens, then turns on the hot water too. I raise my brow, halfway expecting a tiny cement mixer to roll out of the cabinet doors any minute.

Jonah turns off the water and mumbles something stupid under his breath. He's always using pseudo curse words he makes up to keep from cussing. I tell him it's the same thing since he means it in that context, but he disagrees on the grounds that he makes up a new word each time.

He wipes his hands down his pants and sighs. "I need to check the pipes. Can you get me some tools?"

"Sure thing." I go to the toolbox while he bends to the ground.

Jonah folds his long body and halfway disappears under the sink. Only his legs stick out, like the Wicked Witch on *Wizard of Oz,* trapped under Dorothy's house.

"Can you hand me a wrench and turn on the water when I say to?"

"Yep." I lift the toolbox and hobble over, carrying it at my knees. It's just heavy enough where I can't lift it properly. I set it beside the sink for easy access to whatever Jonah might need and retrieve the wrench.

"Here." I shove it in the opening.

He takes it, and I straighten to cut on the water when he cues me. A mumbled "now" comes from below, and I turn the knob.

The pipes squeal and the faucet shakes. My legs soak to the point that I wonder if I've peed myself. If so, chugging Diet Coke really is a hazard. I look down and see water gushing out from underneath the sink.

"Kill it!"

I shake to attention and jerk the knob the opposite direction. Jonah slides out beside me, soaking wet. He sighs and shakes his head. "I'm gonna need to beat that back in place. When I tell you to, hand me the hammer."

I nod. Yes, I'm back to nodding. Partly because I know now is not the time to sound amused and partly because I'm desperately trying to keep my eyes off Jonah's wet T-shirt. Something is terribly wrong with me today. I need to go home tonight and kiss Daniel to cleanse my head of Jonah.

Oh wait, that's not an option, since Daniel thinks Jonah and I are in love!

Jonah sighs and wipes a hand over his wet hair. I bite my

bottom lip. In a weird, redneck sort of way, he resembles one of those shaving cream commercials where the hot, recently showered guy stares in a mirror to shave. He dips his head back beneath the sink, saving me from continuing that train of thought. I stare down at his wet jeans and then feel the tightening of my own when I bend to get the hammer.

"Hammer."

That's my cue. I stick it inside the cabinet and wait for him to grab it. A second later, he complains, "No, Carol. Not the sledgehammer."

"My bad, that's all we've used so far." I pull it back and fumble for the smaller hammer.

I understand why he's annoyed, but I'm soaked too. We're in this stupid sinkhole—literally—together. A little irritated at his attitude, I jerk the hammer from the toolbox and shove it under the sink.

"Son of a basset hound!"

"What?" I twist to see Jonah holding the side of his head, which is inches away from the hammer in my hand.

Blood starts pouring through the cracks of his fingers.

"Oh no." We were maybe seven when I first learned the word hemophilia. Of course, I couldn't pronounce it until much later. All I knew then was when Jonah got a bad boo-boo, it wouldn't stop bleeding. Meaning his cuts and scrapes were way more serious than mine.

He holds his head tighter and scoots out from under the sink. I snatch the larger rag from the pile and dive toward him. I'm all but sitting in his lap, squeezing the rag against his head. "Move your hand."

He does as he's told, and I tie the rag around his head in a makeshift tourniquet. "Hold that." I take his hand and place it on his temple. "I'm so sorry."

"It's not your fault. I shouldn't have raised up." He shakes his head slowly.

I steady his head with my hands. "Don't move. I need to get you to the doctor for stitches."

Jonah snarls. "No, it'll soon slow down enough to super-glue it."

I balk. "Jonah Jackson, you are not supergluing a head gash."

"I know. You're gonna do it."

I sit back on my heels and cross my arms in protest. "No, I'm not. This is your head we're talking about. Not a tin can covered in macaroni."

"Gee, thanks. You could've at least compared me to a birdhouse."

"Birdhouse quality would be stitches, which is what you're getting." I reach out and offer him my hand.

He takes it, and the warmth of his palm calms my nerves. Weird, I should be the one calming him in this situation. "Come on." I wrap my other hand around his and pull so he can get his footing. He leans against the sink as he stands.

"Hold on to me." I drape his long arm around my shoulder and lead him toward the front door. I stop when we get to the step up. "Easy here."

He clears the step fine but shuffles across the threshold clumsily, almost taking us both out. I shut the door behind us and take my time leading him down the porch steps.

On the last step, he leans into me, his weight pushing me to the side. I reach out to brace him from falling, but he shoves me aside and throws up right in front of the porch.

I turn my head and cough while he finishes. That's the upside to having a boy best friend. You never have to hold his hair back while he pukes.

"I think you may have a concussion."

Jonah spits, then lifts his head to me. He laughs. "Nah, just shook up."

"Uh-huh." I reach for his arm and help him straighten

before looping it around me again. We stagger a bit but make it to my car with no further incidents.

I open the passenger door, and he falls inside. His big boot is hanging out, so I shove his foot inside and shut the door. Then I circle around to my side.

"Are we going to get ice cream?"

I laugh. "We can afterwards at the hospital cafeteria if you're a good boy at the ER."

He moans, then holds his head. I reach over and buckle him like he's an overgrown toddler. My chest rises and falls as I brush against his wet chest. I fumble around with the buckle a little longer than necessary.

Back off, Carolina. The man just puked. And this isn't a man, it's Jonah.

I back out of the driveway and buckle myself as I head toward the hospital. Now, I'm really regretting drinking that Coke so fast. I could use a bump of caffeine right about now.

CHAPTER TWELVE

Jonah

I turn the air vents my way and set them on high. So what if I'm wet as a stray dog in a rainstorm and it's January? My body is on fire thanks to my throbbing head.

I just had to sit up to get the hammer myself. Why couldn't I have waited?

My vision blurs as I lean against the headrest of Carol's car. She's driving unusually fast for her, or for anyone in Apple Cart on a Sunday afternoon. I close my eyes and fake curse under my breath. Me and my stupid bleeding problems.

A simple scrape for most people leaves me bleeding for a country mile.

Carolina freaked out the first time she saw me bleed. It was the summer after first grade. We were playing in my then-new treehouse Daddy built. I scratched my shin on a nail climbing down the steps. Blood gushed out, and I started running toward the house to find Mama.

By then, I knew to go find an adult to patch me up. Carol ran after me, screaming and crying. She later told me she thought I was dying.

Bless her heart.

I smile at the memory. That smile is quickly wiped away by shock when the car jerks into park and my head bobs forward.

Gentle fingertips brush my cheek. "Sorry, Jonah. I was in a hurry."

My eyes open to Carol leaning toward me. She studies my head and strokes the side of my face. Her lips are mere inches from mine. For a split second, the only thing stopping me from kissing her is the fact that I lost my lunch fifteen minutes earlier. And that my head won't stop bleeding. And that I may have a concussion.

I give her what I'm sure is a stupid grin, because she returns the gesture with a giggly smirk. "I'll help you out."

Just like that, she moves away from my view and gets out of the car. I wait for her to open my door, as I'm still dizzy from the injury, mixed with reckless driving.

"Come on." She takes my hands and helps me stand. One hand is soiled with dried blood from holding my head.

I hate that she has to do this for me. At the same time, there's nobody else I'd rather have taking care of me. My vision blurs as I stand beside Carol in the midday sunlight. She shuts my door and locks the car, all while holding a death grip on my arm.

Her slim fingers putting pressure on my forearm feel a little like tiny blood-pressure cuffs tightening. Still, it's Carol's hand, and she's holding me tightly to try and support my large frame. So in a weird way, I like it.

She shuffles me toward the revolving door, which is a hassle for me on a normal day. Her head sways back and forth as she waits on an opening, not unlike a cat watching its owner swing a toy feather. I have to stop watching her before I get nauseated again. I've all but centered my vision when she shoves my back with her free hand, slamming me into the door.

I make it inside the opening, but I fall. A young couple stares at me from the lobby. I get the feeling they're waiting for me to move. Except I can't. Or at least I can't without stumbling. Thanks to the bloody rag on my head and my soaked clothing, I'm sure I resemble a lanky excuse for Rambo.

They stare down at me as I spin the other direction. When I get back to Carol, she jumps in sideways with both feet like she's skipping rope. I dab my head with my palm, thankful no fresh blood comes back when I look at it.

Carol works on lifting me to my feet and apologizes to the couple as we turn by them once more. The third time I pass, the guy steps in with us and hoists me to my feet. I stumble back a step, but he steadies me and helps Carolina ease me out.

"You gonna make it, buddy?"

I nod. "I reckon so, thanks."

He nods back and offers us a sympathetic face. The woman just stares at us like we fell out of a horror movie, but I'm sure we look the part.

Carol leads me to the front desk, where the receptionist is already aware of our presence. "We need to see a doctor. He needs stitches."

"You'll have to go to the ER. It's Sunday afternoon."

"Yes, which way is that?" Her eyes widen, and I know she's fighting to keep her patience. Whether with the receptionist or me, I'm not sure. Maybe both.

The lady points toward the left wing. "But you'll need to go out and enter through the ER door."

"Seriously?" Carol's forehead wrinkles as she glances back at the door that almost did me in.

The woman sighs and picks up the phone. She punches a few numbers, then says, "I have a young couple up here needing to come back there for a head injury." I try not to grin when she refers to us as a couple. We're a couple of drowned rats right now, but I'll take what I can get with Carol.

The woman pauses a beat. "I'm afraid he may injure himself further going that way."

We wait in awkward silence as she fumbles with her glasses frame and stares at nothing. "Thank you." She raises her eyes to us and adjusts her glasses on the bridge of her nose. "Go on to the left. They'll open the door."

"Thanks." Carolina smiles. She starts tugging me toward the door, then stops and turns her head. "Miss, do we need to say we're the ones you sent?"

"Oh, I'm certain they'll know." She purses her lips, then drops her gaze to her computer screen.

"Of course," Carol mutters as she leads me to the ER.

We stop in front of the glass doors. A woman in scrubs who looks vaguely familiar stands on the other side, as if waiting for us. She presses a button, and the doors slide apart.

"Hey, I didn't expect you to be the guy all injured." I blink. Five minutes here and I've managed to create a reputation for myself. And not a positive one. "What happened?"

"Hi, Brooke. Jonah had an accident with a hammer. I think he needs stitches."

Brooke, of course. She went to school with us. She dated that baseball guy. Uh, Nate the Great. My vision is too blurry to recognize her. Ugh, I need to sit down. I shrug free from

Carol's grip and stagger toward a chair, almost collapsing on my way there.

"Whoa, careful there. Let me get you a wheelchair." Brooke pats my shoulder like I'm pathetic.

Carol sits in the chair beside me and makes a puppy dog pout that lets me know I *am* pathetic. "I need your insurance card to check you in," she says.

Without giving it a thought, I hand her my wallet. She smiles and lifts her eyebrows, as if she thinks she now holds my entire life in her hands. In a way she does. She just doesn't know it.

I watch her go up to the window and talk to the nurse behind it. She gives the woman my information and lets her copy my card before coming back to sit with me.

"I really am sorry, Jonah."

I fight back a smile and put on a downcast face. I'm not at all mad, but it's fun to see her grovel a bit.

"I'll make it up to you."

"Okay." This time I do grin. Then I turn my back to her and rest my head in her lap. She smiles down at me.

I try to focus on her perfect face, but it's hazy against the florescent lighting. My head spins at the lights, so I turn away from her and stare at the floor. The dots in the tile run together, so I close my eyes.

Carolina must sense my discomfort, because she strokes the back of my neck right below my hairline. It soothes me, tickles me, and heats up my insides all at the same time. Maybe I should've had her hit me with a hammer years ago?

As I contemplate how long I can milk this, Brooke returns. "All right, Jonah. Let's get you back."

Carolina's chocolate eyes lock on my face when I raise my head. She reaches for my hand to help me into the chair. Instead of letting go of her hand once I'm in the wheelchair, I hold it tighter. She massages the back of my hand with her thumb.

"Are you in pain?" she asks.

"A little," I moan. Sure, my head is throbbing like . . . well, like someone hit it with a hammer. But aside from that and smelling like someone in soaking-wet work clothes with puke breath, I'm good.

All good. Too good now that Carolina's petting me like a long-lost puppy. I shouldn't take advantage of this, but I'm a desperate man.

Brooke wheels me away with Carolina by my side, my hand resting in hers. She parks me in a room. "Sit tight and I'll get the doctor."

Carolina squeezes my hand one last time, then pulls away. My hand cools at her touch, and the warm current flowing from my body ceases. It's as if she cut off my lifeline. I've gotten way too used to her comforting me. She sits near me in a chair and rests her elbows on her knees.

"At least we're close to dry now," I say in a joking manner.

She frowns at me and shakes her head. "Jonah, I—"

I hold up a hand to shush her. "I told you, it's fine. Accidents happen."

She stands and squeezes my shoulder. I grab hold of her hand and try my best to focus on her eyes. "Thank you for taking care of me."

"It's the least I could do."

"No, really."

We share a moment, and that warm current resurges inside my body. After a few glorious seconds, we're interrupted by voices in the hallway.

"No, ma'am, you do not need to work outside until that sprain heals."

"But doctor, the *Farmers' Almanac* says—"

"No, ma'am. Even if it's the only day in the year to plant cabbage, you need to rest for a few days."

I bite back a laugh at both that conversation and the smirk on Carol's face that tells me she's doing the same. A man in scrubs who looks to be in his early thirties comes in.

"Hi, I'm Dr. West. Nice to meet you."

"Hi," Carolina and I answer in unison.

"My radiology tech says you had a run-in with a hammer."

"Something like that." I immediately regret my answer when Carol winces. She feels bad enough already, and my sulking isn't helping.

"He has hemophilia, so I knew he'd need stitches," she says.

"Yes, best get that taken care of right away."

"And we think he may have a concussion."

"I see." The doctor narrows his eyes and peeks under my head dressing. "Deep cut. A hammer did this?"

Carol nods. "It was my fault. I shoved the hammer under the sink the same time he raised up."

The doctor glances at her, then back at me. "I thought you two looked a little wet."

He gets out one of those little tools with a flashlight on the end and shines it in my eyes. I look this way and that best I can as he directs me, then try and follow his finger.

"When was the last time your husband had anything to eat?"

"I'm sorry, did you say my husband?"

The doctor turns red and holds up his hand. "Oh, I apologize. Your boyfriend."

"No, we're not . . ." Carol moves her hand from my shoulder for the first time since the doctor entered and motions between us with her finger while shaking her head.

"Apologizes again. I just assumed."

My head starts throbbing again and my hearing is muffled. Either that or my heart has climbed up to my head, since I can feel it beating between my ears. Maybe it's retreating to my brain for support after Carolina shot down any notion of us being together in two seconds flat.

"We're not together." She rests her hand on my shoulder again, which does nothing to prove her point. "Not like that."

Now my stomach has decided to spin with my head. The doctor looks in my mouth and ears and tests my reflexes. I'm numb to everything, my body gone limp at Carolina's firm rejection.

It's not like I should expect her to claim me as her significant other or even pretend for the doctor. Heck, why would she? He's a young doctor. No wonder she cleared up our status pronto.

"Have you ever had head trauma before now?"

Maybe it's the crappy lighting of this place, Carol's touches messing with my mind, or the fact that I feel like I've been run through a woodchipper. But when I open my mouth to answer, all that comes out is whatever is left in my stomach.

Right on the doctor's shoes.

Carolina

In the last few hours, Jonah has bled like a stuffed hog and thrown up twice. Oh, and let's not forget falling into the rotating door at the hospital entrance.

Given his nauseated state and inability to keep his eyes

focused, the doctor had Brooke give him a CT scan. I stayed in the room with the nurse, replaying the hammer scene in my head for the hundredth time. Then I wanted to beat my own head in when they wheeled him back looking like death warmed over.

I draw my shoulders in and slide down the wall, resting my damp bottom on the cold floor. Of all the people to hit with a hammer, it had to be Jonah. The person I least want to hurt.

Not that I want to hurt anyone. But if I had to pick somebody's head to whack with the back end of a hammer, Jonah wouldn't even come to mind. I watch from across the room as the nurse finishes cleaning around his fresh set of stitches. The side of his head resembles Frankenstein's, and it makes me want to cry.

Dear God, please don't let him have brain damage.

No sooner than I finish my silent prayer, the doctor comes in with a clipboard in hand. "Good news, no internal damage. Just a good old-fashioned concussion."

Jonah shakily stands from sitting on the edge of the bed. He rocks backward a bit. I instinctively stand to try and catch him like a mother would a baby learning to walk.

"Easy there, cowboy. You're still dizzy," the doctor says. "You need to take a few days off and rest."

"I have a lot to do tomorrow," Jonah protests.

"Well, you're going to have to rest. I'm sorry." The doctor frowns at him, then turns to me. "Make sure he rests."

I nod, then slant my eyes at Jonah in a silent warning. Yes, I've been pampering him and will continue to. But that turd must mind if he's going to get better.

The doctor gives us a few more instructions, and the nurse brings Jonah something to take for his nausea and headache. Then the doctor steadies him and leads us to the back door. The one that we should've went in earlier, which doesn't spin like a fair ride. I help Jonah to the curb and have him sit on a bench while I pull the car around.

He allows me to lead him to the door and help him inside. It must be hard for him, independent as he is, but he's been a good sport. I'm shocked at how he's allowing me to help him so much.

We drive in silence on the way back to the mansion. I park in front of the house but don't cut my engine. In all the commotion before, I didn't take time to lock the doors and turn off the lights. "I'm going to lock everything up, including your truck. Do you have your keys?"

"Yeah." He pulls them from his front pocket to show me. "Why are you gonna lock my truck?"

"Because I'm driving you to Jack's."

"And we'll leave the truck here?"

"Just until tomorrow when you're less loopy. You're going home to bed, and I'll stay there until the morning."

"What about your job?"

"I'll call Audrey when we get to the house. She'll understand."

Jonah rests his head against the seat and stares at the roof of my car. I hop out and take care of the house and his truck. He's in the same exact spot when I return to the car, except now his eyes are closed.

I ease out of the driveway to not disturb his rest. The whole time I'm driving out of town to Gamer's Paradise, I'm brainstorming how I'll get this big lug into the house.

By the time I turn down the dirt drive to Jack's place, Jonah is snoring. Just great.

I don't bother him until I park in front of the house. And I mean right in front of Jack's house. I couldn't get any closer without pulling onto the porch.

"Jonah." I shake his arm and he flinches. I duck when he swings his big hand my way. If I go down too, I'll have to call my mama to come take care of us both. Considering I don't want to spend the evening getting my temperature taken and being spoon-fed chicken broth and Jell-O, that's not an option.

I cut the engine and go to Jonah's side of the car. He's curled against the door, and his head falls when I open it. The only thing still holding him in is the seat belt. I squat down and shove his upper body back into the car with full force.

He wakes up and jerks his head toward me. Fear glazes across his face, then gives way to his signature goofy grin when he recognizes me.

"Hey there. We need to get you in the house."

"Huh?"

I point behind us to Jack's house. "The house. You're home. Or at Jack's."

He scratches his head and yawns.

"Just help me out here." I lean across him and unbuckle his seat belt. His shirt is only a little damp now, and I try not to think about what's beneath it.

Now for the hard part. Getting him up the few wooden steps just outside this door. I glance back at the steps, then at Jonah. His long frame is folded into my car like a cheap lawn chair. "Take my hands."

He does as he's told, giving me a lopsided grin. Between his increasing drowsiness and extra-goofy expressions, I'd say the medicine has kicked in.

"Stand gently."

He minds me on the standing but not so much on the gently. His head hits the roof of the car, and he falls back into the seat, taking me with him. On the way down, he hits my car horn. If he's not fully awake by now, that should do the trick.

"Jonah, your stitches!" I jerk my head toward his to make

sure they're still intact, then sigh with relief when I see they are.

He laughs, calling my attention to his mouth. Which is right below mine. My body tingles as I realize I'm lying on top of him in my car, our damp clothes plastered together like one of those paper mâché projects from vacation Bible school.

I clear my throat and press my hands against his shoulders to lift myself off him. When I do, my eyes meet Ms. Dot and Paul staring back at me through the driver's side window.

I jump off Jonah and out of the car. "Ms. Dot, Paul. What are y'all doing here?" My words come out fast and clipped. I smooth my hair down and grin.

"We didn't mean to interrupt anything," Paul answers, craning his neck to get a better look at Jonah.

"We were out doing some Sunday driving and heard a horn. Thought we'd best check out the commotion."

I should ask what two old people are doing driving dirt roads right before dark, but my mama taught me to respect my elders. Even those who swap prescription pills and mooch off every catered event in town.

I laugh nervously. "Of course." I point to the car way too casual for having just climbed off Jonah. "Jonah hurt his head, so we've been at the ER the last few hours. I'm trying to pull him out and get him into the house to rest."

"Oh, poor dear." Dot puts a feeble hand to her mouth. "Paul, go help her."

Paul follows orders and opens the driver's side door. Jonah waves at him and smiles. "Hey, Paul. Nice shirt."

I wipe my hand down my face. Yep, the medicine has definitely taken effect. Paul shuts the door and circles the car to the passenger side. "Best to pull him out by the legs."

I step back and let Paul take the lead. He grabs Jonah by

the belt and starts sliding him toward us. His long legs slink down to the ground like honey from a Mason jar. Then his bottom hits the dirt with a thud.

Watching it makes me wince. "Are you okay?"

"Uh-huh." His voice is loopy and distant.

"Get on that side, Carolina."

I get on Jonah's left and mimic Paul in lifting him by the armpits. Jonah starts squirming and laughing.

"He's really ticklish under the arms," I say.

Paul shakes his head and removes his hands, causing Jonah's right side to fall back on the ground. "Sorry, son." He lifts him by the waist this time.

I've always heard adrenaline can kick in at a time of crisis and give a person unnatural strength. That must be the case here, as scrawny old Paul lifts Jonah to his feet and steps away from the door.

"There, shut that door, darlin'."

I shut the car door and rush to Jonah's side. Paul and I get under his shoulders and walk him up the steps. We only have one minor stumble, so I'll call it a win.

Ms. Dot follows us, her hands over her mouth. I can hear her muttering "bless his heart" among other worries as I unlock the door and we walk Jonah inside.

Once we drop Jonah onto the couch, Paul pulls a handkerchief from his shirt pocket and wipes his brow. "Whew. Dot, I worked up an appetite."

I ignore Paul hinting to eat with Dot. Or the fact that he's riding around with a recently widowed woman. "Thank you," I tell him.

Paul nods as he folds the handkerchief and returns it to his pocket. "You just help him take it easy. That's some gash. His head will look like a melon come morning."

I frown. All because of my lack of tool knowledge.

"Thanks again," I say, walking toward the door. It's my subtle hint for them to leave.

Paul follows, but Dot stays cemented in the center of the room, holding a hand to her chest. "Bless his heart."

"Come on, Dot. It's getting dark," Paul says.

"Call me if you need anything, sweetie." She pats my arm on her way to the door.

"I will," I say, although I don't intend to. The last thing I need is her spreading around town that I stayed all night at Jack's house with Jonah, while Jack was on his honeymoon.

They let themselves out, and I lock the door once they've made it off the porch. I turn back to Jonah, whose head is thrown back against the top of the couch. He's staring at the ceiling fan like a six-month-old.

Chocolate and Brownie mosey in from the laundry room. It's as if they waited for Paul and Dot to leave before making an appearance. "Hey, girls." I pat them both on the head. "Jonah, have they been fed today?"

"Yeah," he says way too loud for indoors. Then he jerks his head forward, meeting my eyes. "I fed everyone after church."

"Great." I totally forgot Jack usually keeps young deer in a pen. My shoulders relax. I've never had to take care of a pet. Unless you count the time Tanner and I rescued a turtle. Turns out it was already dead when we found it. We somehow assumed he was sleeping for four days. Or was it a she?

Jonah starts to wobble to his feet. I leave my post by the door and rush toward him.

"Careful. Let me help you." I duck under his arm and hold tightly to his hand after his arm loops around me. "Where do you want to go?"

"The bed."

I start toward Jack's room.

"No, I'm staying in the other room."

I turn into the spare bedroom. Two large duffle bags sit in the corner, which I assume are Jonah's. As soon as we make it to the bed, he collapses in it.

"Jonah, your clothes are soggy and nasty. You need to change before you fall asleep."

He groans and sits up. Then he pulls his shirt off and flings it my way. It hits my face and falls to the floor. I've never gone to a strip club, but according to movies, that's the sort of thing that happens there.

Just when I'm reminded of strip clubs, he jerks down his jeans.

"Jonah, no!" I drop my head to a pair of Wranglers on the floor. I'm afraid to look when a pair of hunter orange boxers lands beside them.

I squeeze my eyes shut. "Jonah, get under the cover, now!"

I hear the covers rustle but refuse to lift my eyes. He's too out of it for me to trust he knows what he's doing. I keep my eyes to the ground and walk in the direction of the duffle bags. I rummage through one and find a pair of boxers. I'm not sure if they're clean or dirty, but I'm not about to sniff them and find out. Anything is better than commando.

Since I'm not the best aim, I best walk them over to him. With my hands over my eyes, I shuffle forward until I hit the bed. Then I dare to peek. Thank the Lord, he's under the covers.

I take the boxers and drop them on his chest. "Put these on." Then I turn my back to him. This day has turned into quite the unexpected.

"Done," he shouts behind me in a groggy voice.

My body tingles as I turn around. I peek again, and sure enough, he's covered up and the boxers are nowhere in sight. Which I hope means they're on him.

I slowly ease myself onto the edge of the bed. Maybe if I pin down the cover, he can't toss it back. "Jonah, I'm going to sleep on the couch tonight. If you need anything, yell for me. Do you want anything now? Any food, water?"

"Water," he mutters.

"Okay, I'll be right back." I stand and walk to the door, then turn and point a finger at him. "Stay under the cover."

"Yes, ma'am." He salutes me and grins.

I shake my head on the way to the kitchen. Thanks to Bianca, Jack keeps some groceries on hand now, aside from his usual sweet tea, Mountain Dew, and dog treats. I grab two bottles of water and go back to the bedroom.

Jonah is propped against the headboard with the cover pulled up under his arms. He smiles. "Thank you, Carol," he practically sings out as he takes the water from me.

I open my own water and sit on the edge of the bed. "How's your head?"

He shrugs. "Been better, but I don't feel it as much." He yawns. "Thank you for taking care of me."

"You're welcome." I tuck a piece of loose hair behind my ear and drop my gaze. My cheeks feel flush. Oddly enough, I'd take care of him even if I hadn't been the cause of his injury.

"I only want you to take care of me," he slurs.

I laugh. "As if you had a choice today."

He shakes his head. "No, you could've called Mama or Alex or left me at the hospital."

I laugh even harder. "Left you at the hospital?" I get calling his mom or sister, but I'm pretty sure an overnight stay at Health Cross Medical Care wasn't an option.

He nods. "You're always so good."

"Thanks." My cheeks grow a little warmer, and I find myself moving an inch closer to him. "I'm going to go in there and eat something. If you need anything, call me. Okay?"

He nods and grins, then stretches out his arms. "Hug?"

I smile and lean into his hug. When we're a few inches apart, he turns his head and presses his lips to mine.

I freeze. My body stiffens like stone. I'm petrified in this stance, my arms around Jonah's shoulders and my lips against his. What do I do?

My heart races as I anticipate him kissing me. Really kissing me. Then he pulls back and smiles. I blink. Not what I was expecting. But then, what was I expecting?

Do I want him to kiss me?

Lightning bolts shoot through my body as a tornado of emotions swirls inside. I pull my arms from around him and stand, then take a long drag of my water. This is too weird. He's being weird. He's had a concussion and now heavy medication. I mean, his head is already swelling. Clearly, he's not in his right mind.

Not knowing what to say, I back away from the bed and tiptoe toward the door.

"Carol?" he calls before I leave.

I twist toward him, my hand on the threshold. "Yeah?"

"I love you. I always have."

CHAPTER THIRTEEN

Jonah

Either the woodpecker I've developed a love-hate relationship with since staying at Jack's is outside my window, or my concussion has morphed into an audible drumming noise.

I raise onto my elbows and massage my temples. The room isn't spinning and I'm well rested, so I assume it's the bird. I stand up and yawn, then wince.

It's got to be bad when you smell your own breath. I remember barfing—a couple of times—yesterday. As I stagger from the bedroom to the bathroom, I try and remember what else happened.

Let's see. Sink burst. Hammer to the head. ER visit. X-rays and meds.

For some unknown reason, I recall seeing Paul. I flip on the bathroom light and blink into the cabinet mirror. My eyes widen as I inspect my forehead. A wide row of stitches covers my right eyebrow. The area around it is bruised and a little swollen. I dab my fingertips against it, then notice some dried blood left on my hand.

Maybe I should take a shower. I try and step inside the tub and almost fall back on the toilet. Nope, I'll settle with brushing my teeth for now.

As I reach for my toothbrush, another scene from last night flashes through my mind. I'm pretty sure I kissed Carol. My tongue sticks to the roof of my mouth, and I suddenly find it hard to breathe.

Holy ninnimuggins. I kissed Carol! And I wasn't even coherent enough to remember it. I take my frustration out on the tube of toothpaste, squeezing a fresh strand of goo across the brush bristles and half the sink.

I wash the rogue glob down the drain, then brush my teeth with full force. The minty flavor is like a healing balm to my mouth. Wait . . . was my mouth this ratchet when I kissed Carolina?

I certainly hope not!

My stomach buckles as I continue brushing in quick, firm circles like the people who prep your windshield for the carwash. I spit the minty mush down the drain and wipe my chin before washing my hands. I really could use a shave too, but my stomach begs me to feed it first.

For the first time since I can recall, I don't have to pee after waking up. That probably means I'm dehydrated.

I head toward the kitchen at a snail-like pace. My head is past the headache stage but still sore. When I turn the corner, I'm shocked to see the back of Carolina's head.

"Carolina?"

She jumps and turns around, startled. Then she glances down at my boxer shorts and turns her head back toward the coffee pot. "I expected you to sleep late."

I scratch the back of my head. "So did I." *And I expected you to not be here.*

I stagger to the table and pull out a chair. "What all happened last night?"

She stares out the kitchen window above the sink. "Could you please go put on some pants?"

"Oh, right." I stand and saunter back to the bedroom. Maybe the decency part of my brain is injured. Or at least the part that cares.

I rummage through my bag for some gym shorts and slip those over my underwear. Then I pull on a T-shirt for good measure. When I return wearing clothes, she smiles.

"Want some coffee?"

"Sure, thanks." I return to my chair and rest my elbows on the table. I barely have time to get comfortable before she joins me with two cups of coffee. "Thanks."

I take a sip and relax. She always adds the right amount of cream. My eyes follow her hand as she lifts her own mug to take a sip. I allow my gaze to linger on her lips even after she lowers her mug, then look away when she meets my eyes. Heat rises up my neck and behind my ears. Does she remember the kiss?

She's got to remember the kiss, right? At least one of us should. Unless it was awful, and she chose to forget it. But how can she act so casual now?

"Thanks again for taking care of me yesterday. I know I was a handful."

"No problem." She waves her hand dismissively. Yep, way too casual.

"I wasn't a problem, was I?" I raise a brow in question. Maybe I can ask enough vague questions to lead her into sharing exactly what happened.

Carolina rubs her lips together, causing the heat to travel down my neck to my stomach. I brace myself for her to mention the kiss. Instead, she says, "I had some trouble getting you in the house. Paul helped."

I blink at my coffee before taking another sip. "Yeah, I vaguely recall seeing Paul. What was he doing out here?"

Her face goes deadpan. "Having a Sunday drive with Ms. Dot."

"Oh." I raise my chin, then grin. She laughs.

"They just happened to be in the area." She rolls her eyes.

"And they stopped by?"

She sips her coffee and shifts a little. "Only after you fell back in my car and set off the horn."

I grit my teeth. "Uh, I don't remember that part."

"You were highly medicated. I suspect you don't remember much." The way she draws out the word "much" leads me to believe she's hinting at the kiss.

My palms get a little clammy, so I close them around the mug. At least best I can. The mug has antlers for a handle, which makes it hard to squeeze.

"I remember seeing Paul. Then I think you helped me get into bed."

"Yeah, that's before you started stripping."

"Stripping?" The heat goes from swirling inside my stomach to other areas, embarrassing me further. Exactly what all did I do last night?

"Don't worry. After you threw your shirt in my face, I turned my head." Carol grins around her mug and starts to laugh.

I groan and drop my head in my hands. "Ouch." I lift it after touching my stitches. "Carol, I'm so sorry. I didn't know what I was doing."

"Clearly." Her eyes widen as she downs the last of her coffee.

A thin line of moisture beads across her top lip. I consider rubbing it off with my finger. Maybe even with my tongue. *Stop it!* I can't think like this. I've got to quit fantasizing about my best friend. I've already embarrassed myself enough and I'm not even sure exactly how. Other than the impromptu striptease while I was delirious.

I scratch at the back of my neck to try and stop the jolts of heat traveling from there to my bare feet. This is too much. I must know. "What exactly happened last night, Carol?"

She toys with the antlers on her own mug and stares at the table. "Well, for one, you kissed me."

I feign shock, but she calls me on my bluff. "Come on, Jonah, don't give me that fake face. You've got to remember it."

My shoulders drop. "So I somewhat remember kissing you, but no details."

"It was just a quick peck." She fans in front of her face. I pretend it's because she's now flushed too, and not because she's trying to brush it off as nothing. "No worries. You were drunk on whatever pain pill the nurse gave you."

A small part of my heart chips off. The pain travels all the way to my toes, as if that broken piece bounced down the stairs inside my body and landed in the basement with a crash. I've dreamed of kissing her for ten years. It took me being basically unconscious to get up the nerve. Even worse, I had barf breath and didn't even move my lips enough to consider it making a move.

I rest my cheek on the table and stare at the outdated cabinets. I can't face Carolina right now. Then I close my eyes, hoping when I reopen them, I will realize this is all a bad dream. An alternate universe where I make a fool of myself and have a head knot worthy of an ogre.

A gentle touch tickles my scalp as Carolina's fingers gently caress my hair. My eyelids pop open in surprise, then droop when she continues the circular motion. "Jonah, there's nothing to be embarrassed about. I know you didn't mean it."

Those last words take a sledgehammer to what remains of my heart. That's just the problem. I did mean it. Whatever pill I swallowed must've had a truth serum attached to it. All I've wanted to do since middle school was kiss her. But I purposely waited until we were both out of braces, both mature enough to have kissing experience and appreciate the moment.

Only to squander it on a time when I had hideous breath and a head injury.

Easy as it would be to keep my face planted on the table, the wood cooling my cheek and her hand in my hair, I lift my head. Her hand falls to the table, and her face falls into that sympathetic stare—emphasis on the "pathetic" part.

Since I've dug quite the hole for myself, I may as well go a little deeper and dig my grave. "What happened after the kiss?" My lips tingle as I ask, partly from the idea of having them on Carol's and partly from fear of what she'll say next.

She shrugs and stares down at the table, tracing a wood-grain line with her fingernail. My head gets a little jealous, longing for that gentle scratch against my scalp. Why exactly did I lift my head and beg for more answers?

Without looking up, she gives me those answers. "Well, after I helped you in bed, we hugged. That's when you kissed me. Then you pulled away, and I walked out of the room, and you went to sleep."

"Oh." Knowing that I did nothing else crazy, I should feel relieved. Instead, my injured mind clings to the fact that I was the one to pull away. I bite back a grin. Does that mean she didn't want to pull away?

Maybe it's false hope on my part, or the logical side of my brain lies behind the aching knot. For whatever reason, I let those words give me a snippet of hope that one day, I'll get the chance to kiss her again.

And when I do, I'll make darn sure I remember it.

Carolina

It was nearly dark when I left for Auburn. Jonah slept on and off throughout the day, so I caught up on Netflix and made sure all the animals were fed. Jack only had a few baby deer in the pen, so that wasn't too much trouble with Jonah's instructions.

I endured a mild panic attack when Jonah questioned last night's events, but getting it out in the open made the rest of the day more normal. Like ripping off a Band-Aid. At least most of it. I left out the part where he told me he loved me. That tidbit is too sticky to rip off just yet. I didn't have the gumption to pull that many hairs off my arms at once. Maybe one day I'll peel off the rest of the Band-Aid.

However, I'd much rather it eventually come off on its own. I mean, *if*—and I mean a big *if*—Jonah is in love with me, he will tell me eventually. Right?

I turn on the radio to try and stop the tennis match in my head. My thoughts are a jumbled ball bouncing between "does he love me" and "does he not." If I were an eight-year-old girl, I'd be picking petals off a flower right now to determine the fate of our relationship.

But I'm not. I'm a twenty-three-year-old woman who's trying to decipher the layers of his response. Of course Jonah loves me, and always has. I love him too. He totally embodies the "brother from another mother" cliche, and I can't imagine my life without him, to the point that I dread him getting married one day. Because unlike my real brothers, he's more considerate of my feelings.

I sigh and punch the button to mute my radio. This isn't

helping, especially with every station I turn to playing some sort of love ballad. I'm closing in on Opelika and have analyzed the whys behind Jonah's love confession the whole way. That's long enough to get a college credit.

That is, if they had a class in Jonahology. Which I'd totally ace, by the way. At least I think I would.

Maybe I don't know Jonah as well as I claim. Could he love me in *that* way? Is Daniel right? He's right about a lot of other things.

I yawn as I exit the highway. As soon as I left Jonah to sleep, I called Audrey and then called both our mamas to let them know what happened and why Jonah and I would be MIA for a bit. Then I ate a bowl of cereal and attempted to fall asleep myself. I tossed and turned for hours before finally giving up and watching a movie.

It didn't help that the movie I decided on turned into one of those rom-coms where the friends fall in love. Go figure.

At some point, I dozed off and slept decent until the sun woke me up. Well, as decent as one can sleep on a worn-out couch with two dogs snoring nearby and a man who's just confessed his eternal love sleeping less than thirty feet away with a head injury.

After our little chat over coffee, Jonah acted normal. I made some eggs and bacon. We ate, he slept some more, then we talked and watched reruns of *The Office*.

By the time I dropped him off to get his truck and went to Mama's for a quick shower and my clothes, I'd forgotten about the whole "love" thing. Then she and Daddy told me "I love you" when I left, sending my mind back to last night with Jonah.

I pull up to my apartment and cut off my car. With my hand on the door, I hesitate and sit in the dark silence. All day, I lay around and checked on Jonah. Then I've been in a car alone. I simply need to stay busy to get this nonsense of Jonah loving me out of my head.

With newfound resolve, I open the door and retrieve my bag from the trunk. Then I march toward the apartment with all the confidence of a runway model. Not that any of them are five-foot-four with messy hair and sweats, but I've got the strut down pat.

I give myself a quick pep talk as I rummage through the bottomless pit known as my purse. *You love Jonah, and he loves you. Just not like that. You'll go inside, relax, and think nothing more about a romantic relationship.*

A smug smile crosses my face as I unlock the door and swing it open to Kendra sitting on the couch. Only she's wearing a wedding dress. At least I think that's a wedding dress. Perhaps one that's been mauled by a rabid dog. My smile flattens when she jumps up and twirls around like a toddler taking ballet. So much for not reminding myself of romance.

"Don't you love it?" She flips her sandy blonde hair over one shoulder and bats her eyelashes.

I've known her since freshman year but still can't decide if she's serious half the time. Often to my own detriment.

"Do you love it?" I settle on playing the politician card and answer her question with a question.

"Yes, it's vintage and classy."

I bite my bottom lip and nod slowly. Vintage, definitely. But I think she's confused classy with classic. Or maybe class-less. I gather the gumption to fake smile, which satisfies her enough to ramble on without me having to say anything more.

"I found it at this antique place. They have the quirkiest finds. You'd just love it."

I doubt that, but I continue smiling for my friend. If

she's into this dress, she'd obsess over some of the crap Paul brings into the General Store.

Kendra steps closer and fans out the lacy skirt. It certainly smells like an antique. I wrinkle my nose and take a seat on the chair across from the couch, a safe distance from the musty dress.

Kendra reaches for a massive binder behind her, which I recognize as the dreaded wedding planner. Then she skips across the room and drops it on my lap, closing the distance between me and the mothball scent that lives in that hideous frock she's wearing.

"I've always admired the vintage look." She points to a page of magazine clippings with lace-covered dresses. "And now I can wear my dress as the something old."

My eyes trail from the binder weighing down my legs to Kendra. As her friend and roommate, can I allow her to wear this down the aisle?

"You know, a lot of brides are doing something similar, but by repurposing their mother's dress."

Kendra plops down on the arm of my chair and sighs. "I can't do that."

"Does your mom not have a wedding dress?"

She shakes her head. "Not that. Her dress is cursed."

I laugh, then stop when she shoots me a serious glare. "My parents are divorced."

"And?"

"And why would I want to wear something that ended in divorce?"

I shift best I can underneath the barrier of the binder. "Kendra, I don't think that has anything to do with it. I don't believe your mama's dress is jinxed."

"No, cursed, I said cursed." She narrows her eyes as she corrects me.

"Well, that either."

I stare down at the dresses on the page in front of me. Kendra makes small sniffling sounds that grow louder by the second. Before I can lift my head to check if she's crying, she slides onto my lap and starts to sob.

She's always been the emotional type and cries on my shoulder now and again. But I've never had her sit in my lap. I pat her shoulder and try to not inhale the mothball bomb surrounding her.

"It's okay, Kendra. You'll be beautiful in anything, and Brandon and you will have a great marriage. You could get married in overalls and it wouldn't matter."

She lifts her head from my shoulder and sniffles. "That's a great idea."

"Repurposing your mom's dress?"

"No, marrying in overalls. I'd be like the first bride to do so. I can stick flowers in that little front pocket." Her face fades, and I'm certain it has everything to do with my reaction. "Maybe I should look for dresses with my sister when I go home next weekend. You know, just in case."

I nod. "I'm sure she'd love that."

Kendra sighs and relaxes more of her weight onto me, digging the edge of the binder into my hip. I grimace and try to ignore the slight pain.

"I'm just so nervous, you know." She sniffles some more, then wipes her nose across the sleeve of the dress.

I'm more worried about her nose than the dress. If a disease can be caught through the nostrils, she's as good as dead.

"My parents divorced, and Brandon's parents divorced. If we put our marriage in one of those Punnett squares, the odds are divorce is the dominant trait."

I blink down at the faded lace across my lap. My parents love each other to the point that it's sickening. Aside from Hannah, nobody I'm close to has been through a divorce.

And from what I've picked up on through her and Tanner, she did everything in her power to prevent it from happening. I wish I had some consolation for Kendra, but all I can offer her is my support and the love I sense between Brandon and her.

"Kendra, I don't know where you're coming from, but I do know that you're not your parents or Brandon's. He loves you. It's so evident. The way he watches out for you, knows all your little quirks and preferences, cheers you up when you're sad, always puts you first. If that's not love, I don't know what is."

Kendra's lips wiggle at the corners before turning into a smile. "Yeah, he does love me."

I nod. "And you him. That's all that matters."

"Thanks, roomie." She wraps her arms around me, squeezing me in a hug. I turn my head best I can when the snot sleeve reaches across my face. That only makes her squeeze me tighter, and the iced coffee I chugged on the last leg of my drive starts to make its move.

"Uh, Kendra. I really need to pee."

"Oh, sorry." She hops off my lap with the ease of a circus performer, which isn't far-fetched given her attire. I lift the binder and hoist it toward her before hurrying to the bathroom.

Once I'm on my throne for the time being, I relax for the first time in hours. My heart aches for my friend. I sure hope she can realize just how much Brandon loves her, regardless of their family history.

I close my eyes and sigh, recounting my novice advice. "Oh crap!" My eyes pop open when I realize that everything I said about Brandon with Kendra also applies to me.

With Jonah!

CHAPTER FOURTEEN

Jonah

As if waking up to a bruised boulder on my head wasn't enough, I realize it's Tuesday. I'm supposed to help Daddy at the store before going back to Auburn.

I take a shower to wake myself up since I didn't get to that yesterday. With all the lying around, I could wring the oil out of my hair and use it to fill my truck. Poor Carolina had to deal with my nasty self all day.

I shudder as I massage shampoo onto my scalp. She deserves some sort of reward for hanging around all day, especially after our talk about the kiss.

Of course, she casually commented that I was out of my mind. Maybe to the point of not remembering tossing my shirt at her or stripping off my underwear. But kissing her? That, I remember . . . sort of.

The fact that I have any recollection of it lets me know it was intentional. But I didn't let her know that.

When I wasn't asleep yesterday, I analyzed her actions. Paid close attention to her expressions for any clue that she didn't mind me kissing her. Or, just maybe, that she wanted me to kiss her.

I hop out of the shower and dry off, carefully blotting the sore spot on my head. Chocolate and Brownie meet me in the hallway on the way back to the bedroom. "In a minute, girls. Let me change."

Jack has gotten them spoiled to his schedule. One morning, I slept in after working late on the house. They came in my room and scratched at the blinds until I woke up.

As if understanding me completely, they stay in the hallway, but continue staring my way. It's a little awkward having two female dogs watch me drop my towel and put on clothes.

"Stalkers," I mumble as I head to the laundry room for their food. They wag their tails, happy to ignore me now that their bowls are filled with kibble.

I shrug on my coat and go to the pen where Jack has baby deer. There are two right now weaning off bottles. I mix some milk and feed them both half a bottle, per his instructions. He's transitioning them to grasses.

Once my animal duties are done, I load up my duffle bags and lock up the house. I reach for the Auburn cap I keep on my truck dash and try best I can to fit it on my head. With one side swollen, it doesn't quite fit like usual.

I plan on driving straight to Auburn after I leave the store. Jack and Bianca get back this weekend, which means I'll go back to staying with my parents. On a positive note, that means no more animals to feed. On the negative, my daddy will know just how much time I spend at the mansion. He's already made several snide comments about how I'm wasting time when I could simply work at the store and get paid right away.

What he doesn't get is that the risk is part of my reward. Fixing up a place someone left for rubble and having some family fall in love with it, all while making a hefty payday, is a huge adrenaline rush for me. I want to build something I can be proud of. To take someone else's discards and turn them into a winning hand.

Helping someone decide what type of nails are best for a smaller, personal project isn't going to cut it for me. Not forever.

I'm halfway to the store when my stomach growls. In all the commotion of feeding animals, I forgot to feed myself. I pull into the gas station for something quick. Either that, or I'll get stuck eating peanuts and beef jerky from beside the cash register. Several old men hover around the coffee machine, so I grab a Mountain Dew and a biscuit. Rumor has it we're getting a Jack's down by the highway, close to Outdoorsman Oasis. That would put a hurting on the Quick Stop's breakfast business.

The cashier tilts her head as if trying to get a better look at my forehead. I drop my head until I'm done so I don't have to explain the hammer situation. Thanks to my ER visit, I'm sure it'll be all over town soon enough. Especially since Paul witnessed my inebriated state.

Five minutes later, I'm chewing the last bite of my sausage biscuit and parking at the side of the store. I crumple the silver wrapper in my hand and toss it in the bed of my truck on my way inside.

Aside from a few shuffling noises, the store is quiet. I walk past the break room to Daddy's office. He's behind his desk, glasses in place, opening mail.

"Jonah."

How does he do that? He hasn't looked my way and I haven't spoken a word, but he knows it's me.

"Yes, sir?"

He raises his eyes to meet mine and frowns. "Why didn't you tell me about your injury?"

I cup the bill of my cap as if I can hide it. "In my defense, I was out of it until I showered an hour ago."

"Carolina called your mother last night. Said she didn't want us finding out through the grapevine."

I move my hand from my cap and shove it in my pocket. Daddy adjusts his glasses and focuses back on the mail, but continues talking. "You need to take your time on this house, son. When you rush things, you're not careful. That's how people get hurt."

"Daddy." I take a moment to swallow and compose myself, so I won't raise my voice. "I wasn't in a hurry. The sink pipe burst, and I kinda jerked my head up too fast, right where Carol was holding up a hammer."

He leans back in his chair. It squeaks, and I smirk, imagining Papa Rat laughing. Do rats laugh?

"You think this is all fun and fine, but you're wasting your time."

My smile fades. "Excuse me?"

"This house stuff." Daddy pulls his glasses from his face and wipes his finger across the bridge of his nose. "I know you like your projects. Lord knows, so do I. So I've kept quiet and not asked you to work here unless I need you." He returns his glasses to his face and gives me the stern stare he reserves for when I'm in trouble.

I'm a grown man about to graduate college and now stand two inches taller than him, but he still intimidates me with that face.

"Jonah, your time would be better spent here getting to know our main vendors, building camaraderie with the staff. I'm willing to retire soon, but not until I know the store will be in good hands."

His glare has nothing on his words when it comes to

intimidation. I shrink back against the door frame, suddenly eight years old again. Right after I wrecked the lawnmower into the shed.

Tell him! My inner thoughts scream for me to just come clean and tell Daddy that I don't want to run the store. But I can't. At least not now.

"I'm sorry. This is really important to me, and I'm about to graduate. Could I please work on the house, just until graduation?"

Daddy's face softens as he leans forward and sighs. "I suppose so."

I stand a little taller, as if the shift in his tone has given me back the six inches I lost earlier. "Thank you."

He nods. "Sure, son. I was young once too." As I turn to leave, he calls out again. "And Jonah?"

I twist my head. "Yes, Daddy?"

"On one condition." Oh, here we go. "If I need you here to meet someone or do something important to your future, you will come."

"Yes, sir." I force a half-smile before marching down the hallway. The farther I get from his office, the lighter I feel.

I don't want to be groomed to take over the store, and I get the sense that Daddy will find a lot of insignificant reasons for me to show up more. Even worse, I've upped the ante on my deadline. Not only do I need to finish this house and make a profitable flip to bring Carolina back home, but I also have until graduation to prove my capabilities as a builder to my father.

Sighing, I slide past Uncle John's office into the extra office, which doubles as a junk room for files and other miscellaneous items. All the things we can't throw away but don't know where to put. This is my makeshift workroom for now. Daddy drops hints all the time that I can move into his office when I'm ready.

All I can say is he best WD-40 his chair and settle in for the long haul. I flip on the lights and frown at the stack of files waiting on the desk. Inventory. My least favorite task, yet the one Daddy so eagerly passed on a few years back.

It's one of those repetitive chores where you think you've finished, only to have to start all over. Like mowing grass or washing clothes. Never-ending busy work.

I rub the side of my head, then fix my cap back best I can. I could use a good brain freeze right about now.

Some guys drown their problems in beer. I drown mine in a pint of Blue Bell Homemade Vanilla. If that makes me a teenage girl mourning a breakup, so be it. I like my ice cream.

Before diving into the dreaded first folder on a stack as long as my forearm, I pull out my phone to text Carolina. I find the ice cream cone emoji, which makes me even more of a teenage girl. Then I add the word "tonight?" She replies right away.

That bad?

I follow with one of those worried/stressed smileys. Her response is the movie camera emoji. A huge grin stretches across my face.

Today may be filled with a mountain of inventory work and playing pretend heir to the family business. However, tonight I get to indulge in my three secret guilty pleasures: ice cream, rom-com movies, and Carolina.

Carolina

Today, I had to play catchup on spreadsheets, thanks to being out Monday with Jonah. For once, I don't mind the busy work. All the mundane information has helped me keep my mind on something other than if Jonah's in love with me.

And if I'm possibly in love with him.

I've always found Jonah attractive, but never viewed him in *that* way. A lot of girls have asked me about him over the years, especially at Auburn. For some reason, I've always discouraged them from dating him. My reasons were shallow and silly, such as "If you knew what a goof he was, or how aggravating he could be . . ." I'd follow my argument with saying he's like my brother, I should know.

Now I'm wondering if on some subconscious level, I was combating potential suitors out of jealousy. When he dated Sasha, there were no random texts like this morning about hanging out later that day. I missed that so much.

Maybe I didn't want a girl to date him—even a great girl —because it meant less time he could hang out with me. Or maybe, just maybe, I really do have deeper feelings for him.

I drum my fingertips on my desktop. They tingle with numbness as my nerves tense. Not long from now, we'll be in his trailer, alone, watching a romantic movie. Do I bring up him saying he loved me, even though he was doped up on pain meds when he did? Do I prod him for clues on how he really sees me? Or do I act like usual?

This is so strange, and all new territory to me.

The phone in my cubicle rings, jolting my attention away from Jonah. I stare at it like a ticking bomb for a moment before picking up.

"Home-Sweet-Home Designs, this is Carolina."

"Hey, Carolina, it's Audrey. Can you stop by my office before you head out for the day? I have some exciting news."

"Yes, ma'am."

The phone clicks off, and I sit like a statue as the dial tone moans in my ear. Exciting news? I return the landline to its receiver and stare at my computer screen. Could this mean an end to my career as master spreadsheet checker?

I stretch out my hands, then resume typing. My fingers tingle even more now, thanks to Audrey's looming secret. Between my curiosity about the "exciting news" and my anticipation of how things will go tonight with Jonah, it takes every bit of focus I have to finish the last half hour of work.

A little before six, I shut down my computer and rub my eyes. Many of my cube mates have gone home, and the front door closed to the public at five.

It's customary for Audrey to work until six, leaving after everyone else. I slide back my chair and collect my purse and coat, then head toward her office. My heels echo as they click on the wood floor, reminding me how very few people remain in the building. With no clue what Audrey's news might entail, I wanted to wait as late as possible. In a pathetically loyal sense, I decided to get as much work done on my current project as possible in case she promotes me off spreadsheet duty.

I rap my knuckles against her open door, and she looks up from her computer screen.

"Come in, have a seat."

I take a seat in one of the two stiff office chairs facing her desk. She clears her throat and pushes her blonde hair over one shoulder. "Carolina, you've done a great job so far keeping me organized."

"Thank you." I lace my fingers and squeeze my hands together in anticipation of what's coming.

"I know spreadsheets aren't glamorous, but we haven't had many brand-new projects since you've started."

I nod and squeeze my hands tighter. Visions of me taking a hammer to my computer screen and smashing through a spreadsheet swirl though my head. Then the scene transitions to the all too real scene of hitting Jonah with the hammer. I flinch and unlock my fingers, running them down my pants leg.

"Are you okay?"

"Yes," I answer, pulling my hands back in my lap. *Focus, Carol. You're about to get a real job.*

"As I was saying, we've had a few new projects come in recently. I want to put you on one of the teams."

I shove my hands under my hips to keep from flailing them in the air. This is happening. I'm getting to work on an actual project!

"You'll be helping Rhonda on this fun new remodel."

My stomach flips. Maybe I can incorporate some of the ideas I had that won't work for the mansion. How fun will that be? Two remodels at the same time. I really am like Joanna Gaines.

Audrey smiles and leans across her desk. "You'll be turning a spare bedroom into a puppy nursery."

She did not just say dog nursery. The one project file I've come across that sounds like a bad joke. Would it be rude to decline? Probably so. I plaster on my fakest smile.

"And I have even better news."

Dear Lord, I hope so!

"You get to design the potty area all by yourself!" By the enthusiasm in Audrey's voice, you'd think she worked for Publisher's Clearing House.

Someone pinch me, shoot me, anything. Just wake me up from this nightmare. I have no trouble holding my fake smile, as my face is now frozen in shock.

"Only a few more days of straight spreadsheets to catch

me up, then you can meet with Rhonda on Monday." Audrey smiles and nods.

I mimic her nod like I'm a puppet on a string. In a way, I am, and Audrey is one disturbed puppet master. Not knowing how else to respond, I stand slowly and lie. "That sounds great." It comes out sing-songy, like I'm a kid actor in one of those after school specials.

Before Audrey has time to analyze the sincerity of my answer, I turn and walk out of her office. Thankfully, the hallway remains void of anyone who might notice the snarl on my face as I head for my car.

I reach for my keys and unlock the door, then grab my phone and text Jonah two ice cream cone emojis before typing, "Better make it a double."

Dots appear, and I climb in my car as I wait for his response. My phone dings, and it's a photo of two gallons of Blue Bell sitting on his linoleum counter.

If that isn't love, I don't know what is.

I'm by no means a health nut, but I do make it a point to eat regular meals instead of diving headfirst into a vat of ice cream. However, some days call for a sugar fix.

That's why I drove straight to Jonah's trailer park, not bothering to stop by my apartment or even a restaurant for actual takeout. I'll eat ice cream and whatever else he's dishing up tonight. I've got more important things to worry about than food. Like whether Daniel's delirious hypothesis holds any weight. Oh, and how to design a potty area for puppies.

Ugh. I roll my eyes and slam my door shut in front of Jonah's trailer. I lock it behind me, since a few people had tools stolen last month. It's mostly college kids living here, but not all are honest.

I climb the wooden steps to his door and knock on the metal frame.

"It's open," he calls from the other side.

I push open the door and grin at Jonah standing in the kitchen, scooping up two large bowls of heavenly vanilla.

"How'd you know I'd be coming right away?"

He grins back. "Your text sounded a little desperate, especially since it's not yet your time of the month."

My neck warms, and I run my finger under my collar to separate it from my collarbone. Is it weird that he knows that about me? Absolutely. But Jonah can read my moods better than anyone, and I'm pretty sure he's had that week marked on a calendar someplace for a while. For his own safety.

As a reminder of how much I hate him mentioning it, I toss my keys at his head. He ducks and they land in the sink. "Wow, maybe you shouldn't have given up your basketball career so soon."

"Haha," I snark. He and Tanner always give me a hard time about my lack of coordination.

I drop my purse and coat on the couch by the door. The bowl of ice cream calls my name as it glistens underneath the ugly kitchen light fixture. Jonah slides one bowl toward me, then reaches under the counter. He lifts a brown paper bag with a circular logo sticker on the front.

"Is that?"

Jonah's face lights up as he nods. "They were parked by the gas station on my way into town. So I decided to treat you—and me."

I lick my lips as he pulls two small Bundt cakes from the bag. One is red velvet, his favorite, and the other is strawberry, mine. He slides it my way, and I grab for the clear container like a football player recovering a fumbled ball. I may not can do sports but I at least know how they work.

Jonah laughs, and our fingers brush as I pull the cake my way. My pulse speeds up for a split second, and I can't decide if it's because Jonah's hand is against mine or the anticipation of eating my favorite dessert.

"I'll get some spoons, and we can eat on the couch."

"Sounds good." With my Bundt cake in one hand and my bowl of ice cream in the other, I plop down beside my coat.

Jonah lives alone and has one couch and a recliner. In addition to squeaking every time the legs lift, the recliner is right beside the TV, making it impossible to watch while in it. When it's just us two watching TV, we share the couch. That makes so much more sense than pulling up a five-gallon bucket. He keeps three of them stacked in the laundry closet for extra guests.

I settle onto the well-worn cushion and tuck my legs beside me. Jonah sits on the opposite end, then scoots a little closer as he hands me a spoon.

"Thanks." The word comes out so raspy that it embarrasses me. I switch the direction of my feet, pointing them toward Jonah so I can shift toward the arm of the couch. I sit by him all the time. But that was before he kissed me and said he'd always loved me.

If this were a movie, Dolly Parton and Keith Whitley would break out in a love ballad while I awkwardly debate if I want to sit closer or farther from Jonah. Or say screw it and go get a bucket seat.

My neck heats up again, so I take a generous bite of my ice cream. He turns on the TV and scrolls through movie titles. I'm convinced both Jonah and Tanner use me as an excuse to watch rom-coms. Of course, Tanner now has Hannah for a movie buddy. Neither of them likes to admit to the other that they watch this sort of lovey-dovey fluff, as they say, but I know better.

However, both have threatened me to secrecy.

Hmm . . . note to self, if I really want answers out of Jonah, I can blackmail him with his movie preferences.

"Oh, here's a classic. Let's watch this one."

I'm too busy getting lost in my Bundt cake to answer, but the irony of his choice makes me a little uneasy. *My Best Friend's Wedding.*

At least he didn't choose something like *Friends with Benefits.* I sink into my cushion as the movie starts. Jonah takes off his cap and starts rustling his hand through his hair. Fresh man smells funnel my way as he does.

Like a bloodhound, I sniff the air, taking in the scent of pine mixed with mint. I catch him looking my way out of the corner of my eye and drop my gaze to my bowl. As I scoop some ice cream, his hand comes toward me. I freeze as his spoon lands on my Bundt cake.

I slowly lift my eyes, then blink when I realize his face is mere inches from mine. He swallows and lifts his lips in a slight grin.

Crap! Is he going to kiss me?

I close my eyes, not sure what to do. Should I let him? Do I want to let him? Should I just go ahead and make the first move?

"Can I have a bite of your Bundt cake?"

My eyes pop open to his begging face. "Uh, yeah, of course. You bought them." I giggle like a schoolgirl as he spoons out a generous bite and pops it in his mouth. He still hasn't moved his face. Instead of moving my own, I study the motion of his jaw as he chews. My chest tightens as I imagine what it feels like inside his mouth.

His eyes flicker to me, and my cheeks heat up. Jonah's

good at guessing what's on my mind. I hope he's not trying to analyze my thoughts at this moment.

As if I couldn't get more flustered, he licks the corners of his mouth before sitting back against the couch and facing forward. I try my best to focus on the movie too, but all I can think about is whether Jonah wanted to kiss me and what he meant by saying he loved me.

Even worse, I think *I* may want to kiss him now. Like for real kiss him. And for the rest of the night, all I can think about is how great it could be since his face is freshly shaven and he has strawberry Bundt cake breath.

CHAPTER FIFTEEN

Jonah

Something happened Tuesday night, and I'm not sure what. Carolina was quieter than ever, especially for her. Even though she often had a mouthful of Bundt cake and ice cream, still, uncharacteristically quiet.

I hoist a box of nails onto a shelf in the hardware store's stockroom and move on to the next box as I replay my movie night with Carol.

We talked a little about our work, and she mentioned getting promoted to designing a dog toilet or something like that. I guess that's why she didn't have much to say. There can't be much more humiliating things than planning a place for dog poop.

I thanked her for calling my parents but left it at that. No need to worry her with my own work drama. Sitting beside her with a bucket of Blue Bell and a mindless movie that delivered laughs and a happy ending was all the therapy I needed to destress.

We've texted some the last few days, but I haven't seen her since she left my trailer Tuesday night. After the movie, she lingered by the doorway when I stood to let her out. I kept getting the sense she wanted to say something important. But she just stood there, staring at me for a long pause before saying good night.

Whatever it is, I might can pry it out of her tonight when we meet at the house. More than anything, it bothers me that something might be bothering her.

"Son, I need you to make a delivery."

I turn to Daddy standing a few feet behind me. "Sure, where?"

"Paul needs some things." He pulls a folded receipt paper out of his front shirt pocket and hands it to me. I scan the page, noting the various types of screws Paul ordered.

"Okay. Does he want them right now?"

"Yeah. You know Paul. Once he gets something on his mind, it's then or never. Go ahead and take them, then go on home."

I narrow my eyes. Is this a test? Just in case, I answer with, "I can come back afterward if you need me."

"No, it's Friday. Go on and start your weekend."

I half grin. "Thanks." I'm not sure if he realizes my weekend plans all revolve around the mansion. But hey, I'll take all the extra hours I can get. Even a little less than two at the end of the day.

Daddy walks away without saying anything else, as he often does. I'm not sure I've ever heard him say the word "bye" before. He just sort of meanders off once he's said his piece.

I continue stacking the few boxes nearby, marking off my

inventory list for each one I've stocked. Once I finish with the nails, I revisit Paul's list to gather his supplies.

Paul is a unique character, and in more ways than simply owning a store with the most miscellaneous junk. He mooches off all the events in town for free food. Mama said he once showed up at a baby shower to hoard some of those little square cakes women make. He's also been known to pull up at the Pig and honk his horn. Someone comes out, gets his grocery list, and shops for him. Paul had people shop for him long before the invention of Instacart.

He has some kind of entitlement thing going on, in my opinion.

It's in Paul's best interest that I don't take over the store one day. I'd keep deliveries to large items like lumber and tile, then charge a delivery fee. He'd probably boycott us.

However, I hope to avoid all that and make my future in building rather than managing a store.

With that hope in mind, I box up Paul's screws and take them to my trainwreck of an office, totaling the price and printing an invoice before heading to my truck.

I suck in the crisp air and the freedom of having the rest of the weekend on my timetable. That is, after this delivery.

I drive the few blocks to Paul's store and park in his gravel lot. Despite going inside hundreds of times, his store still gives me the creeps. It's that stupid sign above the door that reads, "From a cradle to a coffin." As a little boy, I'd grip my parents' hands so tightly every time we went inside that my knuckles looked like white marbles.

A jingle rings out when I open the door. That's new, but not unusual. For here, at least. Paul likes to demonstrate doorbells and other gadgets he has for sale. Part of his marketing scheme is to use the things he sells. The curtains and rods on the dressing rooms are all for sale, as are the shoe racks holding up discounted boots.

I once noticed a price tag on his cash register.

"Paul?" I crane my head to find him, since nobody's in the store aside from an older man examining coffee mugs.

Paul pokes his head around the corner and grins. His belt buckle glistens in the light of a nearby floor lamp. It's not far from weighing as much as him.

"Hey there, Jonah."

"I brought what you needed from the store."

He claps his hands together loudly as his face lights up. "Perfect! I've got a few loose screws that need fixin'."

No kidding . . .

I chew the inside of my mouth to keep from saying something sarcastic.

"Come with me." He motions for me to follow him to the back. We pass the infamous wall of boots and go through the door leading to the back, where I've never gone before.

The lighting is dim, and shelves of funeral flowers and gardening tools go on for what feels like miles. I don't like it back here.

We travel past rows of anything and everything, from drink tumblers and fly flaps to bathrobes and blue jeans. At the very end of the room is my worst nightmare.

Every fear of this place I've conjured up as a child comes to fruition when I lay eyes on a coffin.

"Is that?"

"Yeah." Paul lays his hand on the hood like it's a car. That brings a whole new meaning to the phrase, "Ride or die."

I swallow. "So the screws are for the coffin?" Just to clarify once and for all that they're not for Paul's head.

"Yeah. It's not staying shut. Those things can happen when you get a used model."

I cough, barely able to choke out, "Used?"

"Yep. A feller wanted cremated, but his wife just had to have him on display so she could take one last family photo.

So they rented it for the funeral only, then did the whole urn thing afterward."

This is now beyond my worst nightmare. Eight-year-old Jonah couldn't have imagined someone renting a coffin for show, then selling it to Paul. My hands start to sweat, and the box of screws slip out, hitting the concrete floor.

"Whoopsie, I'll get that." Paul moves his hand from the coffin casual as can be. Good thing too, because I'm frozen, unable to bend.

He picks up the box and straightens, holding his back. "That box is heavy." He draws out the word heavy for emphasis.

I stare at his belt buckle, no longer shining in this dimly lit area. If he can hold that thing up all day, my box of screws shouldn't send him to the chiropractor. And why I had to come back here with him is beyond me.

"If that's all you need, I'd best get back to work." I lift my eyebrows in question.

"Oh right." Paul chuckles and sets the box of screws inside the coffin.

My skin itches like I've napped in a live ant bed. He pats me on the shoulder with the coffin-touch hand, causing my shoulder to burn. I shrug his hand off as we start toward the front of the room. I keep my gaze forward after accidentally locking eyes with one of those porcelain dolls on a random shelf.

At last, we reach the doorway. Paul opens the door, and it takes everything in me to not kiss the ground after I pass the threshold.

I breathe in the weird scents of his store, happy to replace the musty funeral vibes with the mixture of fruity incense and gardening mulch.

The older guy meets us at the cash register with a couple of coffee mugs. "Just a second there, Jonah," Paul says to me before circling behind the counter and checking out the man's merchandise.

I stand by as Paul rings up a mug shaped like a hound dog's body and another that reads, "Farts are always funny."

The man laughs about giving this to his brother-in-law, and then Paul shares a corny joke with him. Finally, Paul pays me for the screws. I reluctantly collect sweaty cash and change, then thank him. I ask him for an envelope, which he gladly gives me for fifty cents.

Then I tuck the money inside and try not to read too much into why it's so sweaty. Who knows where it came from? A woman's bra, a meth head's stash, or the coffin in the back.

I shudder at the idea of touching something from any of those, then abandon the creepy store for sunlight and freedom. Time to escape to my dilapidated mansion now that I'm scarred for life.

Three hours into gutting the back bedroom, I hear a car park out front. I glance through the window at Carolina. It's dark outside, so I hurry to the front of the house and flip on the porch light.

She stands and pulls a bag from her passenger side. I open the door, and my heart beats faster with the excitement of the only barrier between us now removed.

"I bought some food from Big Butts on the way in. Figured you'd be hungry."

"Always, thanks." I take the bag from her when she makes it up the porch steps. "I have us some drinks in the cooler."

"Great." She smiles and a playfulness glimmers in her

eyes. Before my brain has time to decode that look, she turns and hurries down the porch.

I stand holding the food, hoping her cheerfulness is about seeing me and not something stupid, such as designing dog toilets being more fun than she expected.

Carol returns with a duffle bag on her arm. "I've still got to change. I left right after work."

I motion for her to pass me and soak in the scent of her shampoo as the top of her head waves under my face. Then I close the door and turn off the porch light. The last thing I want is anyone stopping by "just wanting to say hi because the light was on." One of the most annoying traits about small-town living. That and when people leave town and say, "Go with us." I'll never understand that one for sure.

We go to the kitchen, and Carol grins at the walls. "I see you finished taking down the fruit."

"Yeah, not an easy task, but I got 'er done."

"Looks good." She smiles, and I smile back. She blushes a little, making my heart jump.

There's a flirty something in the air between us, and I'm certain it started Tuesday night. I don't know how or why, but I choose to enjoy rather than question it.

I put the food on the counter and start unpacking the Styrofoam boxes. "Wow, one whole box of ribs."

"Yeah, I caught them right before closing. Billy Bob topped us off with half a slab he didn't want to take home."

"Sweet." I grab some paper plates and plastic forks from the cabinet nearby, then pull a Diet Coke from the cooler for Carol.

"Thanks." She takes the can from me, brushing my hand with hers. There's always a bit of energy that lights up whenever I touch Carol. But this time, I swear it's as if she feels it too.

She slowly pulls her hand away and walks to the counter.

We fix our plates in silence. Then I top off my tea and hoist myself onto the counter. Carol does the same a few feet away, though with much more effort than me.

"I really need to bring in some chairs and maybe a small table."

She shakes her head. "I don't mind eating on the counter. I'll just pretend it's a log and we're camping."

I frown. "Like you ever went camping with us."

She balks. "There was that one time in your backyard."

I stare at the popcorn ceiling and try to recall. "Oh yeah. Jack and Tanner and me set up that tent. You came to eat s'mores, then fell asleep in the tent while we played Uno."

We might've been ten at the time. It was before the days I might've freaked out at having Carolina Nash sleep next to me. In movies, they often have the cheesy scene where the guy sees the girl differently for the first time and realizes he wants her for more than a friend. Well, cheesy as it is, that's exactly how it happened for me in middle school. Only there was no background music for my montage of feelings, and I'm pretty sure she never had that moment about me.

Or has she? Given the shift in our relational climate this week, it might be worth pondering.

"Yeah, see, I camped." Her voice brings me back to reality.

"Not on purpose." I laugh, then chew a bite of rib.

"So? I still slept outside in a tent." She arches an eyebrow and tosses back her Coke.

"I bought some paint samples at the store today." Wow, that came out of nowhere. I shove a forkful of baked beans in my mouth to keep from rambling.

Even with carrying the torch for Carolina so long, I've never acted nervous around her. I'll blame it on my near-death experience with Paul and the used coffin rather than her sudden flirtatiousness.

"That's exciting. For any room in particular?"

I sip my tea, then waver my head. "Mainly this front area. You mentioned liking pale blues and neutrals, so I poured a few small cans for us to try."

"Fun, can we test them after we eat?"

I laugh. Her enthusiasm is adorable. "After you change clothes." I point the rib in my hand toward her dress pants and nice shirt.

She glances down and frowns. "Yeah, I probably should've done that before eating barbecue as well."

"You'll be fine. Now your brother . . . he'd already be wearing sauce for sleeves."

"No doubt." She laughs.

We chat about the paint a few more minutes, then I tell her about my encounter with Paul and the coffin as we finish eating. I enjoy the metamorphosis of her expressions as I relay my worst nightmare played out in the General Store.

Carol laughs so hard that she sloshes some of her drink onto her shirt. Without thinking, I grab a handful of paper napkins and pat them against her collarbone. Once my hand shifts a little lower, I realize what I'm doing and drop the napkins.

"Uh, sorry," I mutter, dropping my head to hide my embarrassment.

"It's fine. I'll go ahead and change."

I refuse to lift my eyes to check if she looks fine. Instead, I stare at the bones on my plate while she scoots down from the counter and grabs her duffle bag.

The last thing I wanted was to accidentally grope her. I've hugged her, carried her, and held her many times for fun, comfort, and any other reason she might need me. But I've never crossed into the area of her forbidden fruit.

What was I thinking trying to clean a Coke stain in that area? I feel like a creep.

I busy myself bagging up the trash to try and ease my mind. When she comes back into the room, she's dressed in a baggy sweatshirt that's also dry. Her face is neutral.

"Carol, I didn't mean—"

She walks up to me and puts her finger on my lips to shush me. A gesture she's done many times before, but one that feels more sensual somehow in this moment. "It's okay, Jonah. I know you didn't mean anything. You were only trying to help. You're always a gentleman."

With her finger still on my lips, I answer, "Thanks." That's all I can say, because what else can I say in a moment like this? One where I'd really like to simply kiss her finger instead of talking. But I refrain.

She slides her finger down my chin, which is much more intimate than her usual movement of jerking her hand back after a moment of shushing me. This makes my head spin, and I draw my lips in once her finger is gone. They tingle from missing her touch.

"I promise, it's fine," she whispers as she brings her hand back up to my face to rest on my jaw.

All I can think about is how much I want to pull her in for a kiss . . . and how I should've shaved this morning.

Before I can respond either by words or actions, she pats my jaw and drops her hand again. Then she turns on her heels and shouts over her shoulder, "Now let's get to work!"

Easier said than done, since I'm soooo focused on wall paint and flooring after all that.

CHAPTER SIXTEEN

Carolina

My vision blurs as I stare ahead at the aisle of light fixtures. Normally, shopping for home supplies makes me giddy. Today, my head's not in the game. Instead, it's less on the job and more on the client.

Jonah may or may not be in love with me, but I'm almost certain I'm in love with him. And that's a big problem.

According to all the romance movies, it's the best kind of happy ending. Girl meets boy, and over time, they become best friends. Then they eventually realize they're in love and live happily ever after.

If only real life were that simple.

Because I have no clue how he feels about me. Jonah's the same no matter how I approach him. I can flirt, smile, or simply stay quiet. He's the same. Solid as a rock.

Short of making the first move or point-blank asking him

if he's in love with me, I have no way of knowing how he feels.

During my little epiphany on the toilet earlier in the week, I'd decided everything he did and said pointed to love. I'm sure it does, but I'm not sure it points to *in* love.

Jonah's a loving person all around. He cares deeply for anyone and everyone in his life—including me. One might say especially me, but I could argue it's because we're together so much. I've become an extension of his family. A surrogate sister of sorts.

Why else would he have not made a move by now?

He's not a shy person, and he's dated other women. Add to that the fact that we're together all the time, and alone more than ever. Why wouldn't he make a move? I all but planted myself within kissing range on his couch Tuesday.

Then there's last night. I basically fondled his kissing mechanics with my finger, only to have him stare back at me with that goofy grin. Did he mistake my moves for aggravation? Am I that off my flirting game?

Maybe I should call Daniel and fondle his face to see if it works. Nah, not worth it.

"Earth to Carolina."

I blink as Hannah swipes a hand in front of my face. "I thought I lost you there for a moment."

"Oh," I laugh, happy she can't read my thoughts. We're looking at light fixtures and potential appliances for the kitchen.

Jonah and I decided on some flooring and paint colors last night before stripping the carpet from the back bedrooms. He had worked hard on the walls in there too.

He really doesn't need me on the grunt work, as I'm probably more of a hinderance than help. But I'd like to think he enjoys having me around. I've enjoyed being there.

"I'm thinking a modern chandelier for the dining room,

but more common fixtures for the rest. I want to keep the regal feel, but make it still seem homey, you know?"

Hannah squints up at the fixtures hanging overhead. "Yeah, I agree, especially if you want to try and sell to a family. Nobody wants multiple chandeliers for kids to swing on and shoot Nerf bullets through."

I grin at her. "Are we talking about Taylor or my brother?"

"Both." She laughs and rolls her eyes. "And any potential future children."

My face lights up. "You two better have children one day! I didn't get to know Taylor as a baby."

She blushes. While I have no problem thinking about my brother and Hannah having kids one day, I sense that she finds it an awkward conversation with me. "We'll try, but slow down. We're not even officially engaged yet."

I nod and decide to focus on that instead. An engagement and wedding, I have no problem pressuring them about. "It's about time you two tie the knot."

She smiles. "I'm glad you think so. I just want to make sure everything is right, you know?"

I offer her a sympathetic face and refrain from pointing out what she already knows. There's no way Tanner would ever leave her or cheat on her the way her ex did. However, I admire her for taking precautions after what she's been through, especially with a young child.

Heck, I can't even decide what to do about Jonah. Should I tell him about the "I love you" and ask what it means? Or should I let it go since he was literally out of his mind when he said it? Or should I just say screw it and kiss him?

My chest heats up at the thought of surprising him with a kiss. One that doesn't involve him being heavily medicated.

I inhale and exhale to bring my train of thought back to the station from its trip through lala land. "Let's ask about that chandelier and then look at some ceiling fans for the bedrooms."

"Sounds like a plan," Hannah agrees.

She follows me to the nearest counter to speak with someone about the lights. The employee shows us the various sizes and variations for that type of fixture. I snap a few photos and text them to Jonah with a question mark.

I'm game for whatever. You have complete creative control. Just don't blow the budget.

He follows that with a winky face emoji. I try not to let myself get excited about the emoji. That doesn't mean he's flirting. It could be typical Jonah teasing.

Instead, I relish in the fact that until Monday, I have complete creative control of a mansion rather than input on two square feet of a dog nursery.

Jonah

Not long after I settle onto the couch beside Tanner, the front door opens.

"Hello, darlin'." Tanner smiles at Hannah, who's carrying a large food box.

Carolina walks in behind her with another box. "Eww, stop calling me that."

"Haha, and hello, little sister." Tanner stands and takes

the box from Hannah as he kisses her on the cheek, completely ignoring Carol's box.

She puts her own box on the counter. "We brought Italian from Tuscaloosa, but I'm sure it could use some warming up by now."

"All right." Tanner smiles. "I'll fire up the microwave."

"Sweetie, just put the oven on low broil. It will taste better like that."

"'Kay." Tanner grins at Hannah like a lovesick puppy, then follows her directions. She pulls tin containers of pasta from the boxes and uncovers them.

I sigh as I watch Tanner and Hannah hug in the kitchen. They stare at one another like he's been off at war for years, rather than helping me on the house for one day while they shopped in town.

I'm jealous of Tanner. Has my life really come to this?

Carol elbows him as she passes them to get to the refrigerator. He ignores her and hugs Hannah tighter. I turn around and focus on the TV.

"Jack comes in tomorrow, right?"

"Yeah," I answer Tanner without turning around.

"I hope he's sunburnt." Tanner laughs. He lives for anything he can rag us about.

I'm convinced the reason he hasn't gotten married yet is because he doesn't want us to somehow ruin it. After all the aggravation he's dealt Jack and me over the years, you better bet we'll get him back with the bachelor party, and possibly the wedding too.

Okay, probably just the bachelor party. Hannah shouldn't have to suffer for his harassment. Marrying him will be insufferable enough.

The ice maker buzzes behind me, slightly drowning out the narrator on this hunting show. Not a big deal, since I can only take in so many random facts about fox hunting in one thirty-minute sitting.

A few minutes later, the oven beeps and I hear plates shuffling behind me. Tanner's house is so small that noises in the other rooms easily carry over, not unlike Jack's house. The mansion is more like the lodge, with plenty of floor space between room entrances. Although it does have a distinct echo without any flooring or furniture.

"We're ready to eat."

I stand at Hannah's announcement and walk toward the kitchen. Carolina is busy putting drinks around the table, and Tanner is sticking spoons in all the pasta. My stomach growls as I eye the lasagna and chicken parmesan. There's also Alfredo, which is always Carol's go-to.

I help myself to a spoonful of everything and grab a baguette. Hannah passes out napkins as we all sit. If it weren't for having to endure her and Tanner's PDA, I'd eat with them more often. She's very maternal, always giving out extra napkins and asking if anyone needs drink refills. Bianca has a much more "get it yourself" approach. As they say, you can take the girl out of the city, but you can't take the city out of the girl. Or something like that.

Tanner asks the blessing, then immediately downs half his tea. "Aw, that's good. I'm tired."

"Yeah, you're not used to working like me."

He narrows his eyes my way, then grins. He knows I'm right. I refrain myself from also mentioning that he's put on a few pounds since dating Hannah. Between her and her mother's cooking, he doesn't eat near as much cereal and frozen pizza.

My grandma used to call it happy weight when someone put on pounds after getting in a good relationship. I glance at Carol from the corner of my eye. She's the only girl I could imagine getting fat for.

We fall into conversation about our various jobs and the house. Hannah points out several ideas to make it great for families. I take mental notes, as she brings up things I've never thought about, like maybe a fence around the pool so little kids can't wander by and fall in as they play outside.

Carol smiles a little wider whenever Hannah mentions her daughter or kids. I've always known she likes kids, but it's not something we talk about. As everyone around me chatters, I sit back and allow myself to picture Carol and me in the future.

I imagine us married with a kid, maybe two. She could do her design and wedding thing. If she wanted. If not, she could stay with the kids and possibly help me with houses. I'd be building and remodeling homes, having built whatever house she dreamed up for us. She could want an underground mansion with orange brick on the front, and I'd build it. I'd live anywhere she wanted if it meant the two of us building a life together.

Even someplace that isn't Apple Cart.

My hand shakes a bit as I reach for my tea. This whole time, I've concentrated on finding ways to get her back to Apple Cart. It never occurred to me that I could leave. I don't necessarily want to leave this place, but I'm not exactly married to it either.

The only thing—or person—I really want to be married to is Carol.

I sip my tea and watch her face light up when she talks about how she plans on transforming the dining and kitchen area of the mansion. Tanner jokes with her about not knowing how to shop for appliances since she rarely cooks, and they share a little sibling banter. Hannah swats his arm after a few minutes, and he stops nagging Carolina.

From an outsider's view, this looks like a double date. Carol and I sitting by one another, passing bread and chatting with the other couple. The women have gone shopping together, while we men stayed home and worked on the house. It's almost more like two married couples. Like I'm having a casual dinner with my wife and brother-in-law and his wife while the grandparents keep their daughter.

At some point, Tanner mentions Carolina's internship. This leads to her rolling her eyes and detailing her week working on the dog potty. We all share a good laugh as she explains how the dog owner has changed the color scheme three times and wants a farm theme now to make the puppies feel as if they have a natural habitat. As if all puppies were born on farms like pigs.

I get lost in the conversation and relax back in my chair. Without thinking, I rest my hand under the table on Carol's knee, then start to rub the spot right above her kneecap.

Her leg stiffens, and I realize what I've done. Not once, but twice now, in two days. What is wrong with me?

I draw back my hand and hide it under my arm like its covered in leprosy. It's as if all the restraint I've managed over the past decade has come uncoiled in one weekend. I stand. "I gotta go to the restroom."

Whether any of them picks up on my awkwardness, I don't bother looking. I keep my eyes locked on the hallway as I make my escape for the bathroom door. This should buy me at least a few minutes of solitude to get my act together.

It's not like I can burst out apologies this time with Tanner and Hannah there. They'd want to know what I did. And I'm sure Tanner would love to know I was feeling up his sister's leg underneath the table.

Just great, Jonah.

CHAPTER SEVENTEEN

Carolina

"Carolina, you've got to squeeze your thighs, so the toilet paper doesn't fall!"

I push my legs closer together to give Kendra a more stable target for threading the broom handle between her legs through the toilet paper roll between mine.

Yeah . . . we're at her bachelorette party. The one I refused to help plan and didn't want to attend. My idea of a bachelorette party is having a nice meal, then hanging out at the lake. Not playing immature games that would be better suited for middle schoolers. Well, if they weren't filled with innuendos.

"Not that much. I need a target!" Kendra yells like a coach about to lose the game of her life.

I unbuckle my knees, causing the toilet paper to drop and roll across the room. Kendra drops her broom and sighs as the other team claims the victory. Their prize is a bag of

M&M's that they must share. Proving my point that whoever planned this party has the maturity of a thirteen-year-old.

This is the first weekend I've stayed in Auburn since Jonah bought the house. I offered to go home and help, but he said I needed to go to Kendra's party.

I tried not to read too much into that and assume he wanted rid of me. It did make me feel better when he explained how he didn't enjoy Jack's bachelor party, but stayed for Jack. Even after JoJo nearly injured him on the go-karts.

I'm not sure if my head is clouded with mixed feelings or if I'm losing my touch, but I can't seem to read Jonah at all lately. He alternates between what I think is making a move and being awkward. Extra awkward, not just Jonah awkward.

Leaning in like he's going to kiss me, then eating a bite of my cake. Freaking out whenever his hand touches me for more than a millisecond. Giving me a look that says he wants more, then dipping his head when I meet his eyes. Super strange.

My biggest fear is that maybe he's picked up on my flirting with him, and he's caught between being nice and letting me know that's not what he wants.

The girl who's apparently in charge of this circus announces that it's time for Kendra to guess her panty line. We gather in the living room of the apartment where this shindig is hosted and stare at a clothesline of panties strung in front of the TV.

Prior to the party, we were instructed to each buy Kendra a pair of panties that reflected our personality. I snort-laughed when I read that on the back of the invitation. I'm not sure they make panties that mean dry sense of humor, super organized, and not a fan of going out. So I bought a pair of solid red, which is my favorite color for most clothing accessories to add some pop to neutrals.

I take a seat on the couch beside a girl stuffing her face with chocolate-covered pretzels. Kendra sits in a chair beside the TV that is decorated with balloons and streamers. She's wearing a veil with a crown on top.

Kendra is the perfect roommate. We're friends but not super close. She pays her part of the bills and keeps her space neat. Aside from her fiancé, I haven't met a lot of the other people in her life. But given her crunchy vintage vibes and artsy flare, I'm not at all surprised by her friends. Let's just say they seem like the type to encourage her to wear the mothball-infested dress.

She goes down the line guessing panties, and gets most of them right. It's in my favor that most of the women brought panties made of hemp and other materials that I can't pronounce. Apparently, my satin isn't eco-friendly.

Hey, I go for comfort in my clothing and assumed Kendra would want that too.

After the panty game, we fall back from middle school entertainment to elementary school by playing pin the lips on Brandon. Someone has printed a life-sized photo of Kendra's fiancé and cut out paper lips. We have to try and pin our lips on his.

The pretzel-packing girl wipes crumbs down her pants and ties a scarf around my eyes. Then she spins me several times until I feel like I've jumped off a merry-go-round. Yet another indication this is elementary school all over.

"Okay, pin your lips on Brandon's."

I fumble with the lips in my hand, trying to keep the tape on the back from sticking completely to my fingers as I feel for the poster with my other hand. I reach it and run my finger across the poster to find what I assume is the top-center. Then I peel the lips from my hand and plop them on the picture.

Everyone laughs as I untie the scarf and survey my work.

I've kissed Brandon on the nose. More like right on the nostril. Oh well, I didn't want to kiss Brandon anyway—real or fake—or play this game.

I resume my seat on the couch and pull my phone from my back pocket. Jonah sent me a photo earlier of one wall painted in the living room. I can't wait to see more, but don't want to pressure him, so I keep my text vague.

How's it going?

To my delight, he texts a photo of the living room. It's dovetail gray and gorgeous. He must've painted on it all day. He comments that he has only one wall left, then sends me a selfie with him holding up a bag of Doritos. I laugh.

"What's so funny, Carolina?" Kendra's question comes out of nowhere.

I raise my eyes from my phone to see that they've finished the kissing Brandon game. One girl is holding an unopened candy bar, so I assume she won.

"Nothing," I mutter, surprised to find everyone's attention on me.

Kendra walks over and glances down at my phone. Instinctively, I tuck it under my arm. "Oh, I see, you're texting your boyfriend."

"Am not," I protest, giving her my sternest face.

She pouts and shakes her head. "Just admit it."

"Admit what?"

"You miss him."

I scoff. "Miss him? I saw him two days ago."

"So you're not denying he's your boyfriend."

"He's not. We're doing a big project together."

"Are you talking about Daniel?" This comes from the tiny girl with dreadlocks who's said nothing the entire night.

"You know Daniel?" I'm now more interested in how she knows Daniel than I am in defending my reasoning for texting Jonah.

"Everyone on campus knows Daniel. But yes, we worked at a charity event together."

Of course they did. Perfect Daniel, always doing for others. The guy I should love but don't. Instead, my long-time lanky friend has my heart fluttering suddenly.

"No, not Daniel. Jonah." Kendra grins mischievously as she practically sings his name.

"Oh, I don't know him," Dreadlocks replies.

And she wouldn't. Jonah's way too unconcerned about the environment to cross paths with her. Just last weekend, I picked up several sweet tea jugs and chip bags he'd stuffed on the edge of the patio to "throw away later." He was too busy pressure washing around the pool and cleaning up tree limbs to care about trash. I put a trash can outside the next day to help him out.

"He's Carolina's best friend," Kendra sings again. She makes air quotes around "best friend."

"That's enough," I say a little too harshly.

Kendra's head jerks back. "Whoa, Carol, I'm just messing with you."

"Sorry." I pout at her and shift the phone farther toward my armpit in case she tries to grab it.

Kendra half-smiles, then drops her confrontation in favor of getting more spinach dip. I return my phone to my back pocket and debate when would be a safe time to go home without everyone thinking I left because of this. They can't have any more games to play, can they?

We've already rung toilet paper, guessed panties, and kissed Brandon's photo. What else could be left?

As if reading my mind, the girl who ran the toilet paper game jumps up and announces its time for Kendra to open her presents. Good, that's usually the end of all gatherings.

I relax against the armrest as Dreadlocks and Pretzel Packer gather all the gifts around Kendra's chair. She returns to her makeshift throne with a mouthful of chips. After swallowing, she smiles and chugs a sip of her punch.

My cup is still hanging around somewhere in the kitchen. One sip, and I'd had enough. It tasted like someone spiked peach juice with essential oils. Given the crowd, that's not too far-fetched. I'm certain I'm the only one here who isn't wearing a beaded piece of jewelry and who didn't take my shoes off at the door.

Toilet Paper Person announces that whenever Kendra opens a gift, the person who brought it must give her a word of advice for her marriage.

Seriously? I only noticed like maybe one or two other diamond rings in the room. I mean, we're all early to mid-twenties here. None of us can have that much experience. Especially me.

For as much as I love weddings and the idea of having my own wedding—and marriage—one day, I freak out whenever I imagine that with whoever I'm dating at the time. Even Daniel, who I for sure assumed might be The One when I started hanging out with him.

At the end of the day, I wasn't willing to possibly move back to his home state, or anywhere with Daniel, for that matter. In all my relationships, no matter how long they lasted, I've never dated a guy who was worth sacrificing my own plans.

One by one, Kendra opens boxes of lingerie and cute pajamas. Each girl gives out advice. Some silly, some pretty solid. Maybe I should take notes?

My gift is last. She plucks the tissue paper from the bag

and pulls out my pink and lime striped short set. It's cheeky and cute but not embarrassingly skimpy.

"Aw, Carolina, I love it." She holds the cotton set close to her chest and smiles.

"Thanks."

"Now, what's your advice for me?"

My skin tingles with nerves as all eyes in the room shift to me. When it comes to love and relationships, I have nothing. I've turned down the campus heartthrob for no real reason at all other than there aren't the sparks between us that there should be, according to all the movies I watch. On top of that, I'm currently conflicted about my new attraction to my best friend.

All I have to give is common-sense, solid life advice.

"Uh, I'd advise you not to wear the antique store dress?"

Jonah

For the first time in close to a month, I'm sitting at Jack's kitchen table with poker cards in hand. Thanks to Jack spending half a month on his honeymoon and me working at the house nonstop, we haven't played poker together in a while.

"What you got, Jonah?" Tanner makes the face he makes when he's trying to be serious but is really hiding something.

I lay out my cards, and he grits his teeth. "You won again," he says.

I laugh and collect the chips. Then I dig into the bag of Doritos. "I'm glad y'all talked me into taking a break," I say around a mouthful.

"I'd say you've earned it. I can't believe what all you did while I was gone."

"Thanks, Jack."

"All while going to school and taking care of my babies too." He bends down and pets Chocolate and Brownie, who have planted their butts beside him. "Yes, my girls stayed with Uncle Jonah," he coos like a new grandma talking to a baby.

Tanner rolls his eyes and smirks my way. "And let's not forget who fed them the days Jonah was in Auburn."

"Sure, thanks, man."

Tanner frowns at Jack's nonchalant thanks, and I laugh. "If we're thanking you, then we have to also thank your sister for feeding them when I had a concussion."

Jack's face scrunches. "Yeah, Uncle Jeremy told me about that. Sounded brutal."

I shrug. "It wasn't that bad after all the bleeding stopped. I had plenty of medication and slept most of the time."

Tanner buries his head in his hands and laughs loudly. After catching his breath, he says, "What I wouldn't give to see Carol's face when it happened."

"She was a real trooper. Hopped up and grabbed a rag to wrap around my head."

"Yeah, we're all used to you bleeding out by now," Jack adds, sipping his tea.

"She didn't come in this weekend, did she?" Tanner is notorious for having to ask me the whereabouts of his sister.

"No. Kendra had some kind of bachelorette thing last night."

Tanner rolls his eyes. "I'm sure that was a blast."

"Yeah, probably about as fun as JoJo almost killing me in the go-kart."

"Oh, come on. It couldn't have been *that* bad," Tanner says.

Jack and I exchange a glance. JoJo was the one who shot Jack in the back of the neck at the beginning of paintball. We're both a little afraid of him now.

I shuffle the cards a few more times, as I tend to do while we talk. The older we get, the more we talk than play. I blame it on living in Apple Cart. This place eventually turns everyone into busybodies. It's just a matter of time before we transition to sitting at the corner table at Mary's, chatting around our coffee mugs.

"Anyway, I told her to just stay in Auburn this weekend. She's helped every weekend so far."

Tanner shakes his head.

"What?"

"Nothing." He gives us his signature dimpled smirk, meaning he's up to something.

"I call bull." With Tanner, it's never nothing.

"I just don't see how you can work with her around all the time."

"Who, Carol?"

"Uh, yeah."

"She tries whatever I ask her to do and is decorating the place for deferred pay. She's actually a big help."

He laughs. "Yeah, like try to hand you the wrong hammer."

"That was on me." I usually ignore Tanner and Carolina's bickering, but have the urge to take up for her right now.

"Whatever, man."

Jack shoots me a look that communicates he's missing something. "Did you two buy the house together?"

"No. She agreed to help me decorate it and volunteered to work on it with me."

"Oh. You plan on selling it, right?"

"Well, yeah. It's not like I'm going to live in it." I scratch my neck as my hairline prickles. A flash of Carolina inside the totally restored mansion pops in my head. I immediately look at Tanner to kill any daydream of myself married to his sister. Then I ask Jack, "Do you want to buy it?"

He laughs. "No way. I need to stay by the lodge. We're fine here. Besides, if Bianca ever did want a bigger house, we'd just build someplace on the property."

"Makes sense." I turn to Tanner. "What about you? Hannah sounded excited about it having a pool."

He laughs more than Jack. "Too much wasted space. We'd have to have triplets to fill that place up."

"You never know," Jack teases.

I deal the cards, realizing if I don't, we'll never get in another hand. Jack goes to the freezer and the dogs saunter after him. They wag their tails when he pulls out a few Popsicles.

"When are y'all getting married?" Tanner hasn't officially proposed to Hannah, but we all know they're on track to get married.

He shrugs. "I dunno. She's already had the big wedding and all that. I don't care to. Maybe I'll bring home a ring one day and take her to the courthouse."

"Quite the romantic," Jack jokes, as he breaks up the frozen stick for his dogs.

"Coming from the man who went iguana hunting on his honeymoon."

"Hey, it was an excursion. We did plenty of other stuff too."

"I'm sure you did." Tanner wiggles his eyebrows, and Jack slaps his arm. "Ouch."

"What about you? Sasha still in the picture at all?" Jack is always behind on what's going on with me. Not that I mind, as long as he doesn't ask these sorts of questions while we're at a family gathering. I try and keep my personal life on the DL, or my mama will get excited and start wanting to plan meetups with whatever girl I'm dating.

I shake my head. "That's been off for months now."

"Oh, I thought you two really liked one another."

"We did. Just irreconcilable differences, as they say."

He nods. I leave it at that. Nobody knows the irreconcilable part is that she gave me an ultimatum about Carolina. Sasha point blank said, "Either quit hanging out with her so much or we're done."

For as much as I liked Sasha and enjoyed dating her, that was an easy choice. She was my backup plan. The one I could easily love if Carol never came around to loving me. But I couldn't do it if Carolina wasn't in the picture.

Even if I never have her the way I want, I still want her in my life.

"He'll goof around until he's thirty, then marry my sister."

I choke so hard that sweet tea comes out my nose. I rush to the counter for a paper towel as Tanner bursts into laughter. "Hey, I get it. The thought of marrying her would choke me too."

I sit down and clear my throat. "No, I'm shocked—I just —what makes you say that?" Did Tanner somehow see the perfect family picture swim through my brain minutes earlier?

He fans out his cards and smiles. "You two seem like the type that would make one of those lame pacts." In a mocking voice, he adds, "If we're not married by thirty, we'll just marry each other."

"No." My own voice is squeaky, so I take another sip of my tea. "You're one to talk. At least I've had more real relationships."

"Ohhhh snap." Jack leans forward, enjoying this exchange.

Tanner raises his palms, not realizing he's showing us his hand. I take mental note of his cards before he sets them down. "All I'm saying is some people do that sort of thing. And for what it's worth, Carol could do a lot worse than you."

"Thank you." That's the nicest thing Tanner's ever said to me.

"How about we up the ante on this one." Jack raises one eyebrow and glances back and forth from Tanner to me.

"How's that?"

"If Tanner wins this hand, you have to confess if you have feelings for his sister."

"Whoa, whoa, whoa. Who said I had feelings for—"

Jack lifts his hand to hush me. "If you win, Tanner has to propose to Hannah."

"Like now?"

"Yeah." Jack nods.

"Fine by me." Tanner smirks my way.

My whole body heats up like I'm weed eating in August. I feel exposed, and not in a good way.

"What if you win, Jack?"

"I get all the chips and win the money."

Tanner and I exchange a glance, then he narrows his eyes. His lips slowly curve into a smile. He has good cards. I saw them. Better than my hand.

"I'm game." Tanner nods to Jack.

My throat knots up so that I can't speak. If I decline the wager, I'm indirectly admitting that I have feelings for Carolina by not wanting to make a bet that might end in me having to admit I have feelings for her.

Against my better judgment, I nod to Jack. My eyes plead with him to please have the winning hand.

He cups his hand around the bill of his cap and lifts the corner of his mouth. I'm pretty sure he read my desperation.

If so, that means he now knows my deepest secret. I'm in love with Carolina Nash.

I take a deep breath and lay down my cards. Tanner grins as he lays his down next. We both turn to Jack. Does he have the winning hand?

One by one, he lays down his cards. Each time a card touches the table, my heart pricks with a sliver of hope. The last card down reveals he has a royal flush.

Tanner slaps his hands on his head as Jack rakes in the chips. While Tanner still has his face hidden, Jack winks my way.

Oh yeah, he totally knows my secret.

CHAPTER EIGHTEEN

Carolina

We've accomplished more in the last month than I ever dreamed possible. The house is coming along nicely, with most of the walls painted and Jonah having installed the support beams. We're laying the flooring and working around the outside some now that the weather's nicer. Only the bedrooms remain bare.

That's more than I can say for my paying job. The client has shot down all three of my dog potty designs so far. I swear, some people have too much money and time to waste on the dumbest things.

Coming here and making progress on something that makes actual sense is like sucking in a breath of fresh air after suffering through one of Tanner's room-clearing farts.

It's spring break week at Auburn, so Audrey gave me half the week off. I volunteered to work the whole week, but she pointed out that I'll be an adult soon enough and should enjoy my time off while I can. Although I like most of my coworkers, and of course Audrey, I didn't hesitate to agree. It's to the point where I dreamed of portable puppy potties last night.

If that's not a sign I need a break, I don't know what is.

For the last hour we've been sprucing up the area near the pool. I shove a flower bulb into the hole I dug and surround it with soil. Jonah walks by with a wheelbarrow full of mulch. "Here's the mulch when you're ready."

"Thanks." He starts to walk away, but I catch his attention. "Hey, I'm still leaning toward carpet for the bedrooms." We've painted the entire upstairs and updated all the light fixtures, then installed new tile and a new tub in the master bathroom. But we moved back downstairs since we had a hard time agreeing on flooring.

He stops and removes his cap, then wipes his brow before putting it back on. "If you think more buyers will like that. You know I hate carpet with my allergies."

"I'm surprised you're not sneezing up a storm now."

"I took a bunch of nasal stuff before I got here."

I plant another bulb and dig a few more holes. A fence guy is coming by later this week to give Jonah estimates about putting one around the concrete patio. We agreed that a fence would not only be a good safety feature for kids, but also shield anyone sunbathing from nosy neighbors.

In particular, Ms. Dot and Paul, who make it a point to ride by on the golf cart regularly. I don't know what those two have going on, but if they decide to get married, that's one wedding I will not help plan.

"If we don't go with carpet, we'll need to put down a bunch of floor rugs. People tend to walk barefoot in their bedrooms and like the space warm."

Jonah nods. "Carpet is cheaper than hardwood, especially with adding rugs."

"Good. Just pick something less fuzzy, and you'll be fine." I grin, and Jonah wipes at his nose as if to highlight the point of having allergies.

"Maybe our buyer won't have my issues."

I laugh. "Do you really want me to comment on that?"

"Nope." He smiles, and my pulse picks up a notch.

For the last month and a half, we've had this back and forth dance of our usual aggravation and teasing lined with a hint of flirting.

More than once, I've almost made a move. Kissed him myself, held his hand, something, anything. I'm just not sure how he'd respond. More like I'm scared.

I have the suspicion that Jonah knows how I feel, and I'm not sure he shares those feelings. He will graze his hand across my leg or let it linger against my back when helping me up the steps of that dreadful dungeon of a basement, only to pull it away once I start to respond with a smile or lean into him.

Either he doesn't like me in that way and is afraid of leading me on . . . or he's just afraid.

The bell on the back door dings, alerting us that someone's upstairs. Jonah installed a doorbell that rings a little quieter at every main entry whenever someone comes to the front. That way, if the owner is out back, he or she will know when someone's at the door.

I suggested we may need to also install a camera. In Apple Cart, you may not want to open the door for some neighbors. Even if they come by under the ruse of bringing food.

I stand and take off my gardening gloves, letting them fall where I was kneeling. Jonah and I walk together up the hill leading to the front yard. Two men wearing uniforms stand out front, one holding a clipboard.

"You must be the owners," the older of the two says.

"Yes," Jonah answers, without clarifying that he's the only owner.

"I need one of you to check this receipt and make sure your order is correct."

Jonah takes the clipboard and holds it where I can scan it with him. He sure treats me like an owner, for someone who hasn't spent a dime on this place. The list is a rundown of all the kitchen appliances we ordered. With some help from Jack, Jonah finished the cabinets about two weeks ago. Now all we need is to move these in so I can start decorating the kitchen.

"Look good to you?"

I turn my head to Jonah's face tilted toward mine. For a split second, I imagine us as a real couple, making these decisions for our own home. I swallow before answering. "Yeah, looks great." I look back at the man in front of us before Jonah realizes I'm not talking about the appliance order.

"Good to us," Jonah says to the guy, who I now notice has "Eugene" sewn across the pocket of his shirt. Eugene takes the clipboard and calls to the other guy, "Okay, Slim, unload." Slim, which I doubt is his real name, nods and adjusts his sunglasses before opening the back of the van. Then they both grab dollies and start unloading our order.

Jonah and I stand back as they push the pieces up the porch and into the house. Then we follow them inside and direct them to the kitchen.

"Nice place y'all got here," Slim says. His eyes gravitate toward the high ceilings in the living room. "Whoa."

Before I can say "thanks," he falls headfirst onto the new hardwood floor. The oven rocks back on the dolly, but miraculously comes to a standstill.

"I'm sorry, man. Are you okay?" Jonah helps him to his feet, which isn't hard considering he's the skinniest person I've known to move appliances.

Slim nods, blushing from apparent embarrassment.

Jonah turns to me. "I should've taken out that stupid step down."

"It's fine." I pat his forearm. "That would've been more work and money," I assure him.

He smiles down at me and nods. Since there was only the one right past the doorway, we decided to leave it. That made more sense than leveling up the rest of the floor to match, especially when it ran seamlessly into other areas of the home.

After Eugene and Slim recenter the oven on the dolly, they follow us into the kitchen.

"You two just move in?" Eugene wipes his brow with a handkerchief pulled from his shirt pocket, then runs a hand over his gray hair. He's just as unlikely an appliance mover as Slim, but quite the opposite. Approximately forty pounds overweight and way past his prime.

I open my mouth to say we don't live here and prepare to explain that we're home remodelers, but Jonah beats me to it. Except he lies.

He throws his arm around my shoulder and gives it a light squeeze. "Yeah. Our first home."

Okay, so technically it is our first home. But not in the way Eugene implied.

"Great for you kids. Much better than what the missus and me started out in."

"Oh yeah?" Jonah grins, giving my arm another squeeze. I'm not sure what game he's playing, but I lean into his embrace, soaking up the attention. It's been a while since he hasn't acted like I have cooties.

Eugene laughs. "You ever heard of Pine Tree Village?"

We simultaneously shake our heads.

Eugene laughs harder, making his stomach jiggle like Santa in children's Christmas stories. Only his buttons are already stretched, so Santa's bowl full of jelly is much better suited for a children's book illustration.

"Yeah, trailer park down by the train tracks near Tuscaloosa. All kinds of hobos would get off there after running from the law."

I widen my eyes as Eugene gives a few more details I'd rather not remember. Until now, my only knowledge of train tracks came from the ones near Wisteria that they pulled up when I was a kid and from the movie *Fried Green Tomatoes*.

Jonah drops his arm from around me to point out where he wants everything placed. The sudden loss of his touch sends a shiver across my back. I watch as Eugene and Slim move everything into place. Jonah ends up helping, since Slim has trouble pushing some of the appliances.

Again, how did he get this job?

They situate everything, and I beam with delight at the kitchen falling into place. From the gas stovetop to the stainless-steel refrigerator, it all meshes seamlessly with the updated cabinets and white farmhouse sink Jonah installed.

"There we go," Eugene says as he shoves the refrigerator into its spot. "Now your little lady can cook up a storm." He smiles at Jonah.

I feign a smile and resist the urge to comment that men can and should cook too. Maybe Eugene's wife cooks a lot. Clearly, someone's been cooking for him.

Eugene pulls a pair of bifocals from the same pocket he pulled a handkerchief earlier. The pocket doesn't look big enough to hold all that. Maybe he's a magician on the side?

He puts on his glasses and picks up the clipboard. "All's been paid. I just need one of you to sign here that you received it, and all looks good. You've got ninety days' warranty if anything goes wrong or isn't working."

"Okay." Jonah takes the pen and clipboard and signs his name, then writes the date.

After he gives the papers back to Eugene, he wraps his arm around my waist and tugs me close to him. A jolt of electricity shoots up my spine like the time I accidentally raised my back while squatting under an electric fence.

"Thanks, guys, our kitchen looks great." He grins down at me. Why he feels the need to carry out this act is beyond me.

I stare up at him, then drop my gaze from his eyes to his lips. Without thinking, my mind drifts back to that accidental kiss on the night of his concussion. I want to kiss him again, test the waters. See if how I think I feel is real. If he feels how I think I feel about him.

Without hesitating, I lean up and plant a small peck on his lips. Nothing passionate, but I linger for a few seconds before pulling back. My heart pounds as his short whiskers brush against my face and his lips press against mine. It's a chaste, short kiss, but my insides flip as if we're making out on a blanket in a pasture, beneath a starry sky.

Specific? Yeah, I might've imagined that happening once or twice lately.

Jonah blinks down at me as if in shock, but he doesn't run like he has this last month, anytime something similar happened between us. Instead, he gives me his usual goofy grin.

"All right, Slim. Let's leave these lovebirds to it. Time to pick up our next haul."

Slim waves awkwardly as we thank them, then follows his boss out the door. He cranes his neck once more to the ceiling before dropping his sunglasses back over his eyes. He almost stumbles again but catches himself against the wall as he exits.

As if right on cue, Jonah drops his arm when they disappear. He leaves my side and walks to the refrigerator.

A chill overtakes my body without him snuggled beside

me. And it has nothing to do with the weather, since it's unseasonably hot—the warmest it's been in months.

"Can you believe he thought we were married?" I ask the question nervously, in a desperate attempt to gauge where he stands on all this.

He straightens from plugging in the refrigerator and laughs. "Yeah, that was fun. Nice touch with the kiss. You really had them convinced we were in love."

I cross my arms to keep my heart from falling out of my chest. I guess that answers my question. Up until now, he had me convinced that maybe we were in love too.

Jonah

Yesterday was weird. Carol kissed me. On the lips.

Sure, we were pretending to be a couple, which was all my doing after that old guy assumed we were married, and this was our house. Why wouldn't he? What man and woman do yardwork and order appliances together for a house they don't own?

So I got a little excited about someone mistaking us for a couple. I ran with it and allowed myself to hit on Carolina. Something I've desperately wanted to do but resisted lately. Aside from the occasional slip up, of course.

Then she took me by complete shock when she kissed me.

It wasn't a kiss kiss, but still on the lips. You could say I kissed back. I sure didn't resist. And I very much enjoyed every second of playing house with her while the dudes were here.

I held on to her long as I thought I could get away with it. Then she had to make the comment about how surprised she was that Eugene thought we were married. Is that such an impossible conclusion? Even her own brother suggested we make one of those "when we're thirty" pacts. But I'm not telling her that. Not after she acted as if it's unbelievable for us to be a couple.

Especially not after I mentioned the kiss, and she clammed up. Way to knock me back into the friend zone.

Today has been a mixed bag of emotions. I've somehow managed to lay flooring while carrying on like normal as Carol paints the back bedrooms. I still haven't decided how we can market one as a second master downstairs in case an older couple shows interest. All the downstairs bedrooms are large, but none is larger than the others. It makes even more sense to have a first-floor master option since the laundry is downstairs and the top level has plenty of space for other purposes, like a gym, study, playroom, or all of that.

"Jonah?"

"Huh?" I flinch at Carolina's voice. When I turn my head, she's standing in the hallway entrance looking adorable, with paint spots on her faded T-shirt and her hair tied on top of her head.

"Can you help me with something?"

"Yeah." I stand and stretch a minute, having squatted for far too long. I follow her to the back bedroom, where she's finished all that she can reach on foot.

"Wow, good job, Carol. You're fast."

"Thanks." She blushes slightly. "Painting is a big stress relief for me."

"Wish I could say the same about laying flooring."

She laughs.

"Whatcha need?"

"I'm afraid I don't have this ladder locked out good, and I don't want to climb it until I'm sure."

"Let's see." I shake the ladder, and sure enough, she doesn't have it locked out. I adjust it and lock it in place, then move it closer to the wall. "There. I'll get your paint."

I grab the paint can and climb a few steps to set it in the hole on top of the ladder. "I can hold it steady while you climb up if you need me to."

"Thanks, you know how clumsy I am."

My eyes widen. I can't refute that. She smirks, knowing I silently agree. I hop onto the floor and step aside so she can climb up with her brush. Then I move behind her and hold the ladder steady, trying to ignore the fact that I'm basically hugging the back of her thighs and her butt is dangerously close to my face.

I turn my head and ignore the heat rising up my neck. It intensifies when she shifts her weight to dip the brush in the paint, grazing her legs against my chest in the process.

This torture goes on for about thirty minutes as Carol paints, then says she needs the ladder moved. I scoot back, she climbs down, I move the ladder. Then she climbs up and I do my best to hold it steady since she's nervous about climbing, all while keeping my animal instincts under control.

If this were thousands of years earlier, I'd hoist her over my shoulder and drag her to my cave. But since cavemen didn't have paint or ladders, I doubt they had the temptation of a woman in ripped jeans with her backside in their face. The closest they could relate might be standing on a lower rock as she carved something on the cave wall. Even then, it's not like a cavewoman would have shaved, smooth legs or smell as good as Carol.

The mixture of her signature citrus scent mixed with fresh paint is intoxicating. I need to buy citrus candles and burn them at every house showing. If it has this effect on me, the buyers will love it too.

Of course, to me it's more about it being Carol than oranges and lemons. Back to my caveman analogy, I've memorized her pheromones since middle school.

I could smell the woman coming from a country mile, even if that mile were covered with bahiagrass and cow patties.

We're at the last corner of the room when Carol climbs down the ladder. I'm standing at a respectful distance. She steps to the ground and turns toward me, smiling. "Thanks."

"You're welcome." I smile back and take one step closer.

Instead of shrinking back, she leans toward me. My chest tightens as her smile widens. Is she sending me some sort of signal? Should I go in for the kill or retreat to my own cave, currently the corner of the living room?

I start to dip my head the slightest bit to see how she'll respond. Before I can move in closer, her phone rings, causing her to jump. When she does, her arm hits the ladder and shakes it. The bucket of paint tips and splashes between us. We're covered in a gray-blue color, and I'm super relieved that we painted this room before laying the flooring. I'm also super annoyed that I didn't get a chance to continue the almost kiss.

Carol blinks as she holds out her shirt, now covered in paint. I'm used to paint, dirt, whatever, so it doesn't much bother me.

"Are you okay?" I ask.

She nods. "Man, that paint's cold."

Really? I hadn't noticed since I was sweating from the inside out a moment earlier. "I'll get some towels." Needless to say, the moment has passed.

I go to the kitchen and grab some of the larger rags we keep on hand. Thankfully, the flooring hasn't yet reached the hallway and kitchen, so I can walk freely without worries. I carry the cloths back to Carol.

She stands awkwardly, holding her shirt away from her body as she stares down at her phone in her other hand. She puts her phone in her back pocket, then takes the rag. "Thanks."

"Everything okay?" Her forehead is wrinkled, and I get the sense it's more to do with whatever she saw on the phone rather than the paint on her shirt. "Oh, I have some extra clothes in my truck if you want to borrow a shirt."

"Thanks." She offers me a sad smile, then sighs as she nods back at her phone. "Stupid Daniel."

"On the phone?"

She nods and rolls her eyes.

My stomach pits. I thought that was done. "Y'all are seeing each other again?"

"No. But he recommended me to someone wanting to remodel their apartment."

"Oh." I wipe at my own shirt, so I have something to do with my hands. The nervous energy between us has me stir crazy. Especially when there's nothing I can do about it. "I notice he didn't have the eagle ringtone."

Carol laughs. "Yeah, I moved him to my generic one. He's no longer worthy of a personalized ring."

I grin at the notion of her finding him unworthy of something. Even something as insignificant as a ringtone.

"He left a voicemail, but I'm only going to text him back. Last time we talked, it got weird."

"Oh yeah, what was that about?"

Her cheeks flush and she rocks back on her heels. "Nothing really, he was just being stupid."

"How so?" Why I've suddenly turned into a gossiping granny, I haven't the slightest idea. But I don't like Carolina having something secret with Daniel.

She blushes more and scans the room before looking back at me. Then she laughs so hard, she snorts. "That idiot said you're in love with me."

Well, for once in my life, I agree with Daniel. And if Carol wouldn't have found this so funny, I might prove he's right.

Thank the Good Lord she's so clumsy, or else I might've really embarrassed myself going in for a kiss.

CHAPTER NINETEEN

Carolina

I've never been so relieved to come back to work. Not only did the dog breeder smile at my fourth attempt at the pink pee-pad landing, but I have a good excuse to not be with Jonah.

Things are way too complicated between us.

Thursday evening, we had a moment. One where I believed he might actually kiss me . . . on purpose . . . with nobody around to put on an act.

They say the third time's the charm, so I had my fingers crossed, metaphorically speaking, that this would hold true for us. First attempt: the concussion kiss. Second attempt: we were putting on a show for two appliance movers. Third attempt . . .

I groan and down the last of my coffee. I totally ruined what could've easily been "the kiss." We were perched by the ladder, his head tilting toward mine, my senses on edge as I focused on Jonah and nothing else. Then my phone rang in my back pocket, jerking me to attention, which led to me bumping into the ladder and spilling paint all over us.

Unlike all the movies I binge, I didn't go in for a messy kiss that would end with cute paint splotches all over us. Because this is real life, and Carolina does not do cold, wet paint down her frontside.

The damp liquid plastered my shirt to my body like a slimy pair of Spanx. Add to that my phone buzzing against my butt cheek and Jonah wringing paint from his own arms. What a disaster.

To top it all off, it was none other than Daniel leaving a voicemail. Innocent enough, as he had recommended someone to me for a job. But then I had to go and blab my big mouth about what Daniel had said months earlier.

Jonah's reaction was all I needed to cool my efforts from trying to decipher his true feelings for me. His face blanked when I mentioned Daniel saying he was in love with me. My reaction was to laugh like a high-as-a-kite hyena. Jonah stared at me like I was crazy before laughing along with me.

I somehow managed to muster through the rest of the night, working in separate areas of the house. Then, after crying into my pillow and beating myself up for my clumsiness—both physical and verbal—I came back Friday with my friend-zone game face on.

After that roller coaster of emotions, I needed an escape.

I set my coffee mug aside and concentrate on the pee-pad sketch. Let's see, she wanted a bit more fluff on the corners . . .

As I add more texture to the edges, my phone rings. The landline on my desk, which means there's no chance of Daniel being on the other end. With that assurance, and because it's my job, I pick up.

"Hello?"

"Carolina, could you stop in my office when you get a chance?" It's Audrey.

"Yes, I can come now."

"Thanks."

Audrey hangs up, and I save my progress on the pee pad. To anyone outside of this company, the sketch on my computer screen looks like a large, puffy rug with storage space and a window nearby. But to everyone at Home-Sweet-Home, it's just another section of the puppy nursery several of us have worried with for weeks.

I push back my chair and head for Audrey's office. She's behind her desk and notices me before I can knock. Her door stays open ninety percent of the time, but I make it a point to always knock out of courtesy.

"Come in, Carolina."

I cross the room and take a seat in front of her desk. She steeples her fingers and glances at her computer screen. "I have a friend who's starting a local business." She turns to me. "He and his wife don't have a lot to invest at this time, and they've found an old warehouse downtown where they can put it."

"What kind of business?"

"A restaurant. Think Cracker Barrel but not a chain."

I nod, unsure of how this affects me.

"I told them I could help with the design pro bono, but I don't have time." She opens her hands, then rests them on her desk. "I know you're eager to do more projects, so I have an offer for you."

The word "offer" makes me perk up like a dog hearing "treat." And I should know from the many times the dog breeder has had me over to access her nursery space.

"I can't pay you for this, and it would have to be on your own time. However, if you want, you can have the freedom to work with my friend and design his restaurant. As long as it doesn't interfere with your job here, you're free to work on it."

A project, my very own project. This somehow feels like a trap. "Who's leading the team?" There, a safe enough question to make sure.

"No team, just you." Audrey smiles. "Of course, I'll be in contact with my friend too. But you can have all the control on this one. That is, if you want to do it. I realize it's not a paid job and will take up your spare time."

"I'll do it." The words leave my mouth before I have time to fully consider the offer.

"Great! I'll let him know and get you the info ASAP."

I nod, a little unsure of what I just signed up for. On one hand, I'll be designing a restaurant all by myself. How cool is that? Then again, it might cut into my time working on the house with Jonah.

"Thanks." I give Audrey my best smile considering the circumstances, then walk down the hallway to my cubicle.

I stare at my computer screensaver a minute before wiggling the mouse to refresh my screen. The screensaver is a photo of Jonah and me. Okay, so my brother, Hannah, Jack, and Bianca are also in the photo. It was taken at Jack's wedding. But Jonah and I stand on the end, arm in arm, looking very much like a couple.

On occasion, someone here will comment on my boyfriend based on that photo. I never realized until this past week how many times people actually have mistaken us for a couple. The appliance movers and new ER doctor aren't outliers.

But up until now, I never cared.

Now all I do is try to read into every assumption, every gesture. Do all these people see something we don't? Something I'm finally realizing about us after all these years?

I have no doubt in my mind that I'm in love with Jonah.

It just took Daniel's hypothesis and lots of time working on the house project for me to realize it. However, I can't come on too strong or make the first move.

Jonah's a good guy, and I'd hate to put him in a place where he'd have to let me down gently. I'm not sure he could. If Jonah knew how I felt about him, he'd do one of two things, depending on his own feelings: marry me tomorrow or ghost me forever.

I can't live in a world with no Jonah, and having best friend Jonah who works alongside me and looks out for me like a brother/bodyguard/cartoon superhero all rolled into one beats having no Jonah.

Jonah

My patience is wearing thin. For ten years, I've carried a torch for Carolina, and for most of that time I've sat back, content to love her from afar. Well, not physically afar, but emotionally afar, since she's friend zoned me. Or brother zoned, I guess, too.

Ever since we've started this home remodel together, something has shifted. She's flirted with me on more than one occasion, and even kissed me in front of the Eugene and Slim dudes. An act, but still, a kiss.

Her own actions have revived those achy urges I've felt since eighth grade of wanting to corner her and kiss her, then tell her how I feel. All weekend, I kicked myself for not making another move after the paint catastrophe. But it's kind of hard to just go for it when she laughs in my face about me being in love with her.

That is one thing—possibly the only thing—I can't joke about.

After an awkward few hours Thursday night, we settled back into our usual roles. Best friends, with me secretly loving her but not acting on it. Carol teasing me but not flirting with me. Maybe that's where we're the most comfortable?

Too bad I'm getting uncomfortable with living so comfortably.

I've decided to savor all the time I have with her and make the most of it. That's why despite telling myself it was a silly idea, I'm now at her apartment. Could I have texted her the photos I wanted her to see of the house? Sure. Did I want to? Uh, no.

I hop out of my truck and jog to her apartment door. After a few soft knocks, I hear a muffled "it's open" from the other side.

I can practically feel the disappointment forming on my face when I open the door to Kendra. Her face is covered with some kind of green goop, and she's drinking from a clear glass filled with more green goop. Her hair is tied up in a towel, and she's squatting against the wall.

"Sorry to interrupt . . . whatever this is."

She swats the hand not holding the glass my way. "Nonsense, I'm just cleansing."

"Cleansing?"

She nods, her towel bobbing like one of those hula girls on a dashboard. "Yeah, to get healthy for my wedding."

I raise my chin and decide not to respond to that with words. Kendra's a weird bird, and the less I know about her life, the sounder I'll sleep at night. "Hey, is Carol home? I noticed her car's here." I hook a thumb behind me toward the door.

Kendra takes a huge, audible gulp of the green goop.

When she lowers the glass, there's a fine line between the glistening green mustache from her drink and the already green slime caked on her face. "Yeah, she's in her room."

"Thanks." I cross the living room and stay toward the far wall when entering the hallway. I'm afraid if I get too close to the middle, I might bump into Kendra and get slimed.

Carolina's door is closed, but I hear music playing low in the background. That means she's awake. She's one of those people who can't sleep unless all lights and noise are on lockdown. Me? I could sleep through a tornado riding a freight train.

I knock softly, then say against the door, "It's Jonah."

I expect her to say something back, but instead, the door flies open. She waves her hand for me to enter, a little dramatically, like those people who work the rides at Disney.

"I finished hanging the light fixtures yesterday," I say.

"Oh great. How's the chandelier look?"

"Really good."

She plops down on her bed and crosses her legs beneath her. I start to follow her to the bed, but sit in her desk chair. Given the push and pull between us lately, it appears the safer choice.

On her bed is her open laptop and a ton of papers strewn about. "Whatcha working on?"

"Oh." Carolina claps her hands together excitedly. "This new project from work."

"Another dog something?"

She giggles. "No, a restaurant. But I'm having to do it on my own time, since it's like this additional project." She gathers her shoulder-length hair and ties it back with the band on her wrist.

"That's exciting." The only exciting part to me is the possibility of somewhere else to eat in Auburn, but I want to sound interested.

"It is. I have so many ideas."

"Yeah?" I sway side to side in the swivel chair. "Speaking of ideas, I want to show you some photos of the house." I hand her my phone. "Scroll and you can see all the downstairs. I've still got to lay carpet upstairs, but all that shouldn't take long."

"This looks really good, Jonah. I love the flooring with all the appliances."

"Yeah, I wanted your opinion on staging the place. You know, for furniture and maybe curtains."

Carolina twists her lips and hands me back the phone. I graze my fingers over hers and watch for a reaction. Nothing. She's as solid as Fort Knox.

I return my phone to my pocket and sit back in the chair. She picks at a loose thread on her bed cover, then glances back at me. "I'd definitely go used or maybe even see about borrowing or renting furniture, but you don't have to stage. It doesn't matter to me."

"I thought you said staging is a must, especially in a house this large, to get the full effect of the place."

She shrugs. "I did, but I mean, I don't think not staging will be a deal breaker to anyone."

In all our previous conversations about listing the home, Carol always brought up staging. How it made a big difference in selling a home quickly and showing the prospective buyers what to do with the space. I never expected her to be so complacent about this.

"So would you help me pick out furniture?"

"Yeah, when I'm home I can, or you can send me photos when you're out looking."

I shift in the chair, making the leather squeak. The sound it makes represents my uneasiness perfectly. "I'll be spending all my time finishing the upstairs. I don't plan on shopping any."

Carolina's eyes are locked to her laptop, and I'm not sure she's even listening. After a minute, she answers. "Like I said, you don't have to stage. If it takes too much time, skip it."

I narrow my eyes, as if I can somehow laser focus on her mind and read her thoughts. There's more to this than what she's saying. She can't go from super excited about staging a home to saying it doesn't matter in a few days' time.

"Carol, what's wrong?"

She rubs her fingertips across her forehead. I fight the urge to plop down beside her and scoop her in my arms. Whatever is going on, I want her to know she can come to me with it.

She shrugs and sighs. "I'm just really busy with this project, you know, trying to get Audrey to notice me."

The heck with Audrey, I'll notice you. I am noticing you. I always notice you!

I wipe my hands down my jeans and curl them into fists. It takes every ounce of me to not close her laptop and start my monologue about how talented she is and how she's better off working for herself.

But she's heard it all before, and I know she won't listen. Carolina is scared to start her own business. Maybe a little scared of coming home to Apple Cart, and maybe a little scared of me. She's running from her dream, and maybe from me too. I sense that, but if I say anything, it will only drive her further away.

Instead, I go with the Captain Obvious response. "She'll notice you. How could she not? All I need is some help from you on the weekends."

Carol falls back against her pillow. "Jonah, I may not be coming home much more on the weekends."

I swallow down the disappointment balling up in my throat to keep my voice steady. "Why's that?"

"Well, I have this project now, and Kendra's wanting me

to help with a few wedding things. You know, she gets married a few weeks before graduation."

"Yeah." How could I not know—the freakin' date is plastered all over their apartment like a national holiday. "Save the Date" this and thats everywhere, markings on the wall calendar, that notebook Kendra keeps on the coffee table that weighs about as much as my truck.

"I just thought we could finish this house together, you know, since we're a team." I cringe at using that word. Team describes little boys wearing baseball jerseys or coworkers on a business retreat. Not us. We're a couple, an extension of one another, or at least best friends.

Carol turns toward me from facing the ceiling. "I've picked out everything but furniture, and helped redo the yard. All that's left is for you to finish the upstairs. You don't need me for that."

My face falls, as does everything inside of me—my heart, my stomach, and possibly all those other organs swimming around. It takes every ounce of muscle I can conjure up to curve the corner of my lips into a slight smile. Then I stand and leave her room.

There's no area in my life in which I don't need Carolina Nash. And even if there were, there's no area in my life where I don't want Carolina Nash. She has no idea just how wrong she is—about everything.

CHAPTER TWENTY

Carolina

I'm parked at a coffee shop, playing my new favorite phone game. My fingers hover over the keypad before I close the text thread between Jonah and me. Yep, that's it. No app or Words With Friends, just me daring myself to talk to Jonah first.

After an awkward moment of staring at my phone, I drop it into the cupholder beside me and back out of the parking lot. I just met with Audrey's friend, Reece, who was appreciative of me taking on his project, to say the least. He may not have a lot of funds to put behind this venture, but what he lacks in dollars, he makes up for in enthusiasm.

I pull up to the traffic light ahead. It's my last chance to chicken out of going to Apple Cart this weekend. I packed my makeup and some clothes before work this morning and threw them in the trunk. That eliminates the excuse of needing to run by my apartment.

The light changes, and I can turn to go back to my apartment or keep straight and drive out of town. I hesitate for a split second, which is plenty long enough for the car behind me to honk. Then I stomp on the gas and propel my car forward before I have a chance to turn.

My heart beats against my chest like a prisoner trying to break free. Both from the sudden acceleration and from the anticipation of seeing Jonah this weekend.

Last time we talked, I said he didn't need me anymore. That's true. He never has needed me. However, that doesn't mean I don't want him to need me. I've missed his random calls and texts to get my opinion on something for the house.

And once those disappeared, so did all the other random texts and calls. No more movie nights or ice cream gorges. No last-minute dinners or midnight trips to Walmart because he hates to shop alone for anything other than food.

Oh my goodness. Poor Jonah. The man doesn't like to buy so much as a card table without my help, and I've shoved him away to furnish a full house alone. He must think I'm pure evil. I'm beginning to think I'm pure evil.

Ugh. I blink back a tear, caused more by anger with myself than disappointment in him. I've brought all this on me. I wouldn't text me either after what I said.

My only hope now is to show up and hope he's happy to see me. I pull up to another traffic light and shoot my brother a text when it turns red.

Will be coming into town late. Can I stay with you? Don't want to wake Daddy.

A few miles down the road, my phone dings. His text plays across my radio screen.

. . .

Yeah, come on over. I'll leave the porch light on.

I turn onto the interstate. That's one thing taken care of at least. I've learned the hard way never to show up at my parents' house past ten.

Daddy goes to bed early and doesn't like to be disturbed. Not unlike myself, the slightest sound will wake him. Even when I'm extremely quiet, don't flip on any lights, and use my house key, he hears me tiptoeing in and wakes up grumpy. Then he flies off the handle at anything the next day, because he swears he never got back into a deep sleep. And he loves his sleep.

I punch the radio on to give me a bit of mindless distraction as I drive. It somewhat works, except that every song reminds me of Jonah in some way.

Obviously, the love songs strike a chord with my conflicted emotions. Then there's the songs from the past few years—whether slow, fast, or silly—that my mind somehow relates to Jonah. Where we were or what we were doing whenever the song was popular or first came on the radio. Prom, the lake, that awkward eighth-grade dance. A high school pep rally or Auburn rodeo. Even the Christian station reminds me of all the times I sat beside him in church.

I give up on music and switch to talk radio. Friday night must be a dead space for this genre, because it's an older man and woman discussing gardening. Not the interesting stuff like what plants are best for keeping alive and bloom the longest. They're analyzing the *Farmer's Almanac* on the pros and cons of where to plant tomatoes. In pots, in the ground, on a hill, in a valley, in a shaded area. Blah, blah, blah. I'll suggest this show to Daddy next time he has trouble getting to sleep.

Around the time the hosts move to squash plants, I enter Apple Cart County. It's like a ghost town this time of night. The only sign of life comes from the Quick Stop. Of course, on the other end there's the Wisteria Waffle House and a beer joint at the county line. Luckily, my family is near neither.

I smile when I notice Tanner's porch light glowing as I turn down his street. I'm sure the neighbors might complain tomorrow. That is, if they're even awake after ten. The neighborhood where he rents is full of small, older homes with mostly older neighbors.

I park beside his truck and get out. When I open the front door, he's sprawled out on the couch, wearing a pair of raggedy shorts, watching some hunting show. I'm not sure what channel it is, but that's another one that could help Daddy sleep.

"Good evening," he calls over his shoulder as he turns down the TV volume.

"Good evening, thanks for taking me in."

"No problem." He grins, making his dimples pop. Every girl in town used to swoon at his dimples. Maybe they still do. Only they don't talk to me about it anymore, since they know he's good as married to Hannah.

"Hey, I got you some Diet Cokes in the fridge."

"You did?" Now it's my turn to smile. Tanner can be an aggravating narcissist most of the time, but he has his sweet moments.

I drop my bags in the corner of the room and go to the kitchen. Sure enough, there's a twelve-pack of canned Cokes staring back at me. "Wow, you have actual food in here now." There's enough where I need to shuffle a few things to get a Coke. Quite the change from his usual sweet tea and ketchup.

"Yeah, Hannah shopped for me. She and Taylor eat dinner with me a lot, and she got tired of having to bring over ingredients when they eat here."

"Makes sense." I pop open my can and sit in the armchair I picked out for his house. It's antique, but in a good way. Not in Kendra's crusty dress way. I shift my weight, trying to get comfortable. The stuffing seems to have settled to one side, although the chair still looks great.

"You work late tonight?" Tanner asks.

"Sort of. I met with a guy whose restaurant I'm designing."

"That sounds cool."

"Yeah, but I'm not getting paid."

Tanner chugs a bottle of water then returns it to the coffee table. "Not getting paid? Then why do it?"

I sigh and stare at the ceiling. "It's more of a gaining my boss's recognition thing."

He shrugs. "To each his own."

"Besides, it's not like Jonah's paying me to decorate the mansion."

"Yeah, but he will once it's sold, and he promised you some of the profit."

"How'd you know that?"

"Poker talk."

I lean back in the chair, wanting it to be comfortable since I picked it out. It isn't, but I don't dare let Tanner know. He already hates it. Tanner yawns and stuffs a pillow behind his head.

"You can go to bed. I don't mean to keep you up."

He leans his head back to look at me. "Nah, I'm fine. Besides, it hasn't been just us two in a long time."

I'm suddenly comfortable despite my hips bouncing back and forth on an ancient spring. My big brother wants to spend quality time with me. Who knew? "Yeah, this is nice."

"Y'all are doing good on that house. Hannah and I went out there the other day."

"Thanks. Jonah isn't expecting me this weekend. I hope he isn't mad."

Tanner sits up, his hair standing on end from resting against the pillow. He stares at me like I've grown an extra head, then chuckles. "When has Jonah ever been mad at you?"

I tap my fingernails against the Diet Coke in my hand and shift again on the lopsided chair. "He's acted strange lately. For the first time in my life, it's like I don't know how to read him."

"So? You're not a mind reader."

"I know." I take a sip of my drink, then start to set it on the coffee table. Tanner doesn't have coasters, and it drives me bonkers. I set it in the floor by my seat. "It's hard to read his mood."

"Since when?"

"Like the beginning of February, I guess."

Tanner blinks and props up against the arm of the couch. "Surely he's not weirded out over what I said."

"What did you say?" I raise one brow, giving him my stern "I mean business" look.

Tanner shrugs and grins. "I made some sort of joke about the two of you having one of those deals. You know, the kind where if neither of you meets someone by a certain age, you just marry each other."

Dizziness overtakes me to the point that I'd pass out if I weren't already sitting. I was expecting Tanner to make some smart comment about brain damage due to Jonah's concussion, not tell him to marry me!

"What did he say?" I'm certain my eyes are the size of half dollars, because I can feel my forehead stretching all the way to my scalp.

"Let's just say he literally choked."

My stomach plummets. "Oh."

"You sound disappointed." Tanner leans forward, takes a drink of his water, then glares at me.

I shake my head. "No. Just, I mean, nobody wants someone to choke at the thought of marrying them. Right?" I laugh nervously to try and hide my hurt.

Tanner's voice mellows with a hint of concern. "For what it's worth, I think he's bluffing."

"What do you mean?" I speak lowly to try and hide the emotion in my own voice.

"And I think you are too."

I look down and outline the seam of the chair cushion with my thumbnail, ignoring Tanner. How dare he call me out on something nobody else knows. Not even Jonah.

"Carol? Carol!"

"Hmm?" I lift my head as if I didn't hear him practically scream my name.

"What's really going on with you two?"

I slap my hand to my forehead and groan. "I don't know, Tanner. It's weird. First Daniel accuses us of being in love with each other—"

"Wait, you're in love with Daniel? I thought you didn't like him."

I shake my head and laugh. "No, Daniel accused me and Jonah of being in love. Let me finish." He circles his hand as if to signal me to continue. "I guess that got me to analyzing how I do feel about Jonah and maybe how I think he feels about me. Then Jonah's been acting all strange lately, like he's scared to be around me. Then you tell him to marry me. And now I'm talking about this with my brother. Ugh." I bury my head in my hands and sigh dramatically.

With my head still down, Tanner pats the top of my shoulder. "It's gonna all work out."

"No, it's not," I mumble through my hands.

"Yeah, it will. Either you two will figure it out and start dating or decide to just stay friends."

I jerk my head up, appalled that he would so nonchalantly toss around the biggest decision of my life. "How can you say that? What if I do talk to Jonah and he doesn't want to give us a try? Or what if we want to try and it doesn't work out? He's been my best friend for forever. I can't risk losing him."

"Carolina." Tanner shakes his head as if I'm talking nonsense, and maybe I am. "Jonah's stuck to you tighter than a hair on a biscuit."

I sigh louder. "But what if we decide we want to try and date, and then it doesn't work, and then—"

Tanner smacks his hand to my mouth. "Shut up." He pulls it back and scrunches his nose at his palm that's now streaked by my red lipstick. He wipes it on his shorts. "I don't think Jonah choked because he couldn't stand the thought of marrying you one day. I think he choked because I called him out on something true."

I sit up straight and puff out my cheeks. Then I down the rest of my Diet Coke to try and clear my head from the remainder of my dizzy spell. "You think?"

"Well, I'm no Einstein, but I didn't just fall off the turnip truck either."

Oh boy. I guess there's only one way to find out.

Jonah

I haven't spoken to Carolina since Tuesday night at her apartment. It took me a day or so to get over the initial hurt from her disinterest in staging the house. Especially when she raved about decorating a restaurant. Seriously?

You'd think she could at least help me the last leg of this journey so we can get top dollar for the place.

Bianca was gracious enough to go with me to the nearest furniture store. Her taste is a little too modern and highbrow for my liking, but we found a compromise. What she lacked in homey taste, she made up for with her business savvy. The owner agreed to rent the furniture to us for a steep discount if we keep the tags on full display and mention where we got it. Genius idea.

I borrowed a few wall hangings from my parents' house, and Tanner gave me the cow painting to hang for good luck. I'm hoping it will telepathically speak to Carol. This is the kind of decor that goes down when she's not in charge. Tanner also offered the armchair Carolina picked out for his house. I declined, since it's so uncomfortable. Prospective buyers might get confused and boycott our furniture supplier.

Although I haven't technically listed it on the market, word got around Apple Cart that it's ready for viewers. Whether out of nosiness or a Realtor wanting to make commission, I now have a showing this evening.

My phone reads four forty-five. Most of the store employees will head out at five. I file what I'm working on, then walk down the hall and stick my head in my dad's office. "Daddy, do you need anything before I leave?"

He glances at me over the frames of his glasses and shakes his head. "No, John can help me close up. Go on and do your house thing."

"Thanks." I give a tight-lipped smile, then head toward the back exit. Daddy has morphed from flat-out mad about the mansion deal to encouraging me to get it sold. In his mind, the quicker I sell it, the quicker I can move on to more important things, like taking over part ownership of the store.

Although he hasn't come out and said it specifically, he's told me in code. "John wants to retire soon too. You could run it all by yourself one day. Carry on the family legacy." Sadly, if Jack had shown any interest in the store, none of this pressure would've fallen on me. Or at least not all of it.

I unlock my truck and climb inside. It's mild weather, and a great day to show the house. The flowers Carolina planted are blooming, and I mowed the grass this weekend. With the recent time change, we have plenty of daylight left to show the pool and backyard.

I drive the short distance to the house and park at the edge of the front drive. My stomach knots when I step out and survey the property. For the first time, I view the home as an outsider. Even when I trespassed to snoop around in the dark, I viewed it as my project. That part is over. I've done the hard work. Now I just need someone to see it with fresh eyes and fall in love with it the way I have.

As soon as I go inside, I light a few candles and turn on the ceiling fans to circulate the smell. My throat tightens when a citrus undercurrent passes. I bought these candles from Daisy when Carolina and I were in our flirting phase. The aroma of orange blossoms reminded me of her hair. Now I find it depressing.

Before I get the urge to jump off Broken Bridge—with a rock tied to my foot—I march into the living room and sniff the vanilla candles on the mantel. I fluff up a few throw pillows on the couches and make sure all the furniture tags are turned the right way to show the store logo and the price. As I'm flipping the last few, the doorbell rings.

Ready or not, this is it.

I take a deep breath and open the front door. "Good evening. Come on in."

"Thank you." A middle-aged woman in slacks and heels steps inside. She extends her hand. "Ginger, we spoke on the phone."

I give her hand a shake. "Jonah, nice to meet you."

A tall man around my age follows behind. He glances up at the ceiling, as do most people coming in for the first time, then he looks at me. "Jonah Jackson?"

I narrow my eyes. He looks familiar. Wait . . . if I take away the facial hair and about thirty pounds . . . "Nate?"

"Yeah, man." He extends his hand, and I shake it.

I pull my hand back and stare at it. "Wow, I get to tell my buddies I shook hands with Nate the Great."

He chuckles at my sarcastic tone. "Hey, I'll let them call me anything if they keep paying me."

I laugh. He made Apple Cart history when he got drafted into the Minor Leagues after high school and currently rides the bench in the Majors. That's the farthest anyone around here's ever gone. They hung his senior baseball jersey in a frame at Mary's, right behind the counter where everyone can see it.

"I haven't seen you around in a while. Ball still going good?"

He rotates his shoulder and wavers his head. "Yeah. A few aches and pains, but I can't complain. This your house?"

"For now. But it could be yours." I smirk and raise my eyebrows.

He laughs again. "Well, show it to me. I've always liked this home."

"Yeah, I've enjoyed fixin' 'er up."

"I bet. You've done a sick job on it." He follows the crown molding with his eyes, then hops down the step into the den like a pro. Well, he is a pro, or semi-pro, I guess.

Much more coordinated than Slim, anyway. And a lot less slim too.

The Realtor reads off a notepad in her hand. "It has just over five thousand square feet, four bedrooms, five baths. With multiple rooms upstairs, more bedrooms could be added. All new appliances and new flooring."

"Give me the tour," Nate says to me, ignoring her monologue.

"All right, y'all follow me." I lead them through the kitchen, dining room, bedrooms, bathrooms, and then upstairs. I explain how I added a separate entrance to the extra space across from the second bathroom upstairs, making it accessible as an addition to the master suite or its own room.

Nate compliments how the clawfoot tub looks nice and deep and the master bedroom has enough space for his California king-sized bed. I start to ask why he wants a house here, but he beats me to it.

"I've casually looked at some land to maybe build on one day when I retire. Ginger's been on the lookout for me, and she said I might like this house, so I decided to drive down and give it a look."

I nod. "It's a great estate. Would make an awesome family home one day."

Nate smiles. "It would."

"And next, we can go down and see the pool." I nod toward the window and pull back the curtain.

"The house sits on approximately five point seven acres, complete with blueberry bushes and oak trees," Ginger reads from her list.

"I had that fence installed a few weeks back for privacy." I tilt my head a little farther and notice the back of someone's head in the corner of the backyard. Most likely a nosy neighbor has stopped by to see whose random car is in the drive. "I can take you down to the basement and out back."

"Oh, there's a basement too?"

"Yes, a full basement with a bathroom. It opens to the outside patio." Ginger's more talking to herself at this point.

"Yeah, but don't get too excited. I cleaned out and pressure washed the place and replaced the old toilet, but that's all. Nothing down there except maybe a family of rats."

Nate laughs, and Ginger winces. "Uh, if it's okay, I'll meet you guys around back. I'm going to go out through the front so I can leave my card on the kitchen counter."

"That's fine." Nate and I share a glance when she passes us going downstairs. Had I known the mention of rats would shut her down, I'd have done it sooner.

I give Nate the cliff notes version of Bradley running from Papa Rat as we go through the basement. He laughs so hard, his face turns red. Everyone from Apple Cart loves a good Bradley story, no matter how long they've been gone.

We're still laughing when I open the back door to Ginger, chatting with . . . "Carol?"

"Surprised to see me?" She bounces on her toes like she's either excited about something or really needs to pee.

"Uh, yeah?" I shake my head to dislodge any romantic daydreams of her at this house. Especially since she's all adorable today in a cotton sundress, with her hair down around her face.

"You didn't tell me you'd listed the house already." She grins, but slants her eyes as if scolding me silently.

A mixture of rage and desire kicks in, and I need to get away from here before I go all caveman again. I turn to Nate and Ginger. "Can you two excuse Carolina and me for a moment?"

"Certainly. I'll finish showing Nate around the yard." Ginger clears her throat and stares back at her notepad.

"There are no HOA fees, but you get access to the golf course across from the property with a small fee when it's in operation."

I press my lips together and grab Carolina's elbow. I pull her toward me and fight against the jolt of energy at having her so close. Nate makes some sort of nostalgic comment behind us about learning to catch a pop-fly on that golf course. I continue pulling Carol until she's walking beside me willingly.

Once we're in the front yard, I stop and cross my arms. I start to confront her, but a car passes by slow as Christmas. Nosy idiots. "Come on." I nod toward the house, and she follows me inside.

"Wow, nice furniture. A little uppity for my taste, but . . ." She holds her hands to her mouth and gasps. "No, what is that doing in here?" My wish is granted as her eyes bug at the cow painting hung above the fireplace.

"That's what happens when you leave the decorating up to me." I beam, then go cold when I recall how last Tuesday, she pushed me aside like Daniel's voicemails.

"Well, I'm here now." She turns to me and sways in her sundress, the setting sun reflecting on her dark hair. It's all I can do not to scoop her in my arms and kiss her. Shoot a monkey, I'm such a sucker for Southern belles.

No. I must stay strong. This woman has ripped out my heart, tossed it like pizza dough, then left it in the oven way too long. She's burnt me, and now my heart is black as charcoal crust.

Instead of articulating all that, I simply ask, "Why?"

She stops swaying and blinks. "I want to help you, help us, sell the house."

"You said your part is done."

Carolina wipes a strand of hair from her face and shrugs. "You know you need me."

My nerves coil up like a slinky. I do need her, or I did. But I can't keep putting myself through this torture. Watching her flirt with me as if she wants me, then joke about how absurd it would be for us to be together.

"Look, Carol, I appreciate all you've done, and I'm still going to give you your part of the money I make on the house."

"I wasn't implying you wouldn't." She folds her arms and pouts.

Somehow this gesture makes her look even more desirable, so I focus on the cow painting. Something that has no emotional effect on me whatsoever. "I didn't mean it like that."

"Then what did you mean?"

I sigh and pinch the bridge of my nose. "I meant that the bet's off. Win or lose, you can stay in Auburn." My eyes betray me and drift toward her again. There's a blank expression on her face, which helps me get out what I need to say. "You've got this job stuff going for you, and I want you to be happy. I like you working with me, but I don't need you to do it."

Her face falls, whether from shock or relief, I don't know. My Carol-dar is way off and losing more of a signal by the minute. She nods slowly. "I understand. I'm going to go for now and let you finish the showing."

She brushes past me, her arm grazing mine. For a split second, I lift my foot to move. To run, walk, step, anything to put me on the path toward her. But I freeze and watch her walk toward the sunlight pooling though the front door. She slows down at the threshold, and I let out one desperate cry. "Carol?"

Slowly, she turns her head over her shoulder. "Yeah?"

I try to tell her I love her, now and for as long as I've known what love is. I try to ask her to stay, not in Apple Cart but with me, wherever that may be. I try to ask her to start a life with me, give us a chance. But all I can manage to squeak out of my throat is, "Friends?"

She presses her lips together and swallows, then whispers, "Friends," before walking to her car and driving out of my life.

CHAPTER TWENTY-ONE

Carolina

It's mild weather, but I turn my air on full blast to try and dry out my tear ducts. Despite my usual disdain for cold, it somehow calms me. My body is a sea of emotions, yet numb all at the same time. Like the bay area of an ocean.

I blink back tears on the way to Tanner's house, while silently praying that he's not home. At least I didn't go to my parents' house this weekend. Then I'd be crying in my old bedroom with Mama knocking on the door, asking if I need to talk it out.

No, that's the last thing I need.

Talking only makes things worse. Every time I try and turn the tides with Jonah, he sinks my ship by reiterating how he doesn't need me. The guy should write his own thesaurus on phrases for how to tell someone they're not needed. Or wanted. It's all the same to me.

By the time I pull into Tanner's driveway, my eyes are

itchy from the air combating my tears. I park next to his truck and cut the engine. Almost immediately, the tears begin to flow. I hang my head and watch small, wet dots darken the material of my cotton dress.

I sniffle and pull my hair back from my face, then tie it into a bun with the elastic on my wrist. My only hope of solitude is that Tanner is gone with Hannah somewhere. Either way, I can't avoid him forever.

I get out and slam my door. A huffing sound comes from behind me. I turn to see an older couple walking on the sidewalk, whom I obviously startled with my door. I smile, but they look terrified and rush away as fast as possible.

Did I scare them? I check my appearance in the sideview mirror. Mascara streaks and red blotches cover my cheeks. No wonder they ran. I would too.

My eyes itch again, so I blink, releasing the leftover tears that held back as long as they could. I go to the door, not bothering to lock my car or even get my purse. This is the oldest neighborhood in Apple Cart. Besides, all the residents are too scared to mess with me today.

I open the door and look around. My shoulders relax when I don't see Tanner. I walk to the spare bedroom and plop down face first onto the mattress. Burying my face in the covers somehow comforts me. Another wave of tears floods my eyes and soaks my face against the covers.

I'm not sure how long I lay there or how loudly I sob, but I let it all out until a warm hand cradles my neck and brushes the side of my face. "Carol?"

Thinking it might be Jonah, I raise up. I'm not sure why I expected anyone other than Tanner, since it is his house, but I'm still disappointed. "Oh, it's just you."

Tanner wrinkles his forehead. "Well, I love you, too, sis."

I flip over and prop on my elbows. The combination of

sobbing and smooshing my face in the covers has made my eyes puffy. Tanner is a fuzzy blob version of himself.

"What's wrong, Carolina? Who do I need to kill?"

I laugh a little and sit all the way up. "Nobody."

"You sure? Because I haven't seen you this upset since Daddy wouldn't buy you a pony."

I frown. "It's Jonah." Tanner scowls, and I shake my hands in front of his face. "Don't kill him, but he's the reason I'm so upset."

Tanner sits on the edge of the bed by my legs and frowns. "What happened?"

I pull my knees into my chest and hug my legs. "I thought he'd be glad to see me at the house. Instead, he's all apathetic about it, then gets kind of mad when I try and help."

Tanner sighs as I continue. "Then he starts saying how he doesn't need me. The bet is off."

"What bet?"

I roll my eyes and lean back against the wall, since the spare bed doesn't have a headboard. That's fine. Banging my head against the wall fits my mood better anyway. "When he first talked to me about the house-flip idea, he said if we doubled his money, that I had to come back to Apple Cart and start my own business too."

Tanner grins. "I like that bet."

"Oh, like you care."

"Carol, I do care. I'm not trying to make you live here like the rest of us, but it would be cool to have you around permanently."

"It's just simpler to start out working someplace, you know?"

He nods. "I've always worked someplace, as you say. I don't think I'd want the stress of doing my own thing. But it dang sure worked out for Jack."

"After a long struggle."

"Exactly." Tanner lifts the corner of his mouth. "You need to live your life how you want it. Don't worry about me, Mama, or anyone else. Not even Jonah. Do what you want, where you want, and when it's right, the right guy will come into your life."

I let go of my legs and sigh heavily. Tanner may joke more than anyone, but he has his moments of great wisdom. He's right. And in similar words, Jonah said the same thing to me.

I need to live my own life and not worry about other people. Maybe that's my problem. Everything I do revolves around what others need from me. A wedding, a remodel, a freakin' pup potty. Perhaps the allure of starting my own business has always been a ruse for needing to take control of my own life.

Why limit myself to Apple Cart or Auburn? Why not broaden my job search? As much as I love being close enough to visit my family often, a move might be good for me. I could always come back, right?

"You all right?"

I blink at Tanner, his words bringing me out of my head. "No, but I will be. I think working with Jonah so closely these last few months just confused me."

Tanner slaps my knee and gives it a gentle shake. "That's understandable. You two have always been close. I'm kinda surprised y'all haven't questioned your relationship before now."

That stings. If even Tanner, who notices nothing about anything, could sense that, what's Jonah's problem?

"Yeah, I just hoped he was the one. My one."

Tanner curves his lips into a slight smile, one that doesn't show his dimples. "Yeah, I kinda hoped so too."

Jonah

I stare out the kitchen window, then down at the business cards on the countertop. That makes three more showings. I reach for my phone, wanting to share the news with Carolina, but drop my hand when I remember that's not yet an option.

If nothing changes before this time tomorrow, I will have set a new record. One full week of no communication with Carol.

My stomach sickens at the realization of that. After she left last Saturday, I finished up with Nate and his Realtor. Then I spent the night rehearsing what I might say when I saw Carolina at church the next day, but she didn't come.

With all the weirdness between us, a text won't do. I tried calling her once or twice, but she let it go to voicemail. Then, out of habit, I've started to text her whenever I saw something funny or someone else viewed the house.

I officially listed it Monday. At this point, I'm ready to sell it and move on to the next thing. I've priced it a little over twice the amount I have in it, which is the goal. But I'm not above dropping the price, if need be, especially since our bet is off.

I'll still make a nice bit of money, and I'm sick of walking through it. Every room reminds me of Carol. In the living room, I see her tearing up carpet. In the dining room, she's peeling back wallpaper. Upstairs, she's staring out the window, her hair shining in the sunlight. In the back bedroom, she's on a ladder, tempting me. In the kitchen, she's whacking things with the hammer, including my head.

This whole crummy place reminds me of what we had—or could have. Without her, I don't want any part of it. That's what I need to tell her. In person, or at least with my voice.

I'm old fashioned when it comes to communicating. I've never asked a girl out by text or said anything remotely important for the first time that way either. That's just rude, in my opinion. Men use words, not emojis. Well, except for the occasional ice cream cone, but that's different.

I gather the Realtor cards and stuff them in what will likely become the new owner's kitchen junk drawer. Maybe I'll toss them back on the counter before the next showing to drive up competition and create a sense of urgency.

Before any more memories of Carol conjure up, I flip off the lights and lock everything up. Jack planned a last-minute poker match since Bianca had a business meeting in Atlanta. I'll probably get my butt handed to me, since I'm in no mood to play anything. But maybe it will act as a distraction. When it comes to poker, I have no memories with Carolina.

Except when we played last, and Tanner tried to make me fess up about my feelings. Toad-headed Tanner!

I drive out to Jack's, doing my best to keep a clear head. The stars shine in front of me as I drive farther out of town and turn down the dirt drive for Gamer's Paradise. Jack mentioned that Ronald was here to turkey hunt, which I'm sure has something to do with this impromptu poker game.

The lights are on at the lodge, and two trucks I don't recognize are parked out front. I'm assuming he has other guests hunting too. I haven't talked to Jack all week, or anyone really. Unless you count thanking my mama for supper and answering a few questions from Daddy and Uncle John at the store.

I pass the lodge and pull up at Jack's. Tanner's and Ronald's trucks are already here. Leave it to Ronald to drive the few yards from the big house to Jack's. That guy won't do.

Chocolate and Brownie perk up from their sphinxlike stance on the porch when I open my door. As soon as I step on the porch, they stand and wag their tails. I scratch them both equally behind the ears before going inside.

It smells oddly amazing in here. Not that Jack's place ever smells bad, especially not since Bianca's started lighting Daisy's candles everywhere. But it smells like fresh barbecue.

"Jonah, my man, just in time to eat." Ronald pats his belly.

"I had to make deer poppers earlier for my guests, so I made a few extra pans and cooked them here for us," Jack says.

"Thanks." My stomach growls as if it's thanking him too. I haven't had much of an appetite this week.

I go to the kitchen and fix a plate of deer poppers and Doritos, two of my favorites. Jack pours us all tea, obviously still in hosting mode. Maybe we can get him to pour our refills later. Oh, or fry some honeybuns. My stomach growls again, scolding me for neglecting it so much lately.

Ronald takes the usual empty seat and downs about half his glass before the rest of us can make it to the table. "Ah, that's good."

"Kill anything yet?" I ask.

He shakes his head. "I drove in this evening. Jack said the guests have had some luck."

"Yeah, I have four men at the house this weekend. They've killed two so far."

"That's good," I say.

Ronald slaps Jack on the back, causing him to cough a little. "Jack was sweet enough to save the big room for me."

"Of course, you're my VIP."

Ronald winks at no one in particular. "Marriage has softened this man."

Tanner laughs. "Jack's always been a softy."

I laugh, but when my eyes meet Tanner's, his face straightens. He glares at me a few seconds, then concentrates on his plate.

"I'll deal," I say, reaching for the cards in front of us.

"Sure you don't need any help?" Tanner's voice is more sarcastic than usual, which is saying a lot.

"Uh, yeah." I'm not sure why he asked, since I'm generally the dealer. I can shuffle better than the rest of us. Well, except for that time Michael played with us. He married a woman who used to work at a Mississippi casino. If they handed out certifications for card sharks, he'd have one framed on his wall. And she'd have several.

I shuffle and start to ask if Tanner wants to cut, then decide it's best I ignore him. I deal the cards, then examine my own hand. Not good at all.

"What we playin' for?" Ronald asks around a mouthful of deer poppers.

"I'm assuming money," I say. Best get ahead of any wild ideas Tanner has about making me confess all my secrets.

"How about the rest of the deer poppers," Ronald counters.

Jack laughs. "I'll make you more if you want them. Let's just stick with money." He cocks the side of his mouth up at me, as if assuring me he has my back on the whole not spilling our guts thing.

I haven't talked to Jack about that last poker match, when he saved me with the winning hand. He read my worries about Carolina. It was all over his face. Any other time, I'd have likely confided in him about it. Lord knows I need to vent to someone.

But Jack's newly married and running a business. Besides, I've had my own hands full with the remodel, school, and work at the store. It's not like we've had time to sit on the front porch and shoot the bull.

Ronald laughs. "You'll need it with a wife. Why do you think I've stayed single all these years?" He laughs louder, and we all chuckle a bit to make him happy, even though he's not that funny. "Pretty soon, I'll be the only bachelor at this table."

"Oh, I don't know," Tanner comments, then narrows his eyes at me. "I don't think we can count on Jonah getting married anytime soon."

"Are we really going to do this again?" Heat rises in my face as I glare at him.

"Guys, let's just play the game." Jack pops up as the authoritative voice, and Tanner snaps his mouth shut. He doesn't need to say more, as the look he's giving me says it all.

Ronald glances around at all of us, then shakes his head. "You guys need to get out more. I think your periods have synced."

None of us laugh this time. Ronald hasn't a clue about what went on last time we played. However, the tension in the room is obvious. Jack slants his eyes toward me as if checking my reaction. I curve my lips slightly to let him know I'm okay.

But I'm not okay.

In a matter of months, Carolina has gone from my best friend to my business partner to dangerously flirting with something more to maybe an acquaintance now. And acquaintances come and go in life.

A tingling sensation starts at my scalp and goes all the way to my toes and fingertips as I imagine a life without Carolina Nash. I can't, but I also can't continue as I am. All her recent flirting makes me want her even more. And I can't keep wanting what I can't have, especially when I have no clue if it's available or not.

No more dancing around with almost kisses, public pecks, or flirty smiles. We need to have a serious talk. ASAP.

CHAPTER TWENTY-TWO

Carolina

The last thing I wanted to do was come back to Apple Cart. It's hard enough to avoid Jonah in Auburn, even with him there only a few days a week. My body and mind pull toward him like a magnetic current. I'm afraid after all this time, I've become addicted to Jonah Jackson. The only sure cure is going cold turkey without him.

Too bad it's Easter Sunday. I haven't missed an Easter at Apple Cart Baptist Church since before I was born. Literally. Mama was on bed rest while pregnant with me and had to skip one year. She's told me all about fussing at Daddy to comb Matthew's and Tanner's hair before they left. Then she said she did her hair and makeup from the bed and squeezed into a Lilly Pulitzer dress to get family photos once they came home.

All a little extreme, if you ask me, but that's how much Mama loves Easter Sunday. While I wouldn't dream of missing church on Easter, she wouldn't dream of me going to any other church on Easter besides hers. Even the one I attend whenever I stay the weekend in Auburn.

I wrap another strand of hair around my curling wand and pout at the mirror. Late last night, I drove to Tanner's and slept in his spare room. I've got maybe a few minutes left before he'll want to take a shower and steam the place up. Or worse, use the toilet and stink the place up.

From the corner of the mirror, I can see him drooling on his pillow through the open doors. Growing up with two brothers taught me to wake up early and get all my bathroom time in before they defamed my space.

Even though I technically had my own bathroom, one of them would want to crash mine because the other had taken over theirs. Whoever I marry can't be as bad as them. If he is, I'll make him take the guest bathroom.

My fingers tremble at the idea of marriage. I've done well this week not daydreaming of Jonah. If I don't talk to or see him, I should be fine. But there's a hundred and one perfect chance I'll see him at church.

I sigh and reach for the end of my hair. "Ouch!" I seethe with pain, then suck on my first two fingers. I've got to pay better attention with this stupid wand.

Not trusting my reflexes, I tug my hair loose from the wand and let it fall in a tight curl. This strand is half the length of the others from staying coiled up so long. I set the wand on the counter and finger comb the curl. Forget doing fine concerning Jonah. I almost melted my fingerprints because of him.

I shake out my hand before sucking on the two throbbing fingers once more. By lunchtime, I'll have blisters for sure. Good thing that was the last piece of hair.

I unplug the weapon and carry it, along with my toiletry and makeup bags, to the spare bedroom. Tanner makes a grumbling sound from across the hall. We need to leave a little early since everybody goes to church on Easter.

It's crazy. People literally come out of the woodwork. All the churches in town will be packed, and Mary's Diner will be closed. She takes Easter off to cook for her own family and says the rest of the county should too. I normally help Mama bake bread and dessert the night before, but she's just lucky I'm here this year.

Tanner whistles from the bathroom as I pack up my things and sling my bag over my shoulder. I drop it by the front door, then head for the kitchen to retrieve one of my Diet Cokes. I shift Taylor's juice boxes out of the way to get one. I attempt to push the door shut, but it doesn't budge.

"Hang on." Tanner has his hand on the edge, holding it open. He's freshly showered, in his underwear. He reaches across me for the jug of milk. I frown as he downs the last of it. His throat bulges in and out like one of those creepy-looking lizards we used to chase as kids.

"Ah." He crunches the plastic jug and wipes his mouth with the back of his hand. Then he looks at me. "What?"

"Does Hannah know you're this gross?" He burps in my face, then shrugs. I roll my eyes and head for the couch.

"She loves me, despite all my flaws."

I half smile. I'm happy for them, really, but also a little envious. They really do have a sweet relationship, despite being total opposites.

Maybe that's my problem. Jonah and I agree on a lot of things . . . except for maybe using farm animals in decor. Perhaps I should go for someone opposite of me.

"Let me change and we'll go," Tanner says.

"You mean put on clothes."

"Whatever." He waves his hand in the air as if giving up and disappears into his room.

I pop open my Coke and take a sip. I could go ahead and

leave, but we need to ride together, since finding parking today will be a challenge.

Tanner comes back, fumbling with a tie around his neck. I raise one eyebrow. "When did you learn to tie a tie?"

He smirks. "I didn't. I keep it tied but loose enough to fit over my head. Then all I need to do is tighten it up." He wiggles it closer to his neck and tugs it taut. "Ready?"

"Yeah." I stand and loop my arm through my purse strap.

Tanner picks up my bag by the door. "Good Lord, Carol. What all's in this?"

"Just all my getting-ready stuff and a change of clothes."

He shakes his head. "Women."

I laugh for the first time in a week, causing him to smile. "We can take my car. Easier to park."

He nods and leads the way outside. I open the trunk for him to drop my bag inside, then climb in the front and put on my sunglasses. Easter in Alabama is either hot as a firecracker or cold as a cucumber. No in between. This year it's hot, which I prefer, considering the best spring dresses are sleeveless, like the one I'm wearing.

I smooth out the skirt of my pink A-line dress and back out of Tanner's drive. We ride the short distance in silence. I park under one of the shade trees, not bothering to search for a closer spot. A few vehicles circle the rows of cars like vultures, hoping for an empty space.

My ankles shake as I maneuver through the loose gravel in new heels. The front of the church resembles a flower garden as people wearing all shades of pastels crowd the front steps. Some women have on big hats like extras in a Tyler Perry movie church scene.

Among the sea of spring colors, I spot Jonah. He's wearing a tan suit, with his hair combed neatly. My entire body goes numb when we come within a few yards of him.

Hannah and Taylor find us, and Taylor grabs Tanner

around the legs. "Hey." Hannah's voice sounds like she's ten feet under water, since my pulse has made its way to my head. As Tanner interacts with them, I watch Jonah slip inside. I swallow hard and put on a smile. Then I follow Tanner and his little future family inside.

We shuffle inside the sanctuary among the crowd. I greet Adrianne and Daisy, then a few older couples. Paul waves to me from the foyer, where he's sneaking some communion crackers. I wave, then cringe. I hope they have extra on hand.

Hannah's mother starts moving jackets and purses when we get to her pew. Several people around give her a nasty look for saving seats, but I'm glad she did. Jonah is sitting in our usual spot by Jack and Bianca. Adrianne and Daisy slide in where I would normally sit, and a few families who I never see at church fill up the remaining back pews.

I sit in the center of our pew, between Taylor and an older couple. Another perk to coming with Tanner is not having to come super early with my parents. Mama makes a big deal out of getting her seat on Easter. Not that I think many one-timers would fight for the front pew, but to each her own.

The choir director motions for everyone to stand. Between the Tyler Perry hats and influx of people, it's hard to see the stage. That gives me an excuse to watch Jonah. I slant my eyes so far his way that my head hurts. Finally, I give in and turn my head.

His hands are in his pockets and he's staring straight ahead. I doubt he's noticed me yet. Last night, I tossed and turned, and it had nothing to do with the worn-out mattress. Scenarios of conversations with Jonah robbed my sleep. No matter what, I've got to talk to him as soon as church ends.

With that resolve in mind, I face forward and start to sing. Only when the worship portion is complete and we all take our seats do I allow myself to look back at Jonah. Except he's not there.

There's nobody between Bianca and Daisy. I crane my neck to check out the other pews on that side, but no sign of Jonah. The sanctuary doors are shut, so I have no clue if he snuck out to go to the bathroom.

Without giving it much thought, I stand. People all around stare. I don't want to disturb the older couple beside me, so I shuffle past Taylor, then Hannah and Tanner, and Hannah's parents. All the while, I murmur, "Excuse me." Then I speed walk to the wooden doors and slip into the foyer.

A few deacons stand at the communion table, checking boxes of crackers. I hear one say, "I know we had more than this earlier." Stupid Paul. He needs to go to the altar for that.

I tiptoe to the men's restroom door and put my ear to it. One of the deacons shoots me a scolding look, but I don't care. At least I'm not going in to check. I think I hear someone, so I cup my ear to hear better. The door flies open, pinning me against the wall. I grunt, then squeeze away from the wall when it swings shut.

Earl Ed walks out, adjusting his belt. I sigh and make my way outside. The sun blasts me, and I cup my hand over my eyes to get a better view of the parking lot. I see no sign of Jonah or any other person. Oh wait . . . no, that's Misty. I'd recognize her anywhere. She's standing under an oak tree, smoking one of those electronic cigarettes.

I could walk the parking lot to see if his truck is hidden in the back. But that would take forever. Unless he's volunteering in the nursery, I'm going to assume he's gone.

Defeated, I go inside and slide through the door to the sanctuary. This time, I tap Hannah's mother on the shoulder and ask if they can scoot down. Tanner gives me a half-scolding, half-concerned glare. I shrug at him and sit on the end of the pew.

The deacons open the doors and roll the communion table down the aisle. I puff up my cheeks and exhale. After all that, I could use some communion. Too bad us Baptists drink Welch's grape juice and not something stronger.

Jonah

I've committed the unpardonable sin. At least in the eyes of my mother. I skipped out on Easter Sunday.

She never would've known had Mrs. Ethel not mentioned it on the way out. But it's the first thing Mama mentioned when I showed up to Uncle John's for Sunday lunch.

Easter is one of my favorite times of year. When we were little, our grandparents would hide eggs in weird places like the tailpipe of a truck or a hole in a tree. Jack, my sister, and I would fight tooth and nail to find the most eggs. Then, whenever we got tired of hunting, or the adults got tired of hiding, we'd take the eggs to the gravel road and bust them.

The driveway smelled like sewage for a week. That is, until Grandpa got a hound dog that would eat them all. It worked perfectly until the dog got up in years and passed gas all the time. Then his farts smelled like sewage for a few days after each Easter Sunday.

Those were the good old days. Of course, as we got older, our Easter traditions have evolved. Now we put eggs out for target practice. Jack and I shoot them with guns, while Alex puts them on a hay bale to shoot with her bow and arrow.

That makes it worth still dyeing eggs for Alex. When she leaves for a four-year college, I'm not sure what Mama will do. Probably dye her own eggs.

We polish off the last of the cobbler Aunt Leann made and take our plates to the kitchen. Bianca stands at the kitchen sink, already rinsing off our dinner plates. She didn't eat dessert and doesn't often. Must be a city girl thing.

"Need help?" I ask as I hand her my dessert plate.

"No, I'm just rinsing and loading them into the dishwasher to help out."

"Thanks."

She smiles. "You can go ahead and shoot eggs with Jack."

I laugh. "Perfect." I open the screen door off the kitchen and go to my truck for my gun.

At some point, I'll let Jack know I left church because of Carolina. Although I suspect he already knows. Seeing her in that pretty pink dress, with her hair all curled, was the worst kind of torment. Like a picture-perfect representation of what I want but can't have. I used to stare at cakes in the bakery case the same way as a kid. Even though I couldn't always have a cake from the glass, I'd eventually get to eat one.

Carolina is the cliche of "can't have your cake and eat it too." All these years, I've had her in my life, but never been able to take a bite. I got a small taste of her over the past few months, and now I can't control my animal instincts to eat the whole cake and lick the bowl of icing when I'm done.

Wow, what an analogy. Good thing we had cobbler today instead of cake.

I pull my pistol and a box of shells from behind the seat. Jack is already setting up eggs in a row when I get to the designated shooting spot. Uncle John keeps a dirt pile near the edge of his yard, where the woods part of his property starts. There are usually some old hay bales nearby too, where Alex sets up her eggs.

"Ah, brought the revolver, I see." Jack smiles at my gun.

"Yeah, haven't shot 'er in a while. Thought I'd go old school today."

"Sweet." Jack has a hunting rifle.

"This is a lot more fun than throwing eggs in the road."

Jack laughs. "Yeah. Although that year we played catch for a while before busting them was fun."

I shake my head at the memory. "I think that was when we both decided neither of us would have a future in sports."

"No doubt." He moves back from lining up the eggs and starts to load his gun on the tailgate of his truck. "You didn't stay long at church. Something wrong?"

I scratch the side of my neck and tug at my collar. Jack wasted no time asking me about leaving church. But at least he waited until we were away from the family.

"Carolina." No use beating around the bush.

"Oh." Jack finishes loading his gun.

"Yeah." I sigh and slide onto the tailgate of his truck, setting my gun beside me.

"That night when we played poker. You didn't want to talk about her, did you?"

I stare down at my pants, not caring that the only suit I own is against a rusty tailgate. "No, I didn't."

Jack fools around with straightening ammo to feign busyness. I know he's waiting for me to talk.

Oh, fuddy duddy, I need to talk to someone. Better Jack than anyone else. It's not like I can talk to Carol about herself.

"Tanner was right."

Jack sets down his gun and stares at me.

"Not about the marriage at thirty thing. But I am in love with her."

Jack smiles. "I suspected so."

"Really?"

He nods. "Why else would you do all that you do for her and hang out with her that much?"

"We're best friends."

Jack laughs. "Yeah, but dude, come on. She's good looking and you go out of your way to take up for her. Anyone would have to be blind to not see how you feel about her."

"Then Carolina needs an eye exam."

Jack chuckles loudly. "Maybe so. Sometimes we have trouble seeing what's right in front of us. Like how I was the last one to realize how much sense it made for me to sell the back property to Macon and Ronald."

"Yeah, that was kinda a no-brainer."

Jack shakes his head. "Anyway, have you told her this?"

I rub my palms down my pant legs. "No, not really. I mean, I kissed her, but it was when I had a concussion."

"Yeah, I'd say that doesn't count. Why don't you just have a real conversation with her? Lay it all out and see how she feels?"

"It's complicated."

Jack shakes his head. "How? Either she loves you or she doesn't. Don't you want to find out?"

"I do." I swing my legs to standing and pace in front of his tailgate. "But I don't want to pressure her to change her life for me."

"How so?"

I stop in front of Jack. "I bet her that if we make a certain amount of money on the mansion, she has to come back here and start her own business."

"And she took the bet?"

"Yep, even made a heart swear."

"A what?"

"Never mind." I shake my hand dismissively. "Point is, I don't want to pressure her into moving back here. I don't want her to give up whatever it is she wants for me."

Jack looks out into the pines and sighs, then turns back to me with his lopsided grin. "What if what she wants is you?"

My hands tremble at the possibility of the one thing, rather person, I've always wanted wanting me above all else. "That would be great, but it has to be her decision."

Jack leans against the truck bed and slaps my shoulder. "A word of advice, for what it's worth." He drops his hand and continues. "Bianca and I couldn't be more different. I never expected her to want to move here and never even asked her to. All I knew was I wanted her and had to find some way for us to be together. You've got to lay it all out there, prove to her that you're willing to love her and stand by her no matter what. Then, it's up to her to decide if she wants to take that journey with you, no matter where it leads."

I narrow my eyes at my cousin. "No offense, but I'm not the type to roll a dead deer through the airport."

Jack throws back his head and chuckles. "I think that only applies to my situation. No need for something so extravagant. You already have Carolina's attention. Just talk to her and be honest. Let her know you're all in no matter what the future holds."

I smile, then nod.

Jack pats me on the back. "You good?"

"Good."

"Good, then let's shoot some eggs." He grabs his gun and marches toward the dirt pile.

CHAPTER TWENTY-THREE

Carolina

"You did such a great job on this. Snookie approves one hundred!"

I force a smile, but cringe inside when the client mentions running my pup potty design by her pregnant dog. No wonder Audrey didn't work on this project personally. It's been one big pain in the pooch.

The woman raves about the entire nursery for a few minutes to Rhonda. At least I didn't have her job of spearheading the whole project and working one on one with Giselle—and Snookie, of course.

Rhonda and Giselle shake hands, causing Giselle's bangles to clank like tiny cymbals on her arm. They stand, and I follow suit, along with the other minions on this project. Rhonda offers to walk Giselle out and winks back at us.

I sigh with relief. Once they're out of sight, I go back to

my cubicle. With any luck, I'll never have to see Giselle again. Even though she lives in the area, I'm quite certain we don't run in the same circles.

I'm more Target than Bloomingdale's, and she has an expendable income for a dog nursery while I hang out in trailer parks.

But not lately. I haven't had any contact with Jonah in weeks. Whoever said time heals all wounds is an idiot. I'd hoped that time would make it better, but losing Jonah feels like I've cut off my arm. My dominant arm, at that.

I think it might hurt less to lose a limb than Jonah.

He's grown into such an extension of me that it's hard to function without him. Every time I want to share something with someone or chill after a long day, I'd turn to Jonah. Without him, I've buried myself in work. But the house is complete, the dog potty is complete, and I'm about to turn in my final restaurant report to Audrey.

I shuffle through all my drawings and notes from Reece on what he wants for the restaurant. He approved my designs, but I still want to run it by Audrey since she's both my boss and his friend. Once I'm sure I have everything in order, I stack the papers in a folder and walk to Audrey's office.

She's reading something at her desk. I knock softly, and she raises her head. "Hi, Audrey, do you have a minute?"

"Yeah, what do you need?" She closes the folder on her desk and smiles.

I enter and hand her my folder. "These are all the designs for Reece's project. He's happy with it, but I told him I wanted to run things by you first."

She smiles again. "Thanks for that."

"Of course." I stand at the edge of her desk, fumbling with the hem of my skirt while I wait for her to assess my work, not unlike a student wanting to please her teacher.

"These look great, Carolina."

I grin so wide that my cheeks stretch. "Really?"

"Yeah." Audrey nods. "I can see why Reece was impressed. He told me you were talented beyond your years."

"He did?"

"He did." She winks at me, and I sit back in one of the chairs, now relaxed. "I'm glad you stopped in here. I have something else I wanted to talk to you about."

"Okay." I thread my fingers together and squeeze them gently.

"Your internship naturally ends the week before graduation, but I'd like for you to consider staying on longer, if that's what you want. I know you've probably applied to other places, but I can offer you an entry-level position here. Not much more pay than the internship, but it comes with benefits."

My smile widens at the prospect of not having to go through another interview process or possibly move out of state. Aside from throwing my resume at a few random firms I found one night while upset at Jonah and high on Blue Bell, I haven't really searched for employment. Unless you count posting my resume on Indeed and clicking the option "actively searching," which I don't.

I'd had a hunch I might get an offer from Audrey, and I blamed my lax job hunting on it. However, now that the time has come and she's offering me a real job, I don't feel like I expected. There are no fireworks of excitement or even sighs of relief. Flattery from Reece's opinion, yes, but it ends at that.

In all honesty, I could've probably done Reece's job outside of Audrey's company, charged him a modest price, and come out for the better.

"Carolina, what do you think?"

"Sounds nice." I grin again, unable to elaborate on the offer.

If I stay here, I'd need to find a new roommate or move to a cheaper apartment. Daddy made it abundantly clear that after graduation, I pay my own way. Unless, of course, I wanted to move home until I get on my feet. His subtle way of asking me to come back to Apple Cart.

"Any questions?" Audrey straightens my designs and closes the folder.

"No, ma'am." I spread my fingers, which have gotten clammy balled in my lap. "When do you need an answer?"

Audrey tightens her lips, as if she wasn't prepared for this type of response. Heck, neither was I.

"I'll need to know by your graduation, so I can post the job if you don't want it."

I nod and somewhat smile before standing. "Thank you. I'll weigh my options and let you know."

My options being take this job, move back to Apple Cart and do my own thing, or hope that high-paying job I applied for in Alaska pans out. Ugh, never again will I go on job sites at midnight after downing a pint of ice cream.

Audrey hands me the folder, and I turn and leave before things get any more awkward.

This year has been the year of reconsidering everything in my life. My career options, where I want to live, and most of all, my relationship with Jonah—or lack thereof.

Jonah

Against my better judgment, I go to Jack's to play poker. Bianca and Hannah got invited to ride go-karts with Daisy and Adrianne at Double Drive. Had I known that ahead of time, I'd have suggested we skip playing cards and watch Bianca try to maneuver a bulky frame with a lawnmower engine around the winding track.

She'll probably get the hang of it after a few rounds, but she's also probably wearing some form of spiky shoes.

I've had a few calls about the house, and one person wants a second showing. No firm commitments, but still, plenty of interest to not yet drop the price.

I drove by there today after working at the store to make sure everything looked in order. I should've stayed a while and lit some candles to give it that homey scent before the showing tomorrow morning, but I can't stomach the citrus candles right now or spending too much time in the house. Too many conflicting memories.

Jack and Tanner planned to start around seven and said they'd pick up some barbecue. I purposely pull up fifteen minutes late to avoid any time alone with Jack. I'm in no mood for him to ask if I've talked to Carolina.

Jack may can make some grand expression of love that ends with him riding off into the sunset with Bianca on a stuffed deer, but I'm not him. I need some reassurance that Carol feels the same way. The last thing we said to one another was "friends," and unless I have a clue she wants more, that's where my talk will lead.

I miss my best friend.

Tanner's truck is here, which eases my tension a bit. I get out and climb the front steps, noticing new rocking chairs and a rather colorful doormat. Looks like Bianca's been shopping again.

I open the door to Jack in his recliner and Tanner on the couch. They both stand when I enter, as if I'm to be honored.

"We need to talk," Jack says in a voice that conveys I am *not* to be honored.

I turn to Tanner, who nods in agreement. Uh-oh. Jack must've ratted me out. That turd. Doesn't he know blood's thicker than water?

"Have a seat." Jack motions toward couch before sitting back in his chair. Tanner sits on the opposite end of the couch and stares at me as I slowly lower myself on the edge of a cushion.

"Uh, is this an intervention?"

"Maybe," Tanner replies.

I take off my cap and set it on my knee. My leg bounces so much, it almost falls off. Chocolate sways my way and jumps on the couch between Tanner and me. Smart girl, protecting Uncle Jonah. I scratch her belly with gratitude.

"We're not playing cards until we talk about you and Carolina." Jack puts on his "I'm trying to look intimidating" face. He really looks constipated, but we all know that face means business.

"You told him?" I point to Tanner.

"No, he told me." Jack points to himself.

"Huh?" Now I'm really confused.

Tanner leans toward me with murder in his eyes, and I'm thankful to have a Labrador as a buffer. "You made my sister cry!"

"What? When? I never meant—"

He shakes his head to shush me. "Carolina thought you were sending her signals that you liked her. Like, like-liked her. She tried to flirt with you, then you told her you didn't need her."

A grin creeps across my face. If I'm hearing this correctly, he's saying that she wants me too. Could it be?

"Why are you smiling?" Tanner demands. "This isn't funny!"

"No, it isn't. I'm smiling because you said she like-likes me."

"She did. Who knows now after the mess you've made. Ghosting her, then running out of church like a sinner on salvation Sunday."

"Tanner, Carol is the last person I'd ever want to hurt, trust me. I meant I no longer needed her to help with the house, not that I no longer needed her in my life."

"Does she know that?"

"She should. I mean, we were literally in the house, talking about the house . . ." My words trail off as both Tanner and Jack shake their heads.

"You've got a lot to learn about women, Jonah." Jack scratches his head as his eyes widen. "Never assume they get context. Always overexplain."

Tanner nods. "Even I know that, and I'm not even engaged or married."

I lift my palms, then slap them on my lap. Chocolate shifts her weight at the sound of them slapping my jeans. "Help me out here. Are you saying that you're sure Carolina like-likes me?"

"I'm saying that she loves you." Tanner grins to the point that his dimples pop.

My heart beats so hard that if I were a cartoon, this would be the part where it's visible through my shirt. "Since when?"

Tanner laughs. "I don't know. She didn't tell me the exact moment she started feeling that way."

"No, since when have you known?"

"I dunno, several weeks, maybe a month."

I reach over and smack his face. Chocolate jumps to the floor and runs to Jack. Tanner looks at me stunned, and my own jaw drops, as I've stunned myself.

"You slapped me!" He rubs his cheek. "What are you, a fourteen-year-old girl?"

"No, I . . ." I turn to Jack, who's cuddling his dog and trying to hold in a laugh. Then I face Tanner again. "Why didn't you tell me as soon as she told you this? These last few weeks have been miserable. I've never gone this long without talking to her, and now it's to the awkward point where I don't know what to say."

"Just tell her what's on your heart, man," Jack comments. I detect some shakiness in his words, as if he's still trying to hold off laughing.

"Tell her what's on my heart? What kind of advice is that? A lyric from an eighties love ballad?"

"Man, you've got to talk to her," Tanner pleads.

I turn back to him and sigh. "You're sure she feels the way I do?"

He nods.

"But what if she's mad and refuses to talk to me?"

"Then you've got to *make* her talk to you."

"And just how do I do that?"

Tanner and Jack exchange a mischievous glance. Uh-oh. I have a feeling they're about to tell me how.

CHAPTER TWENTY-FOUR

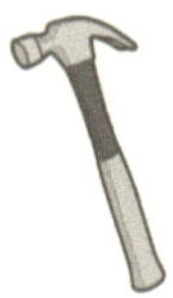

Carolina

"What do you think?"

Kendra's voice catches me off guard. I stand and dust the dirt from my knees. My roommate just had to get married in the middle of nowhere. No kidding. I thought Apple Cart County was the middle of nowhere. That is until last night, when we arrived at Kendra's wedding site.

We all stayed in tents, on the outskirts of an open area between trees, where the ceremony is to take place. According to Kendra, we stayed in yurts, but there was no electricity or running water, so to me it's a tent.

"Wow, Kendra, you look beautiful." The shock in my voice isn't because Kendra isn't pretty, but because her dress is also pretty. "Good job, Adrianne."

"Thanks." Adrianne beams as she fans out the short train on Kendra's dress. The thrift store dress. Somehow, Adrianne magically cut, sewed, and pinned it enough to look normal.

Better than normal—stylish and elegant. Maybe woodland creatures helped her like in a fairy tale, since we're tucked away in a forest. "It helped that I couldn't sleep well in my tent, so I stayed up all night working on it."

"You mean yurt," Kendra corrects.

I shoot Adrianne a knowing look, and she narrows her eyes so much that her fake eyelashes touch. I'm sure she's hiding an eye roll from Kendra.

Adrianne yawns as she opens her eyes wider, and Kendra loops her arm around her. "I'm so glad Carolina brought you. You're like my fairy godmother." She squeezes Adrianne closer.

Adrianne takes a step back. "Careful, hun, that dress is literally hanging by a thread."

"Right." Kendra giggles.

Her hair falls in soft curls around her neck, and she's wearing a pearl necklace with matching stud earrings. Adrianne has a gift for bringing out the best in everyone's natural style. I'm sure it helps that her best friend, Daisy, is somewhat like Kendra.

"The photographer is near the restroom area. I think he's ready for you, Kendra," I say.

"Thanks." Kendra bounces off as I resume my kneeling position by the wooden benches.

Adrianne rushes after her. "You better hold that skirt up when you run across this dirt."

I laugh, which turns into a yawn. Bringing Adrianne was a smart choice. Otherwise, I couldn't have managed to keep Kendra straight and finish all the little details at the same time.

For the next half hour, I tie flowers to the ends of all the benches. By benches, I mean actual logs sawed in half and smoothed down. At last, I stand and study my work. Not bad for a hippie wedding in the wilderness. I snap a few photos with my phone. Quite the unique job to add to my resume. That is if I continue to plan and coordinate weddings.

I've got exactly two weeks from today to give Audrey my answer, and with every day that passes, I have less clarity. I've prayed, made pros and cons lists, and taken numerous long walks on campus to try and clear my head. The only thing out of the norm that I haven't done in a pinch is talk to Jonah.

My stomach aches, and I get a hunch it's not just from the rehearsal dinner meal. Which, by the way, was fully vegan and wouldn't fill up the tank of a push lawnmower, much less an adult-sized stomach. I hold my side to steady my queasiness and pick up my clipboard from the first log bench.

Unlike most weddings in Apple Cart, where the whole town attends and the bride dresses like a debutante, this wedding is simple and earthy. Kendra and Brandon walk arm in arm after the photographer to the archway in front of me. An involuntary smile crosses my lips as I observe their flirty banter from a few feet away.

The photographer muses, "That's great. Keep acting natural," as he snaps away. Adrianne pops in every now and again between photos to adjust Kendra's train.

"I think that's all I need." The photographer snaps one more of the couple sharing a hug, then changes his lens.

"Great, it's almost time for the ceremony," I say, glancing at my phone. Ten minutes until showtime. I snap my fingers toward the tree area where the reception tables are arranged. "We need the band."

Three guys, whose style I'd call dressy grunge, slog toward their instruments by the flower arch. One picks up a ukulele, the other stands behind a keyboard, and the third behind some type of drums. The kind you play with your hands.

I nod with approval as they start playing a soft tune.

Then I hurry Kendra away to wait in her yurt before her turn to walk down the aisle. Adrianne enters, and the three of us stand together in the odd structure, which resembles a giant white-chocolate Hershey's Kiss.

Kendra's face glows as she peeks out of the slight opening. I peek beside her and count as all the parents are seated. Normally, I'd be outside of a closed door—or tent—for a better view, but Kendra begged me to stay with her until her time. I sympathized, as she chose to walk down the aisle alone due to all the issues with her parents' divorce.

Right after her mother makes it to her place on the first log, the music changes. My eyes bug when I realize what they're playing. "No way! How can this happen again?"

Of all the rotten luck. What are the odds that in the last two weddings I coordinated, the piano player bangs out "Great Balls of Fire"? You really can't make this stuff up.

Huffing, I rip open the yurt and step out. As I pull my back foot over the opening, it catches on the flooring of the tent, and I tumble forward onto the mud. I sigh, then lift myself on my arms best I can. A hand wraps around me, and I lift my face to Adrianne helping me up. She's smiling. Odd, since of all people, she'd most likely be the one to share my anger in this situation.

She pulls me to standing and helps me dust off my dress. "Thanks." She nods, still all smiles. Only when I face the front do I realize why she's smiling. Jonah is playing the keyboard!

My jaw drops, and I blink a few times to make sure I'm not hallucinating. Sure enough, it's Jonah. I glance back at Kendra, who's now outside the yurt, smirking.

"Did you know about this?"

She giggles. "It was partly my idea."

I shake my head. "Why?"

"Just turn around, Carolina." Adrianne twirls her finger in my face.

I do as I'm told, making eye contact with Jonah. He breaks off the song, then stands. The crowd claps as if they're at some sort of weird concert. The original keyboard player resumes his post and starts playing slow music again. I nudge at Kendra to walk, as all the parents and her sister, the only bridesmaid, are now down the aisle. She shakes her head. "Not yet."

Jonah walks up to the microphone attached to the arch. "Carolina, I apologize for botching yet another wedding, but Kendra offered when I stopped by your place trying to find you the other night. She agreed that it can be hard to get your undivided attention and wanted to help me—uh, us— out. So here I am. I've been in love with you since the eighth grade, and I'm quite certain you're the sole reason I know the meaning of being in love."

Goosebumps cover my arms as I listen to Jonah confess his love to me, just like in all the movies I envy. This is it. I'm having my own fairy-tale ending. I'm dirty from tripping over the opening of a yurt in the wilderness at a hippie wedding, but I refuse to be a picky princess.

"The last few months have been the best and worst of my life. You've opened up to me and made me think I had a chance at being something more than your friend or brother."

Some of the audience groan and make weird faces at me.

"Not like that. I'm not her brother, but like a brother," Jonah corrects. I laugh, and the crowd goes back to watching him, as if giving him their acceptance once more.

"What I mean to say is you would show me more, then shut me out, and I couldn't handle the rejection. I didn't know how to act around you, and as much as I didn't want to lose you, I could no longer settle for just being a friend.

Then your brother told me how you felt, and I slapped him."

A few people gasp, and I laugh. Maybe Jonah should write screenplays, because this is quite entertaining.

"I did it because he didn't tell me sooner. I couldn't stand being away from you, and I don't want to any longer."

Jonah grins, and before he can say another word, I kick off my heels and run down the aisle. Everyone stands and cheers as I leap into his arms, dirty dress and all.

He kisses my cheek and whispers in my ear, "We've stolen enough thunder. Let's give Kendra back her day." I nod, unable to speak.

The preacher leans toward Brandon and says, "Good luck following that."

Brandon grins at us, and I whisper, "You'll do great," as Jonah grabs my hand and leads me away from the archway and into the trees, where we're no longer in view of the wedding.

The music transitions to the wedding march, and part of me wants to be there to see Kendra walk down the aisle. But this is my moment, at last. And it's with the man of my dreams. Besides, Kendra doesn't need me now. The branches are tied, and the reception is set up. All she has to do now is marry Brandon.

Once we're nestled among the pines, I catch my breath and stare up at Jonah. He's wearing a white button-down shirt that is now stained from my dirty embrace. His jeans are neat, and he's wearing his "church boots."

"You've really loved me since eighth grade?" That's all I can manage to say as years of memories flood my mind, all pointing back to the fact that I've loved him longer than I realized.

He gives me his signature goofy grin. "Pretty much. Every girl I ever dated, I compared to you."

I poke out my bottom lip. That's both the sweetest and saddest thing I've ever heard. "Why did you wait so long to tell me?"

He takes my other hand in his and shrugs. "I didn't want to face rejection or make things weird between us if we tried and it didn't work."

"So what changed your mind?"

He tucks a loose strand of hair behind my ear, then drops my other hand and pulls me to him. I relax into his embrace, his heart beating wildly against mine. "Enough talk." He dips his head and presses his lips to mine.

As he wraps his arm tighter around my waist, I loop my arms around his neck. Jonah deepens the kiss, and my entire body shakes with the release of pent-up emotions I didn't know I'd been hiding.

A weird mixture of excitement and relaxation washes over me as the kiss I've anticipated comes to life, bringing every part of me to life with it. All my senses heighten to the point where it's like if Jonah weren't holding me so tightly, I might float away.

After several minutes, we pull apart. More out of need for oxygen than desire to break the kiss. "Wow," is all I can mutter.

"Wow indeed." He grins and loosens his grip around my waist. I slide my hands from around his neck and hug him as I rest my head against his beating heart.

A smile of satisfaction takes over my face in knowing not only that his heart beats for me, but that it's always beat for me.

Jonah

"There." Carolina lowers her heels to the ground and smiles up at me. I shift my head so the tassel won't get in my eyesight.

She holds up her palm to my face. "Stop moving, I've already fixed your hat twice."

I blow the strings out of the way and frown. "I don't know why we have to wear these stupid things." I've never understood graduation suits, not in high school and not now. You'd think as long as school has been invented, they'd come up with something better to wear by now. For once, I'd rather wear a tux. "And how is yours staying on straight? You can't talk without acting out every word."

She narrows her eyes at me. I grin at her until she gives in and grins back. "Fine, so I talk with my hands, as they say— and it's bobby pins. Would you like for me to pin your hat on?"

"Uh, no." I laugh as she wrinkles her nose. Then I kiss the tip of it because it's so stinking cute.

If Tanner were nearby, he'd roll his eyes or make a mock gagging sound. Like he doesn't want us together. He's partially to thank for us getting together, although I claim I'd eventually have broken down and told Carol how I felt without his urging. But I liked sooner better.

We walk together toward the holding area, as I like to call it. In a few minutes, we'll have to go to separate sections of the stadium to walk with our respective colleges. Carolina made monograms to go on our hats so our families can find us among the crowd. Hers is glittery and mine is simple block letters in Auburn orange—or hunter orange, according to Bama-loving Jack.

My phone rings as we step up onto the stadium steps.

Carol elbows me in the ribs. "Jonah, you need to silence that before we walk."

"Hang on." I dig my phone out of my back pants pocket, which is no easy feat when I'm draped in a thick bedsheet. I wiggle it out and stare at the number.

I almost don't answer, but remember I have to in case it's someone about the house. So far, we've had one lowball offer and one pending contract. The pending buyer backed out when they did a last-minute walkthrough and Papa Rat made an appearance.

Most people would call an exterminator or at least set out some poison, but I've kind of grown fond of the Rat family. In my opinion, the person who isn't afraid of Papa Rat is the right one for the mansion.

"Hello?"

"Hey, Nate Miller here. I wanted to make an offer on the house."

My eyebrows shoot up to my hairline, and Carol gives me a questioning look. I hold my finger up for her to wait. "Okay."

"I think it's just what I've been looking for, and I'm willing to pay twenty above asking price to secure it today, if that's good with you."

"Twenty dollars?" An odd number for earnest money, but I'm cool with that.

Nate chuckles. "No, twenty thousand."

My jaw drops, and I almost drop my phone. Luckily, it falls in my robe as I squat to catch it. I quickly raise it back to my face. "Uh yeah, twenty thousand above asking is totally good with me." I grin as I respond loud enough to get Carolina's attention.

Although that isn't necessary, as she's been impatiently staring at me since I answered the call.

Someone from the graduation event staff steps near us

and calls out to the remaining stragglers who haven't found their place, "I need business grads over here. Education college in the next section. Then liberal arts."

Carolina stands beside me until another girl from her college pulls her in the opposite direction. I give her a thumbs-up as she jerks her head back to me for some sign of what's going on. Then I follow my own herd to the section designated for the business college.

"Hey, Nate, I'm graduating like right now. Can I call you back in, say, a few hours?"

"Yeah, Jonah, no problem. I'm leaving my condo now and heading to Apple Cart."

"Great, see you soon." I hang up the phone and sigh. Then I shoot Carol a text.

That was Nate Miller. He wants the house at twenty thousand above asking.

Eeekkkk!

She follows this with several smiley emojis. A few seconds later, she texts again.

Good thing I told Audrey this morning I didn't want her job offer.

Why? You didn't have to do that.

Yes, I did. Win or lose the house bet, you inspired me to be brave and give my ideas a chance.

. . .

I'm proud of you, Carol.

Thanks.

Kissy heart emoji, followed by every other heart on her phone. Seriously, how does she send these so fast?

So can I persuade you to flip more houses with me? Be the Joanna to my Chip?

Yes. I'll help with anything but basements. Heart swear.

Forever deal.

I wad up my gown so I can reach my pocket and slip my phone inside. The girl next to me shoots me a snooty look as I'm wiggling the material back in place. I mouth a "sorry," then realize I never silenced my phone. She huffs as I repeat my fumbling gesture, but who cares.

In an hour—or several hours, as I've heard these things can last a while—I'll be done with school. Carolina and I have our whole adult lives ahead of us. Best of all, we get to start them together.

No matter how my next building venture goes or the one after that, I've already succeeded beyond measure because I've got the girl.

EPILOGUE

A Few Months Later

Carolina

My phone rings, or rather laughs like a hyena. I roll my eyes. Jonah and I have a new game of putting animal sounds for ringtones on one another's phones. So mature, I know, but entertaining. I answer. "Hello?"

"Is this the number for Apple Cart Turnover?"

"Yes, it is. I'm Carolina. How can I help?"

It took me about as long to decide on a name for my business as it did to decide to start it. Jonah and I made a compromise that helped ease my nerves. We formed the business together to encompass all parts of design and building.

After the mansion sold for a hefty profit, Jonah's dad agreed that he hadn't wasted his time on the remodel. That led to a much-needed family discussion about what Jonah really wanted, which led into what his sister wanted. Alex loves business and bookkeeping and has many great marketing ideas. She admitted to always wanting to take over the store but never thought she'd get a chance with Jack and Jonah ahead of her.

Jeremy and John Jackson agreed to hang on a few more years before retiring, to groom Alex in management while she finishes college. Then, she will eventually have a third equal share in the family business, along with Jack and Jonah as silent partners.

"Yes, sir." I jot down the notes from our newest client. A retiree wanting to renovate his basement into a man cave. "Thank you. I'll speak with Jonah, and we'll set up a meeting soon."

I hang up and walk outside. We purchased an older building on the edge of downtown, and Jonah's been updating it when he has time. Today, he's putting the finishing touches on creating a client seating area on the back patio. I find him on a ladder, hanging artwork I picked out.

"Jonah?"

He stops hammering and turns to face me. "Yes, dear?" He talks around a nail clinched between his teeth.

I smirk. "When you get done with this, I need you to find a time to meet with someone about a man cave."

"All right." He hammers the nail formerly between his teeth, then descends the ladder.

I step onto the patio and tilt my head. "I thought you were going to center it with the windows."

"This is a more stable spot."

I narrow my eyes. "I knew I should've hung it while you were at that other job."

He shakes his head. "Now, you know you don't like climbing ladders without me. And if you want to hang photos, I need to first show you how to find a stud."

"Who says I can't find a stud?" I raise one eyebrow.

He laughs, then pulls me in tight for a kiss. When we pull away, he smiles at me in a way that tells me he's hiding something.

"I have one more heart swear for you."

"What's that?"

Jonah drops his hand from my waist, then shoves his hand into his pocket. I bite my bottom lip as I wait for him to speak. Instead, he lifts his hand and holds up his ring finger. On the end of his finger is a gold ring with a large round diamond and several smaller diamonds and red stones surrounding it.

I cover my mouth and gasp. "Jonah, is that?"

Before I can finish my thought, he drops to one knee. "Carolina, will you heart swear to live the rest of your life with me?"

"Yes!" I fall into his arms and hug him.

He whispers in my ear, "It's not a heart swear if you don't lock fingers."

I giggle and roll my eyes, then pull back and hold up my ring finger. We hook fingers, then he smiles and takes the ring from his finger and slides it up mine. It fits perfectly.

I hold my hand out and let it twinkle in the summer sun. "How did you know what size I needed?"

"Tanner helped me confiscate your class ring for a while."

"Of course he did." I alternate between smiling at Jonah and the ring.

"The red stones are garnets. I know you like red, and I found out the stone means unconditional love and protection for your partner."

I bring my hand to my heart and sigh. "Oh, Jonah, I love it. And I love you." He gives me a quick kiss. "Did you plan on proposing today?"

He shakes his head. "I've been putting it in my pocket,

waiting on the right time, but I've wanted to ask you for a while now."

"Oh really? How long?" I grin and wrap my arms around him.

He sits back on the patio and pulls me onto his lap. "Oh, I'd say about ten years."

That's all he needs to say for me to kiss him again, and again and again, forever.

Want to read Adrianne finding love with grumpy JoJo?
Check out *Cutting out Love*.

Sign up for Kaci Lane's newsletter to receive a bonus scene of Jack and Bianca iguana hunting on their honeymoon!

ACKNOWLEDGMENTS

First, I would like to thank God for giving me creative ideas and placing the right people in my path to help see them to fruition.

My husband, Blake, gets credit next for always supporting my writing endeavors, even if he finds my stories a little too "girly and Hallmarkish." But this one wasn't too bad.

I also want to thank my editor, Joanne, and my ARC team. I couldn't pull this off without all of your help! Each of you is appreciated so much!

ABOUT THE AUTHOR

Kaci Lane is a journalist turned fiction writer who believes all stories should have a happy ending. While unsuccessfully trying to learn Spanish for a decade, she has become fluent in sarcasm, Southern belle and movie quotes. She is married to a Southern Gentleman and has two young children who help keep her humility in check. Connect with her on kacilane.com or follow her on Amazon for upcoming releases.

BOOKS BY KACI LANE

Schooled on Love Series

Taco Truck Takedown

Side Hustle

Buggy List

Off-Season

No Brides Club Series*

No Time for Traditions

Silver Leaf Falls Novellas Series*

A Perfect Match in Silver Leaf Falls

Bama Boys Series

Hunting for Love

Chicken about Love

Hammered by Love

Bama Boys related stand alone:

*Christmas in Dixie***

*Shared series with other authors

**If you enjoyed *Hammered by Love*, you will enjoy *Christmas in Dixie*, which features some of the same characters during the holiday season in Apple Cart County.